OUT FOR BLOOD

There were three of them, all in hunting clothes, all carrying guns. They wore bizarrely patterned ski masks that left visible only the liquid glint of their eyes and the shape of their mouths. They all wore gloves.

Crain heard something and, twisting, looked behind him. There was a fourth man standing there on the rock. This one was openly pointing his rifle at him.

"Aim that some other place," Crain said.

"Don't act so nervous, it's not like you," the first man said. "After all, we're old friends, all of us. We've come to say good-bye."

"Good-bye? Who are you?"

"You'll know us," the man said. Holding his weapon in the crook of an elbow, he used his free hand to pull awkwardly at the wool around his head.

A second man and then the third stripped off their head coverings, and his m̶i̶ back through the years and now he didn't bother to look at the o̶ was in terrible trouble.

THE
DEPARTMENT
OF CORRECTION

Tony Burton

HarperPaperbacks
A Division of HarperCollinsPublishers

HarperPaperbacks

A Division of HarperCollins*Publishers*

10 East 53rd Street, New York, N.Y. 10022-5299

This is a work of fiction. The characters, incidents, and dialogues are products of the author's imagination and are not to be construed as real. Any resemblance to actual events or persons, living or dead, is entirely coincidental.

ISBN 0-06-101309-9

HarperCollins®, ®, and HarperPaperbacks™ are trademarks of HarperCollins*Publishers*, Inc.

Cover illustration © 1998 by Douglas Paul Designs

First printing: July 1998

Printed in the United States of America

Visit HarperPaperbacks on the World Wide Web at
http://www.harpercollins.com

❖ 10 9 8 7 6 5 4 3 2 1

For Anthea,
and to hell with Terry Golway

Although we are reasonably certain that the shocking story revealed in *The Gulag Archipelago* could not take place in this country, the facts of Roy Schuster's case are reminiscent of Solzhenitsyn's treatise . . . We can no longer sit by and permit the state to continue toying with his freedom.

—Chief Judge Irving R. Kaufman
of the United States Court of Appeals
for the Second Circuit

THE
DEPARTMENT
OF CORRECTION

Ruffians, pitiless as proud,
Heav'n awards the vengeance due,
Empire is on us bestow'd,
Shame and ruin wait for you.

—William Cowper

1 ◀

Crain wasn't angry, just rueful because he'd come so close.

The night before, the toothy redhead on TV in Albany had set the colored balls bouncing and when they stopped he was one goddamned digit away from winning $4.7 million. A six instead of a seven and he'd have hit the jackpot.

But, hell, if he'd won, what would he have done with it? A new car, maybe. Have the roof fixed. Give some to the kids, maybe put it in trust for when they grew up. At their age, they didn't have much time for a grandfather. He should spoil them more. If he gave them the money, it might make him seem pretty cool.

What else? He was content with what he already had. The millions wouldn't bring Helen back. The hell with it. Money didn't come close to the pleasure of a day in the mountains.

Even so, twelve hours later, it was still in his mind as he trudged slowly up the slopes toward a spot on the bank of a stream where he planned to sit and wait, shrouded in the noise of tumbling water. He knew where the deer moved; he had carried a gun in these woods since boyhood.

Halfway to his goal, Crain paused to catch his breath and look around. At their peaks, the mountains were bald with snow, but here, on the lower levels beneath the trees, the ground was still brown and crisp with leaves. Cloud cover from the west held back the coming bleakness; there was only a light breeze to carry the smell of pine and maple and of vegetation beginning to rot.

Crain wore high boots, heavy, wide-waled, corduroy pants, and a red woolen lumber jacket with his state license pinned on the back. His thick gray hair was uncovered. He carried the lever-action Winchester mounted with a Zeiss scope that he had bought years ago on a trip out West with Helen before her last time in the hospital. In his deep pockets were a bottle of branch water, the sandwiches he had prepared the night before, and a paperback he would read while waiting for a buck to come to him. He was a man who liked to occupy himself even when he was waiting, and he was not eager to kill. It was pleasure enough to be out in the clean, pungent air.

Crain was satisfied that he had lived an honorable and useful life. But too many of his working hours had been spent in confinement, first obeying orders, then issuing them. Now, with nobody to call master, no responsibilities beyond himself, he could enjoy life as he wished.

He looked down through the black branches at a

small lake cupped in the valley below. His eyes ranged the hillside, and he thought he caught movement where he had climbed earlier, maybe a deer, more likely another hunter. Ever since he had left the road, he had felt the presence of other men with guns. It was the season. Men from the cities would blast away at anything that moved, and the hospitals and morgues would receive their annual harvest of stupidity.

He found the stream, busy now with recent rains, and settled with his back against a low, mossy rock, his weapon across his lap. For a while, he stared around, taking in the clearing across the water, the grassy aisle that escorted the stream down the hill through the trees. When it was all imprinted on his mind so that he would be able to bring up his gun and, in seconds, aim at an intruding animal, he took out his book and began to read about a Frenchman's travels in Arabia.

They came on him silently, although the noise of the water would have covered any sounds of approach. One minute he was engrossed in his paperback, the next he was conscious of them bunched around him. He looked up and lowered the book. His hands went to grip his weapon.

There were three of them, all in hunting clothes, all carrying guns. They wore bizarrely patterned ski masks that left visible only the liquid glint of their eyes and the shape of their mouths. They all wore gloves.

"Any luck?" one of them said.

He shrugged. They could see for themselves.

"Nor us," the man said. The voice was neutral, neither friendly nor hostile. A sense of alarm was growing in Crain and his hands tightened around his gun. They were too intent on him for this to be a casual encounter. It was at least a mile to the road where he had left his car, much more to the nearest house.

"Been here long?" another of the men said.

"A while."

"What you got there, a Remington?"

"Winchester."

"Anybody else around?"

He didn't answer. They were standing no more than a couple of yards away from him on his right so that it would be impossible for him to bring his weapon around swiftly. Once, years before, he had been caught like that. Then it had been a big buck which stared at him as if recognizing his quandary. By the time he shifted to turn his gun, the animal was off and running, an impossible target.

He heard something and, twisting, looked behind him. There was a fourth man standing there on the rock. This one was openly pointing his rifle at him.

"Aim that some other place," Crain said. The mouth of the barrel looked enormous. It remained steady.

"Don't act so nervous, it's not like you," the first man said. "After all, we're old friends, all of us. We've come to say good-bye."

"Good-bye? Who are you?"

"You'll know us," the man said. Holding his weapon in the crook of an elbow, he used his free hand to pull awkwardly at the wool around his head. The mask came off, leaving strands of brown hair pulled upright. Crain stared. He couldn't place the man.

A second man and then the third stripped off their head coverings, and his mind went back through the years and now he knew them all. He didn't bother to look at the one behind. He knew he was in terrible trouble.

"You remember us, PK?" the first man said. "'Course you do. You stole something from us, you and the rest of them. You stole something we can never get back. Now it's payback time."

The man behind moved swiftly. He came down off the rock on the left side and kicked at the gun in Crain's lap. It went butt-over-barrel into the leaves. Crain pulled his legs under him and struggled unsteadily to his feet. He felt very tired, broken with fear. Trying to summon stoicism, he thought that even if he had won the night before, he would never have collected the jackpot. One of them put his boot on the fallen weapon.

"What d'you want?" Crain said. "It was all long ago. It's over and done with." He had difficulty controlling his voice. His gaze went past them in a hopeless search for help. Beyond the group, the woods were still.

"We've had a trial, which was more than you

gave us," the first man said. He seemed to be their spokesman, their leader. "You were found guilty. We've been watching you for a long time, just like they do on death row."

Crain knew they planned to kill him. He had known since he recognized their faces. They were men who saw no great wickedness in killing another human.

He gathered his strength and threw himself at a gap between two of them. They were ready. It was as if they knew what he would do and what they would do. They were younger and stronger. They handled him with ease. They held him, breathing hard into his face from the effort of containing his struggles. There was a horrible intimacy in feeling their breath on his cheeks. He shouted then for help. And shouted again, but in the immensity of the hills the sound was frail, snatched away by the breeze.

They bore him to the ground. They pulled out two wide leather belts. With one they secured his ankles. The other they strapped around his frantically writhing body, pinning his arms to his sides. He was trussed like an animal prepared for the pot.

"You're all insane," he screamed. They forced his mouth open and filled it with an evil-smelling cloth. A dark stain was running down his pants from his crotch.

One of them stood back and removed a glove to take out a pack of cigarettes and a silver lighter. The lighter made a metallic clicking noise when he flicked the top open and closed, open and closed. Just as he was about to put the flame to a cigarette, the leader said, "Christ, Ferret, put that away. Those smokes have done you enough damage. And you can't smoke here. Wait until we're back on the road." The smoker shrugged and returned the cigarette to the pack, but he continued flicking the lighter, open and closed, open and closed, like a heartbeat.

"It's gonna be an accident, just another hunting accident," the spokesman said to Crain, now squirming on the ground. "That's what they'll think when they find you. They won't know it was an execution."

The man called Ferret said, "You'll have company in hell, PK. Your pal, Savage, that cocksucker, is joining you, just as soon as we get around to him."

"Fucker's pissed himself," one said. He had a Southern accent. "First, I'm gonna take down his pants and butt-fuck him, see how he likes that." He reached down to pluck a thin knife, almost a dagger, from his boot and let the bound man see it. He ran his finger along the blade.

"Cuts on both sides," he said. "Neat, uh?"

"For God's sake, let's get it done," another of the men said. "The woods are thick with fucking shooters."

"We got time," the Southerner said. "Time to enjoy ourselves. I'm entitled."

"Only his head," the leader said. "You take down his pants, mess with him down there, they'll find it. There'll most likely be an autopsy."

"He ain't pretty enough, anyway, and he's too

old," the Southerner said with a shrug. "His ass will be bony and wrinkled." He knelt and almost affectionately put a hand at the back of Crain's head to hold it still. The knife flashed down, gouged with a flicking movement, and their victim's right eye was gone. Even through the muffling cloth, Crain's shriek of pain and horror reached them as if it were issuing through his pores. Blood gushed down, turning his face into a red mask.

The knife-man was grinning wolfishly. Again the knife plunged and the other eye was out. One of the watching men turned away and threw up into the leaves.

"You always were too soft, Jackie, you hump," the Southerner said. "Clean as an oyster from its little shell. Those eyes couldn't see the truth, PK. So you don't need them."

"Jesus," Jackie said, wiping his mouth. "That's enough." His face was pale. He scuffed twigs and leaves over his steaming vomit. The Southerner went to hold his knife and hands in the stream and let the rushing water carry the blood away.

The leader said, "Yet who would have thought the old man to have so much blood in him?" His voice was precise, cultured.

They pulled their masks back over their heads. The leader took the hunter's gun from the ground, checked that it was loaded, and flicked off the safety catch. His gloved finger on the trigger, he held the muzzle under Crain's chin, bending from the waist to keep the butt close to the ground. Blood was streaming down, some of it dripping onto the barrel. He hesitated, but it was only to reach out and snatch the cloth from Crain's mouth. He pulled the trigger and the face disintegrated and the sound of the shot went rolling away into the mountains. Blood, tissue, and splintered bone sprayed out and the gunman swore and jumped back, letting the weapon drop to the ground.

Movement across the stream caught their eyes and they turned, astonished, to see a startled deer racing away from the death scene, its white tail darting through the trees.

There was no need to check if the man was dead. His face, the front of his head, was gone. Moving swiftly now, they unstrapped the belts from the body and stowed them in their pockets. They took his flaccid hands and pressed the fingers around the trigger guard and on the trigger itself before letting the weapon fall away to his side.

It had all been planned beforehand. As they moved away, the predators scattered handfuls of dry leaves to cover any marks left by their feet.

"Anything else?" one of them said. There was nothing else. It might be days before the body was found, before a search party came across it, for there were many thousands of acres in the mountains where a man might hunt and have an accident.

The four split into pairs, separated, and walked quickly away from the scarlet mess on the ground, the blood already dulling as it oxidized.

That was the first.

2◄

A large and energetic wave deposited Todd Paige on the sand of the shallows in a flurry of arms and legs. Swearing, he struggled to his feet and pulled his soggy underpants back into position. He didn't know why he had gone swimming so early in the morning. It had seemed a good idea when he awoke with the sun dousing the living room and the couch on which he lay. Probably still drunk, he thought. Now, he was sober, he had grazed his elbow, and there was sand in his ears. Drunk, he had felt fine. Sober, he felt terrible. He moved painfully up the deserted beach toward the house just over the dunes.

The house had been designed by a fashionably-expensive architect who believed that elegance is angular. A riot of sharp edges slashed through the sky-line. Even the obligatory chimney was constructed in a triangular form. Whenever a fire was started, the house filled with smoke. The only bow to conformity with the other beach houses was a long deck over-looking the ocean.

Only one of the bedroom doors was closed. Paige put his ear against it but could hear nothing. In the relentlessly chic kitchen, glittering with high-tech and stainless steel equipment that made it look more like a laboratory, Paige found some Colombian coffee and filled the pot. He switched on the radio and fiddled until he found an all-news station.

Taking food from the huge refrigerator, he tossed strips of bacon and two eggs into a big frying pan. In a bowl, he found some ancient-looking boiled potatoes, cut out the worst of the mold, tipped them into the pan and turned up the heat. As the smell of frying invaded the kitchen, he pondered briefly before cracking another egg and making room for it with a spatula. He was ravenous. Along with his grazed elbow, he had stubbed a toe on one of the wooden steps from the beach, and he could feel the ocean salt drying stickily on his body. When the food was ready, he turned off the stove and, standing, ate directly from the pan, shoveling the food into his mouth with the spatula.

Fortified, he put the coffee pot, milk, sugar, and two mugs on a tray and approached the closed bedroom door. He balanced the tray on one hand and opened the door. It was even brighter in here than in the kitchen. Through the floor-to-ceiling windows, beyond the deck and the barbecue and the empty glasses from the night before, the ocean shimmered. It looked vaguely menacing and it hurt his eyes. He turned away from it and looked at her.

She was sitting up against a pile of pillows in the

king-size bed, a pale blue sheet pulled around her, the telephone at her ear.

"Lunch for three," she said. She looked at Paige's linebacker frame and added, "You'd better give us one reinforced chair. Safety first."

Paige pushed aside a biography of Oliver Cromwell and put the tray on a table at the side of the bed. Also on the table was a photograph of three sweaty polo players with their arms around each other's shoulders. The clothes she was wearing the night before, a short green skirt, white sleeveless sweater, and black bikini panties, were lying scattered on the floor, which was covered with a deep sand-colored carpet.

"In the name of Graham," she told the telephone. "Lady Jane Graham." She put down the phone. "The Blue Parrot in East Hampton," she said. "One o'clock."

"You sure you have a title?" he said, pouring himself some coffee.

"They believe I have and that's what matters," she said. "It does so improve the service. And you quite like the idea, don't you, darling? Pour me some of that coffee. Black."

"You can't prove you have a title."

"One doesn't need to. But one could."

"How? Does Buckingham Palace issue a certificate or something?"

"Oh, my dear. Like a driver's license, perhaps? How very American of you. It's like that Rolls Royce fantasy of yours, sweet but adolescent." In an unguarded moment the night before, Paige had talked about his ambition to own a white Rolls Royce driven by a blond chauffeuse.

"It's more than a fantasy," he said. "It will happen one day."

"Quite," she said. She had Dietrich cheekbones, a thin, arrogant nose, and prominent blue eyes that never seemed to blink. Paige reckoned she looked like a sexy trout. She lived in the ambiguous territory of approaching middle age, and the searching light from the windows picked out the lines at the corners of her mouth and eyes. But she wore her years without deceit, presenting herself with a take-it-or-leave-it flair. Paige wondered vaguely if she did have a title. Sometimes, dismayed by the vulgarity surrounding him, Paige thought that he really belonged on the top-most levels of English society. Maybe he had been stolen from a peer's cradle and shipped secretly to this feral republic.

Certainly, she had a funny accent. You could call it Bermudese, Paige thought, since it seemed grounded somewhere between New York and London. Last night, she had talked about Mummy in Belgravia.

"You like the carpet?" she said.

"Sure." The pile was so thick he could see his footprints.

"I see you wriggling your toes in it. You haven't got sportsman's foot, have you?"

"Athlete's foot? No."

"Your toenails need cutting." They looked all right to him.

"Well?" she said.

"Well, what?"

"What's your excuse for your failure to do your duty last night?"

"I don't remember much of last night after we left the bar. What happened?"

"Nothing happened. That's the problem." She sat straighter and let the sheet fall around her hips. Her bosom, sagging slightly under its extravagance, courted his attention. The sumptuous breasts were as tanned as her arms and face. She was letting him see what he had missed. He felt a familiar stirring in his loins.

"We had a couple more drinks in the Jacuzzi, gazing at the moon," she said. "You were quite poetic. Said it was your idea of heaven, a drink in your hand, a blonde in your tub, and a fat moon above. Then, when we came inside, you collapsed on the couch, out like the tide, leaving me high and dry."

"I was tired. I'll make it up to you now if you like."

"I don't think so. You don't deserve me." She looked complacently at the activity beneath his damp shorts and said, "Too late. And you can't come prancing into a lady's bedroom looking like that. There's a robe in the closet. God, you Americans are hairy."

"Esau was a hairy man," he said.

"Yes, and look what happened to him." Paige wasn't sure what had happened to Esau, so he let her get away with that one. He found the robe and pulled it on. It barely reached his knees and the sleeves ended halfway up his arms.

They had met a few days earlier at a literary cocktail party in Southampton that Paige had crashed for want of anything else to do. She seemed to find him amusing. Then, last night, he had run into Lady Jane, if she was a lady, in a bar around the corner from the motel where he had established temporary residence. She said she was slumming. She had carried him off to her beach house like some strapping trophy, only, it seemed, to have him disappoint her.

Paige, his belongings and his rusty, secondhand Chevy Cavalier—97,000 miles if the clock were to be believed, and still not paid off—were in Suffolk County, the paper's version of purdah, because the city editor, LaFleche, and his cronies had decided he was disrespectful. Page had no great objection at first. It got him away from the office in Manhattan, that snake-pit, and from the oily LaFleche.

The Long Island bureau chief, Stamp, was okay up to a point, and during the week, when the men were in the city, the women were hospitable. Still, the whole thing had begun to pall. Paige found it disconcerting to be covering school board meetings, local courts, and county elections after three years of poking around the underside of Manhattan.

Tonight, for God's sake, he was due at a teacher's strike meeting. His only hope was Savage. Savage could get him back to the city.

After using one of her little razors, Paige was in the shower, trying to get rid of the sand, when the glass door slid open. Lady Jane, wearing a sheet like a toga, stood there examining him as if he were a chestnut bay in the sales ring.

"You need to lose some of that weight," she said.

"I've got the height to carry it off." He reckoned she had changed her mind, was about to join him under the spray.

"Maybe, but this part needs to show a little more stamina."

She reached in to give his penis a fierce tweak. Then she closed the door on him.

Dressed, he telephoned Stamp at the bureau in Ronkonkoma.

Stamp started going on about LaFleche.

"The jerk has discovered *Newsday* is still printing and he reads it every morning now and wants to know why we're not covering every lousy sewer district meeting and PTA complaint and I'm gonna take the phone off the fucking hook and see where that gets him. Where are you, anyway?"

"One of the Hamptons. I'm not sure which. My hostess keeps me so busy I haven't had a chance to find out."

"You keep on using your prick like that and it'll fall off."

"What's going on?"

"What's she like, Paige? She got any chums I'd fancy?" Stamp was embittered that the golden people whirled around his Long Island bailiwick all summer and he never got a glimpse of them. He lived in the certainty that they were snorting cocaine, drinking champagne, and holding twenty-four-hour orgies, and he couldn't get into the magic circle.

"Look," Paige said, "if you don't have anything for me, I'm going to lunch."

"She paying? Okay, okay. Go to lunch. There's nothing much until that meeting tonight. Oh, wait a minute, there was a call for you a minute ago. She left a message. Wait a moment . . . here it is. Some chick called vanAllen."

"She's not a chick. She's a cop. Did she leave a number?"

"Nah, said she was moving around, playing it mysterious. She's calling back. Do I give her your number?"

Paige passed on the number of the beach house and hung up. Detective Lieutenant Sarah vanAllen. Looking for a mention in the rag, he thought. Half an hour later, Paige was drinking more coffee while Lady Jane lazed naked on the deck when the phone rang. It was vanAllen.

"Get your ass in here," she said.

"I'm respectable now. I don't mess with disreputable types like you. I have an important meeting to go to."

"Paige, cut it out. I'm doing you a favor and I don't have much time."

"Shoot."

"I don't know what the hell you're doing lollygagging around the Hamptons, but you'd better get out of your Bermuda shorts and into Manhattan. It's a hot one."

3 ◄

As Paige was emerging from the Atlantic, James "Mickey" Finn opened his eyes and stared up through the bushes at the sullen, milky sky. Across the East River, the sun was already glaring through the haze. It was going to be another hot one, like yesterday and the day before that. He fumbled around in the breast pocket of his jacket, thick tweed spun in the damp chill of the Western Isles, and brought out his last battered cigarette. It was a Pall Mall regular and Finn preferred a filter, but it was better than nothing. In another pocket, he found a book of matches, lit up, and sent a lungful of smoke through the leaves.

He shifted his buttocks into a more comfortable position on the dusty ground and watched a bug climb a twig above his nose. Today he would get moving. He would bum a ride up to City Island and Ronson would give him a job on one of his shrimp boats. All he had to do was pick himself up and find a ride. He didn't move.

The park where he had spent the night lay

between the end of Fifty-seventh Street and the East River. It hardly justified the title of park. A square plot no wider than Fifty-seventh Street, its surface was covered with worn red bricks. In the center was a sand pit, surrounded by iron railings, which the children used in the daytime. A few feet away, inexplicably, stood a weather-worn bronze statue of a wild boar. There were wooden seats around the edges of the brick paving. On the north and south limits were low concrete walls, beyond them behind low railings, patches of earth, and tired-looking bushes. It was here, on the south side, that Finn lay contemplating his future. He came here often, partly because it tickled him that he slept only a few yards from some of the most luxurious bedrooms in the world on Sutton Place, bedrooms where the rich and the powerful lay in slumber no different to his. The handsome brick townhouse of the secretary-general of the United Nations stood directly overlooking the park, and Finn, who liked to think he had a sense of humor if little else, murmured, "Good morning, Kofi. Have a nice day."

Not that he had any respect for the United Nations, about fifteen blocks south. It wasn't the bullshit that poured out of the place. It was the way they treated him. While tourists and foreigners walked freely into the grounds or the buildings, the guards always barred Finn. They would look him up and down and sneer and say, "Get out of here, you bum." Him, a United States citizen.

And the tourists would stare at him and snicker

and walk on past with their cameras and Bermuda shorts and silly white shoes. Once, he slipped through the gates in the middle of a crowd of visitors when the guards were distracted, talking to their fat sergeant. Finn spent a comfortable afternoon stretched out on a bench close to the statue of a muscleman turning a sword into a plowshare. Picked up a couple of bucks from some South Americans, too.

When he left, he walked right past the guards and didn't say a word. He just smiled right at them, but after that they made sure he didn't get in again. Assholes.

Scratching his grizzled jaw, Finn wondered idly when the cop would arrive. He knew who had complained about him. It was the skinny bitch who always wore high heels when she brought her two kids into the park. She never said a word to him, but he had heard her bitching to other mothers, saying he went to the lavatory in the bushes. Maybe it was true, but where was he supposed to go? He remembered his time in the Corps when he had pulled guard duty at the embassy in Paris. There had been these little places all over, pissoirs they called them, and men relieved themselves in front of anybody who wanted to watch. And anybody could go into a bar and use the john even if they weren't customers. In New York, they always tossed him out of bars, except down in the Bowery, and Finn didn't like the Bowery. Down there he saw himself in too many other men.

One day, he had awoken late to see the black-haired bitch standing up on the ramp that led down to the park. She had a cop with her and she was pointing down at him.

"It's disgusting," he heard her say in a nasal whine. "This park is used by children and these men come in and make it a cesspit."

It wasn't that bad. It wasn't as if he used drugs or any of that stuff. He just liked to drink and live the way he wished. Finn knew there were drugs in the little park. On the north side, in the wall, there was a metal door. The padlock was broken and some guys used the darkness inside to deal and shoot up. Finn had gone in once and stumbled down some stairs and found they led straight to FDR Drive. He reckoned it was some sort of emergency exit from the drive in case there was a bad traffic accident in the tunnel below, where cars and vans pounded ceaselessly by.

But now the door wouldn't open. The mothers must have complained. A new padlock had been fitted and the drug guys couldn't get in anymore. He looked over toward the door and stared. There was somebody else in the park already, a guy in brown pants, an open-necked yellow shirt, and sneakers. He was doing something to the door. It looked to Finn as though he was using a key or something, trying to open the lock. Lying among the bushes, Finn watched in puzzlement. He felt obscurely irritated. This time of the day, the park belonged to him, never mind who showed up later. Once, the guy in the brown pants looked over his shoulder as if to make sure he was alone, unobserved. He didn't see Finn in the bushes.

The door was a dull green and covered in graffiti. Finn saw it swing ajar. Brown pants had gotten it open. The intruder looked around again, then put the padlock in his pocket. What the hell was he after? Was he going inside to shoot up? No, he was putting something else in his pocket—the key?—and leaving the door barely open, and now he was turning and moving toward the ramp.

Finn shrank back among the bushes and snuffed out his cigarette in the dust. There was something surreptitious about the whole thing. The guy was fat and he had a peculiar shuffle when he walked. He seemed nervous. What the hell was it all about? Brown pants seemed to stare right at him. He had nasty eyes, narrow and close in his fat face. But the leaves and their shadows concealed Finn and the guy kept going, approaching within a few feet, but then turning to climb the ramp. A moment later he was gone.

For a while, Finn lay there considering the incident, wondering if brown pants was coming back. Finally, he rose painfully to his feet. His shoe touched the bottle he had finished the night before. Bending like a weary housewife, he picked it up and tossed it over the railings onto the broad lawn of the apartment building next door. While he took a piss in the bushes, he stared over at the green door. Gathering up the plastic bag which held his belongings, he left the bushes. The cop could be here any moment, but curiosity drew him toward the door. As he approached, he saw that it had been left so that, to the casual glance, it looked still closed.

Finn pulled it open and stuck his head inside. The roar of the traffic came up at him like a blow. He moved further in. There was nothing, just the darkness and the stairs leading down. The hell with it.

When he stepped back into the park, he saw the cop. The cop was walking down the ramp, looking over the railings at Finn who stood there clutching his plastic bag. As the cop reached the bottom of the ramp, Finn started forward.

"Okay, okay," he said. "I'm going."

"Hold it," the cop said. He was swarthy with pocked features dominated by a beak of a nose. His nameplate identified him as Faso. He had seen the door was open.

"How d'you do that?" he demanded.

"Not me," Finn said.

Faso reached the door, pulled it open, and poked his head inside. When he reappeared, he looked puzzled.

"It's supposed to be locked," he said. "You pick it?" Finn became alarmed.

"It was a guy," he said. "He had a key. A few minutes back, he opened it and he left it open. I was having a lie-down in the bushes and saw it. Then the guy took a hike."

"What guy?" The cop couldn't believe that Finn had opened the door. Finn was a bum, not a break-and-enter artist.

"A feller in brown pants. Fat."

Faso tried to slam the door shut. It bounced back open with a metallic clang.

"You need another padlock to keep it closed," Finn said. He moved closer to the ramp. "The Parks Department . . . they'll have one. Give 'em a call."

"Gee," Faso said, "I really appreciate your advice. It's that sort of thing that makes our jobs worthwhile."

"Just trying to help," Finn said, aggrieved.

"You can help by getting the fuck out of here. How many times do I have to tell you, huh? And zip your pants up for Chrissake, or I'll take you in for indecent exposure."

"I don't do any harm," Finn said, closing his gaping pants. "I'm gone by the time the kids get down here."

The cop was looking at the door and the graffiti. They used their spray cans on everything. Whoever had opened it, it would have to be locked up again. It was the wife of that lawyer on Sutton Place who had complained about the bums and about the addicts shooting up at the top of the stairs. A shyster, but he had connections at city hall, and the women who brought their kids into the park had enough power to break the captain and have every man transferred out of the precinct. Their husbands were surgeons, politicians, lawyers, bankers, diplomats. Plutocrats.

Faso, who came from Flatbush, reckoned that the people who occupied the high-rises and townhouses within four blocks of the park could get together and buy Saudi Arabia, they had that much money. Some of the richest people in the richest city in the world. He would look at the women from this silken enclave as they strolled to the stores or got out of chauffeur-driven limos or, if it was nanny's day off, brought their kids to the park. He thought they were like greyhounds, some of the younger ones, lean and nervous, as if they spent every moment worrying about putting an extra ounce on their cosseted bodies.

Faso sometimes fantasized about their underwear. It would be French, tiny little nothings of pure silk that would cling to the loins and breasts as if painted on, inviting the male to gaze at the smooth flesh underneath. There was a woman who lived in the building on the southwest corner of Fifty-seventh and Sutton, a woman who sometimes gave him a cool, speculative look and once had smiled faintly at him. Tall and dark and long-legged. A model, was his guess. She had a chauffeur who looked as if he had been hired as much for his looks as for his driving abilities, and Faso wondered what went on between them.

Faso had a wife and three children, and his mother lived with them, and things weren't going too well between him and Jean, although they didn't see much of each other now she had taken the job of night cashier in that Bayside coffee shop.

He followed the wino up the ramp. He would have to call the precinct and get that door taken care of.

The little park was one of Charlotte's favorite places. It reminded her of the quiet city parks in Europe, shaded by old trees and far enough from the streets that traffic noises were reduced to a distant hum. She liked it best early in the morning before it filled with children and their custodians.

The twins, released from their walking harnesses, galloped off to the sandpit in a whirlwind of ill-controlled arms and legs. She unloaded the carriage. Two of everything. Two bikes, two toy cars, two plastic baseball bats, even two balls. Sometimes, as she walked the six blocks to the park, she felt weighed down like Mother Courage, and she envied the Sutton Park mothers, probably still in bed while nannies changed diapers and fed the children.

Charlotte went to lean over the curving rail above the East River. The broad sweep of the river always delighted her. Two tugs were squiring a long barge, low in the water, under the cable car that was bringing late-rising commuters across from Roosevelt Island.

She watched for a while, then went to sit on one of the benches. The twins were busily digging in the sand and she hoped they would find nothing unpleasant. Some people brought their dogs to the park.

"Charlotte!"

Melissa was steering her little David down the ramp. The twins raced over to interrogate him while Melissa in her usual black sunglasses gasped dramatically and sank on to the bench alongside Charlotte.

"Quel horreur!" she said.

"Another fight?"

"He stormed out of the apartment like Napoleon turning his back on Elba or whatever it was. My dear, the man was positively screaming. Said he was going to put me on a budget."

"And there's only one answer to that."

"Exactly, darling. I shall go to Tiffany, Chanel, and Bendel this afternoon and teach him a lesson he won't soon forget."

Charlotte laughed. The reports and postmortems on Melissa's fights with her husband, an investment banker with ambitions to become a player in Hollywood, were part of the attractions of the park. While Charlotte was constantly fighting her plumpness, Melissa was sickeningly slim. Today, Charlotte was in a print cotton dress from Macy's, while Melissa wore astonishingly expensive jeans, high-heeled boots, and a silk blouse from Italy that was so elegantly simple it was positively deceitful.

Melissa had everything. A penthouse looking south toward the river and the United Nations com-

plex. A Mercedes of her own in the garage below.
Wardrobes jammed with clothes from the most fash-
ionable designers. A house in the country. A multi-
millionaire husband. And—Melissa was quite open
about it—the occasional lover.

Yet Charlotte was not envious. She liked Melissa
for her careless chatter, for her sense of humor, the
way she could take neither her money nor her men
seriously. And, in spite of her frivolous approach to
life, Melissa was one of the few wealthy mothers
who brought her child to the park rather than dis-
patching him in the custody of a nanny.

Most of the nannies who came to the park were
blacks who took the subway each day from the city's
grim slums to the palaces of the upper East Side.
With the children, they were starting to come down
the ramp in numbers now, and the little square was
filled with cries and laughter and squabbles.

A fat, white-uniformed woman who spoke with
the lilt of Jamaica settled on a bench near to Melissa
and Charlotte, opening a brown bag and taking out a
chicken leg. Charlotte noticed that the old man had
taken his usual place on the bench alongside the
Jamaican. He held his walking stick between his legs.
Even in the heat, he wore his tweed hat. Charlotte
waved at him. Occasionally, when there was nobody
else around, she chatted with him. He was gruff but
seemed nice enough. He also seemed lonely. Once,
when the children were suffering from a persistent
virus, he told her he was a retired physician, but
beyond that, he revealed little about himself.

After removing her sunglasses, Melissa was using her video-recorder to tape the activities of the children. "Hey," she said, looking across the park. "It looks as though that door's open again." Charlotte looked idly toward the green, graffiti-smeared door set into the wall on the north side of the park.

"They've probably been shooting up in there again. I thought the parks people had it locked tight."

"It was locked yesterday. I wonder how they got it open."

"New York," Melissa said, as if that explained everything.

"New York," Charlotte agreed.

It was half an hour after Melissa first noticed the unlocked door that it swung open. At first, nobody paid any attention, even when three men came through it and onto the sun-splashed red bricks of the park.

But, gradually, the casual chatter of mothers and nannies subsided. Somebody whispered, "Oh, my God." All around the park, eyes locked on the men who, in a tight group, were now walking steadily but without haste toward the southern side where Charlotte and Melissa were sitting.

Absurdly, in this heat, the men were wearing woolen ski masks, all decorated with lightning-like slashes, but that was not where the real horror lay. The terrifying thing was that all carried weapons, ugly-looking automatic rifles that affronted the innocence of the park like a vicious slap in the face.

A woman screamed, but the men ignored her.

One of them suddenly stopped, though, his masked head turned toward the railing at the top of the ramp.

"Cocksucker!" he said, the sibilants hissing through his teeth, and now the other men stopped, too, their heads turning as if pulled by a marionette master.

A uniformed police officer was standing at the top of the ramp.

The policeman—beak-nosed, in need of a hair-cut—was as bewildered by the scene before him as the masked men staring up at him. His hands, resting on the railing, made no move toward his gun. He was transfixed.

The men in the masks acted first. All three swiveled their weapons from their hips until the barrels, dull black in the sunshine, pointed at the officer as if in the hands of a firing squad.

A voice, only slightly muffled by the mask, shouted, "Freeze! Everybody stays where they are." The words cracked with tension. The policeman silently stared down. His hands remained in view, clenched along the railing.

The order was obeyed by few of the children. Intent on their games, some youngsters ignored the intruders and the officer above. Some stared curiously at these strange adults who seemed to be acting out some weird game, but, even so, continued riding their tricycles, throwing their balls. A two-year-old walked on uncertain legs toward the gunmen.

But the mothers, the nannies, stared in horror at

the guns. It had all happened so fast. Now, as if a spell had been broken, some shrieked in terror. Some shrank back, their hands going to their throats. A woman in a blue smock screamed, "No! No!" and the words dragged out into an incessant wail.

Charlotte Webster had been wiping the nose of one of the twins when the men emerged from the door and, at first, didn't realize anything was amiss. She looked up as Melissa said, "My God, what's going on?"

Charlotte pulled Ian to her breast and looked desperately for Bobby. He was playing on the bricks with Melissa's David, no more than two yards from the gunmen. In that moment, except for the gradually slowing movement of the children, the scene in the park was frozen as if printed on film: the three men in the middle of the playground by the sandpit, the motionless officer above, the staring, terrified women. One of the men shattered the brittle moment.

"The kids!" he yelled. "Take the kids! That one . . . the blond kid in the gray pants." Instantly, one of the invaders lowered his weapon, turned, and in two strides seized a child holding a yellow plastic baseball bat. As the tot was scooped up, he gurgled with laughter, seeing fun where everybody else saw calamity.

Above the ramp, the officer began to inch backward out of sight of the gunmen. His fingers no longer touched the railing.

"Hold it! Hold it, up there!" shouted the masked

leader. He swung up his weapon and put the barrel to the blond head of the child in his partner's grasp.

"You move out of my sight, shithead," he rasped, "and this kid gets it. I swear I'll do it."

The cop halted as if his back was against a wall. "Fuck you," he shouted. But he didn't move. A dark flush of anger at his helplessness suffused his swarthy features, but he didn't move. The child began to cry.

"And that one!" It was as if the gunmen believed their vulnerability lessened in proportion to the number of child hostages.

Charlotte stood up screaming. "Bobby! Come here. Come to Mommy." With a puzzled expression, the boy half-turned and then he was swept off his feet by one of the men and carried off.

Charlotte began to run, moaning, whimpering, stumbling in shoes that suddenly were too loose. She was halfway around the railing of the sandpit when the chattering thunder broke out. Squadrons of pigeons whirred into the air in outraged flight. At the same moment, something smashed against Charlotte's right shoulder and spun her around. She went off her feet as if lifted by a giant hand before toppling in a jarring sprawl. Even as she lay there, the firing continued and she waited fatalistically for the second blow that would kill her, end it all.

The stunned quiet, when it finally came, was immediately broken by an uproar of screams and shouts and wails. Panic commanded. Women ran to children, plucked them from the ground, held them.

Some turned their backs on the men, now retreating, as if to hide their charges from the wickedness that had ravaged the park.

One of the gunmen was shouting again, but his words meant nothing to Charlotte. She felt no pain. She felt nothing, as if her mind and body had become numb. She sensed somebody near, somebody bending over her, crying.

"Are you all right, darling?" Melissa said. She was clutching her own little boy. "Damn, damn, what a stupid question. It's mad. The world's gone mad. I knew it would happen." Ian, stricken, was standing looking down at his mother.

"Bobby, my Bobby," Charlotte moaned as the desolation of loss flooded through her.

The policeman was moving now, his hand going for his gun as if Charlotte's doomed attempt to run had released him from his prison of frustration. Melissa twisted and looked toward the door. Two of the men and the children they had seized had already vanished into the darkness beyond the door. The third man, though, had not finished.

At the entrance, he turned and thrust his weapon forward at waist level. Again the hammering of shots. To Melissa, crouching with the children over Charlotte, it was like a hurricane. She thought she could feel the raging wind set swirling by the passage of the bullets.

When he was done, the gunman let his weapon fall to his side like a workman at the end of a task. He retreated after his companions.

"Anybody who comes in here gets killed," he yelled from the shadows. "Any, douche bag, you hear me?"

The policeman, unable to use his weapon against the gunman because of the angle of the open door, because of the women and children, was still pounding down the last stretch of the ramp. Suddenly, Melissa was enraged. She set David down. Spitting obscenities, she started toward the door. A woman put out an arm to stop her, but Melissa brushed her away and went at a run into the darkness behind the door. The men had gone. The children had gone. She thought she heard hurried steps, but then there was nothing except the thunder of the traffic on the drive below.

Weeping now, she went stumbling down the steps. Through her tears, she was muttering, "Bastards, oh, those bastards!" Halfway down she almost fell, but she recovered and moved down toward the half-light below. When she reached the bottom step, she stopped and stared blankly ahead. There was nothing but cars and taxis rushing past in a continuous blur, all racing downtown on their various errands.

5◄

"There's been a snatch on Sutton Place," vanAllen said.

"A kidnap? Who's been taken?"

"Kids. At least two, maybe more. Rich kids."

"You're conning me." Paige could see an escape hatch from Long Island opening up.

"There are more cops and brass on the street than the pope gets. The commissioner, chief of operations, the mayor's on his way. That control freak wouldn't miss this."

"Where? Where did it happen?"

"A park. There's a park, a little rinky dinky park at the east end of Fifty-seventh Street where it hits the river. They took 'em from the park. I have to go."

"Has anything gone out on it yet?"

"They're trying to keep it under wraps. You know how long that will last."

"Where will I see you?"

"Christ, I don't know. Oh, hell, if I'm not at the

park, be at the Mayfair at two. No, make it one." She hung up.

Paige put down the phone, stared at the ocean. Lady Jane wandered in from her sunbath. Her smooth and ample bottom and stomach were also tanned. Paige reckoned she was about fifteen pounds overweight, but the excess was in the right places. "I'll get ready," she said.

"For what?"

"For lunchipoo, you forgetful little dreamer, you."

Paige was already dialing the office. LaFleche wouldn't want him back in town. The city editor would order him to give what he had to rewrite. He asked for Savage. LaFleche would be scalding mad but, fuck it. What more could LaFleche do? make him Montauk correspondent?

"Savage. Who is it?" The managing editor's voice was distracted and the line was lousy.

"Paige. Todd Paige. Your man in Suffolk County."

"Suffolk? What are you doing in Suffolk?"

"Transferred. For the good of my health. The air's better out here."

"I wondered why we weren't getting any of your entirely unattributed stories, gang warfare, bodies in trunks, cops on the take. Funny, I miss them."

"Nobody else does."

"LaFleche?"

"That's not what I'm calling about. I'm on to something that will pin your ears back."

"They've gone to the mattresses on Mott Street."

"A kidnap. A big one."

Savage's voice hardened. "In the city?"

"Midtown somewhere. Big money, and a professional job. Kids involved."

"Who? Where?"

"I only have a whisper so far. My contacts are on it."

"Don't bullshit me, Paige. You got more than that."

"I swear . . . I need more time. I have to be on the scene."

"How long will it take you to get in?"

"An hour if I push it."

"Get on it. I'll square it with LaFleche. Better talk to him when you call in, though. Then switch over to me." As Paige put down the phone, Lady Jane came out of the bedroom. She wore white duck pants, a silky white shirt, and she carried a white cardigan.

"Ready, fatty?" she said.

"Sorry. They want me in the city. I'm a star again."

"Bastard," she said. She pronounced it "barstard." She was calm as if she had known it would happen. "I was going to expose you to Mary at lunch, Mary the man-eater. She was a tramp. Then her father died and now she's a rich tramp. What's so urgent?"

"Big story only I can handle. Sorry."

She sighed. "All right. I was getting bored with the beach anyway. I'll take you in."

"I was hoping you'd pick up my car, look after it for me."

"That's going too far. Come on." She dealt with

the dirty frying pan and spatula by arching an eyebrow at them and dumping them in the garbage pail.

As they drove around Brookhaven airport, she said, "I was reading an obituary the other day in that big paper, the one that tries to be frightfully genteel and uses words like paradigm, whatever that is. Said the chap died of lung cancer and made a big point about him being a heavy smoker." Paige was counting the traffic tickets he had found in the glove locker. There were nearly sixty of them.

"My question is: if somebody dies of lung cancer and has never once smoked, do they mention that? Seems only fair."

Paige shrugged. "What time is it?" he said. She pointed to the dashboard clock and said, "Where's your watch?"

"Lost it at poker." Along with a month's pay, he thought, while wondering if Clancy had discovered the Rolex was a fake.

"You don't have any money?" She made it sound like a rare disease. He was trying the all-news radio stations, but they were leading with a bombing in Chicago. As Lady Jane's black Mercedes convertible moved into the fast lane of the expressway, Paige wondered if he could keep ahead of the pack. Christ, if he hadn't been out in the sticks, with a jump like this he would have cleaned up. At least, Lady Jane seemed to have gotten into the spirit of it. She used her horn to clear a path and the speed never dropped below eighty.

Paige crossed the frontier into fantasyland. He

saw himself lolling in the back of his Rolls, chatting with his uniformed, blond chauffeuse who, naturally, adored him. There was a bar, telephone, and TV, of course. The impact of his luxurious arrival on sleazy crime scenes around the city would be considerable. Witnesses and cops would rush to talk to him, give him stuff none of the other jackals had. He could interview them in the backseat, give them a drink if they were worth it. He'd become famous around the city, a celebrity. There would be features about him on TV, network even. He tried to decide whether the chauffeuse should be honey blond or ash blond. Ash, he thought, with her hair cut short so that it would fit neatly under her shiny black cap. The poor girl would fall in love with him, of course, willingly accepting the outrageous hours.

"Hey, Gargantua," Lady Jane said at the Triborough toll, "where d'you want to be dropped?" He told her and she ordered him to write down her Manhattan phone number. "You call me tonight," she said. "We have unfinished business."

They left the FDR Drive at Sixty-third Street, and approached Sutton Place from the north. When she stopped, Paige remained in his seat, patted his pockets, and said, "I wonder if you could help me out . . ." She was staring at him with those unblinking eyes.

"You want some money."

"Well, just a temporary loan until I pick up my expenses." She reached to the backseat for her purse, poked around in it, and thrust some bills at him.

"You'd better be worth it," she said with a hint of
menace. After she had driven off, he stood on the
sidewalk and counted the three $100 bills she had
given him. Perhaps he should have asked for more.
Moving off, he immediately forgot her. The cul de
sac leading to the ramp and the park was closed off
by police barriers. Hell, a team of gorillas from one
of the TV stations was crossing the road, heading for
them. In a minute, they'd be shouting at the cops and
demanding entry with frequent references to the freedom of the press to screw everything up. Another
crew was unloading its cameras from a station
wagon, and he could see Hayden from the *News*
walking across the street, careless of braking cars, as
he headed for the barriers.

No sign of vanAllen. Down Sutton Place, men
in plain clothes with badges clipped to their suits
were talking to doormen. Paige peered at the buildings towering over the park. To the north, he knew,
stood the secretary-general's townhouse. No good.
To the south was a tall apartment building. A photographer, Kaiser, from the rag, was arguing with
the doorman while trying to stuff money into his
hand. No good. There was a flurry of activity at the
barrier. A mobile command post was maneuvering
through the barriers while a TV team tried to slip in
alongside. They were ejected.

He had lost the advantage of the goddamned
tip. Now he was just a member of the snarling press
pack. He saw a woman approaching along Fifty-
seventh Street, leading a toddler by the hand. At

first she didn't notice the chaotic scene, but then she stopped and stared.

"What's going on?" she said.

"Some kids were kidnapped."

"Oh, my God. Not from the park?"

"That's the word."

The woman, smartly dressed in blue seersucker, talked as if her jaw had been broken and wired back into place. She brought the child closer to her side. "I could have been there," she said. "I would have been, only I went to Bergdorf. Oh, my God."

"You take your little boy to the park?" Paige essayed a benevolent smile at the child.

"Sometimes. She's a girl. Jennifer. Can't you see she's a girl? I always thought it was so safe."

"Safe? What makes it so safe?"

"Well, there's only the ramp to get in and out. If you watch the ramp, they can't run out into the traffic." The child was growing impatient, trying to pull her mother toward the park and the fun that should be waiting there.

"No, Jennifer," the woman said. "We're going home. I shall never go there again. Who did they kidnap?"

"You're sure the ramp is the only way in and out?"

"Except for the door in the wall. That's always locked."

"Where does that come out?"

"Come out? Oh, on the drive, I believe. I've never been in, but they say there are steps leading down to the drive. Are you a detective?" She was looking disapprovingly at Paige's rumpled clothing and scuffed shoes.

An ambulance came through the barrier and turned down Sutton Place. Its roof light was on and turning but there was no siren. Paige went looking for a cab. The city was drenched in steamy heat and he was sweating heavily by the time he had walked to First Avenue to find a taxi. It was driven by a man in a black turban who wanted to talk about the Yankees. While he ranted on about Steinbrenner in a peculiar accent, they went uptown and turned on to the FDR Drive, going south.

When they reached the tunnel under the park, Paige saw there was a jam-up. Horns were blaring and cars were trying to filter from the inside lane to the left. Paige told the cabby to pull up behind a police car whose revolving light was throwing an eerie glow into the dimness. A uniformed man stood guard at a hole in the wall. Paige paid off the cabby and approached him.

"Hold it," the cop said. Paige kept moving toward the hole.

"Commissioner's office," he said. The cop hesitated and then Paige was inside. Above him, he could hear footsteps ascending toward a thin blade of light that must be the top of the stairs. He counted twenty steps before, panting, he reached the top. A woman was standing in the doorway, looking out at the park.

"This is the way they came, took them down to the drive?" Paige said.

"I told you I'd see you at one," vanAllen said without turning around. "In the Mayfair."

"They had a car waiting for them," Paige said to her back, "then off they go. Neat."

"A car or a van," vanAllen said. "Two kids. Easy. Down the steps with them. Probably used a van or a station wagon. Must have faked a breakdown."

"You've got a new hairdo, shorter. Very nice."

"You'll have a new face if you don't get out of here. The Mayfair at one."

Over her shoulder, Paige could see into the park. A fingerprint team was working on the other side of the half-open door. Beyond them, detectives were looking upward, pointing. Paige caught a glimpse of two homicide detectives from Midtown South.

"What are Abbott and Costello doing here?" he said, retreating down a step as the fingerprint men turned their attention to the interior of the door. "I thought you said it was a kidnap."

"There was some shooting and an old guy on one of the benches turned belly up. Caught a stray shot or a ricochet when one of the mothers flipped and tried to rescue her kid. She took a flesh wound in her right arm."

"Anybody see it? From the apartments? Where you got all the people who were in the park?"

"You stay here any longer, Paige, I'll lock you up for impeding a police investigation."

"Gollywhoopers, I'm just trying to satisfy the people's right to know. Anybody spot the car, whatever it was, on the drive?"

"Nothing so far. You want me in front of the commissioner? Get out of here."

She'd be at the Mayfair because, like all cops, she wanted ink. She wanted the public to know what a great job she was doing. It didn't hurt if the bosses knew it, too.

The sound of footsteps echoed up the steps. Paige turned and went down, muttering an apology as he brushed past two plain-clothed men coming up with flashlights.

The uniform watched him come out at the bottom with an uncertain glare. Before starting to trudge north on the narrow sidewalk, Paige told him, "Watch out for reporters, officer. Don't let any of those pricks up those stairs. Orders from the commissioner."

In a while, the tunnel would be choked with cars carrying press plates, and reporters and photographers and TV orangutans would be shouting and swearing as they besieged the steps. If the task force in the park didn't put more cops at the bottom of the steps, the lone guardian would be swept away like a piece of blue debris. This was the headline of the month, maybe of the year. Before the pack was finished, they'd have traffic backed up to the George Washington Bridge.

6◄

At the Mayfair, Paige found a corner booth out of sight of most of the restaurant and ordered a Scotch. The place was filling up fast with the noisy lunchtime crowd. The hell with Suffolk County and the beach and the fresh air and demanding women who pinched his cock. Even the booze tasted better in Manhattan.

VanAllen came in, got a soda water from the bar and slid into the booth. "Lucky me," she said. "I get to see you twice in half an hour."

She had intelligent but tired eyes, and faint lines were forming between her nostrils and full lips, lines that had more to do with strain than with laughter. When she smiled it came out as a lopsided grin. Paige reckoned she needed a week marinating on a beach where the only issue was whether to slap on some more sunblock. He wouldn't mind seeing her in a bikini. She always dressed in dark blue or black suits that concealed the subtleties beneath. She was long out of uniform, but she had created her own. Now she was in a blue pants suit with a lighter blue blouse decorated by a bow. She wore flat-heeled shoes. Paige wondered where she kept her gun.

Given her success in the department, inevitably there were many rumors about vanAllen's sex life that usually revolved around her seducing superior officers. Paige had tried to date her a few times, but she always put him off, gracefully enough but nonetheless quite firmly. Each time, he felt as though she had patted him on the head like a little boy who wanted too much candy. He reckoned she must be asexual.

After each rebuff, Paige told himself that he wasn't at all sure he wanted to bed an armed woman anyway. Suppose she had a little ankle-holstered weapon and didn't take it off and he didn't live up to her expectations?

VanAllen had spent more than a year undercover with the narcotics bureau, making buys in some of the most lethal areas of the city. She had been shot once and, more than once, been slapped around by cops when she was in a situation where she couldn't identify herself.

She had taken prizes for marksmanship, handgun and rifle, creating some resentment among her male competitors who said it was a man's game. A few months earlier, vanAllen had come second in the all-state thousand-yard tournament and was determined to take first prize at the next meeting. See how the good ol' boys liked that.

After getting her gold badge, she had set up a

network of women informants that she called "my snitch-chicks." She was tough and she was ambitious. She had already taken the captain's exam.

The department wasn't quite sure what to do with vanAllen after her undercover tour, a long spell with homicide followed by major crimes and then liaising with the FBI. The department was still run by hard-nosed Irish and Italian chiefs who wouldn't say it out loud but nonetheless believed that if women insisted on joining the NYPD their role was dealing with rapes, lost children, and shoplifting. They believed that vanAllen would have trouble commanding a squad of male detectives, so she had been switched to the Organized Crime Control Bureau in an ill-defined role that let her roam the city.

Paige had written up her exploits a few times, made her Superwoman, and there was always a collection time for that sort of literary endeavor. He pushed a piece of paper across the table.

"Draw me the park," he said.

With a silver pencil, vanAllen sketched a rough square. "Here," she said, "on the west side, is the ramp, actually a double ramp, first running north and then turning south down into the park. And over here is the door where you were making a nuisance of yourself."

"Okay, what happened?" In spite of her inexplicable lack of romantic interest in him, he enjoyed looking at her, listening to her. He liked her crooked grin and her low, smoky voice.

"The door is supposed to be padlocked, but they

got it open early before anybody came to the park.
One of the precinct officers, a flatfoot named Faso,
spotted the open door and reported it. But by the time
they had started filling in forms in triplicate to get
something done about it, our chums came up the
steps."

"How many?"

"Three, as far as we can tell right now. Probably
left another man down on the drive with the vehicle.
They took a chance. They could have come down
with the kids and found a prowl car and a helpful
officer trying to get their car started."

"They have one-man patrol cars on the drive.
Not bad odds: four-to-one."

"Yes, well, anyway, they charge into the park
around ten A.M., and all hell breaks loose. They're
armed and they're wearing ski masks.

"No fix on the weapons yet. We're still picking
up lead. Just after they come into the park, this cop,
Faso . . . Joseph Faso . . . shows up with orders to
keep an eye on the door until the parks people can
lock it. He sees the whole thing."

"And lets them get away with the kids? The
commissioner is gonna love that."

"There was a problem, smartass. Faso couldn't
do a thing because of a difficult situation, like guns at
the heads of the kids and a million squawking women.
The bad guys snatch two kids. This woman . . . wait a
minute . . . Charlotte Webster, twenty-eight, mother of
two, Second Avenue, she tries to stop them." Van-
Allen spoke as if reading from a notebook. "They

have her in Bellevue; condition, stable. She'll be okay. It's all over in seconds. They take the kids, haul them down the stairs into the waiting car, van, whatever. They split downtown."

"Whose ticket was punched?"

"A guy named Campbell, retired physician. He's sitting in the park, minding his own business, when the whole thing blows up. Bingo, five of the shots they were tossing around when Charlotte Webster does her thing hit him. It's odd. There were two other people next to him on the bench. Not a scratch on them, just Campbell."

"First name?"

"Duncan. They're doing the autopsy now. He lived alone in an apartment on Fifty-ninth Street, just around the corner from the park. Probably sitting there worrying about his arthritis and whammo."

"Okay, who was snatched?" Paige was getting it down in a scruffy notebook in his eccentric short-hand.

"First, the Webster kid, Bobby, aged three. His twin brother's Ian, also in the park, but they leave him."

"Beautiful. Twins and they've got one of them. Who else?"

"Thor Cardiff, aged two."

"Thor? What sort of a name is that?"

"These people aren't like us, Paige, and they show it with names like that. With their money, they don't care what the peasants think."

"Loaded?" Paige wanted another drink, but that

might interrupt the flow of facts. Without his under-wear, his buttocks were glued to his pants and he shifted uncomfortably.

"The father is Thomas J. Cardiff III, lives on Sutton Place. Close to a billionaire. Steel mills, coal mines out west, he owns a large chunk of General Motors. He's one of those guys who keep their names out of the papers but he's right out of Monopoly, always passing Go."

"Never heard of him. How about the Webster chick?"

"That's where it gets a bit weird. Her husband's name is Charles and he's an architect, but he's rabble like you and me. They've got four rooms over a hardware store."

"They snatched the wrong kid."

"Could be. It was a shambles in that park."

"Who was with Master Thor when they grabbed him?"

"An English nanny, Julie Brompton. We're checking her out. She's been in the States about a year."

"Any ransom demand yet?"

"Nothing. We've got taps on all the phones. Don't use that, though."

"Forgive my hilarity," Paige said. "You think the villains won't assume the phones are bugged? Who's running this extravaganza?"

"The Pill. Pillsbury." Pillsbury was the assistant chief of detectives. VanAllen had no time for him, claimed he was stupid and a publicity hound, which, taking her present companion and activity into account, was odd. The chief, Clarence Davis, rumored to be a mentor to vanAllen, was supposed to be ill, preparing to go in for an operation.

"What do your snitches say about it?"

"Nothing yet. By the way," vanAllen said, "who's your boss these days? Still Jake Savage? What's he like?"

"He's okay, I suppose, for a managing editor. Doesn't bullshit, plays it straight. Why?"

"I'd like to meet him sometime." Before Paige could pursue it, vanAllen finished her soda water and eased out of the booth.

"Don't use my name," she said. "Not yet, anyway. Not until I lock up the perps."

"You catch them, they'll throw the commissioner out and slap you into his chair. Where do I find you tonight?"

"I'll try and call you at your office. Got to go."

"What about the nanny? Where do I find her . . . ?" VanAllen had gone. Paige wondered why she wanted to meet Savage. She was Paige's connection and he didn't want anybody else from the paper horning in. He shrugged, bought another drink with one of Lady Jane's $100 bills, and got a fistful of change. Then he went to work on the pay phone at the end of the bar.

Ejected from New York, he had vacated his Manhattan apartment and now he needed somewhere to stay. He called an unemployed actress he'd met at the Museum of Modern Art a month earlier.

There was no reply, not even an answering machine. An unemployed actress without an answering machine was against nature. Maybe she'd finally found work.

He called LaFleche. LaFleche was livid.

"Who the hell d'you think you are?" he demanded as soon as he heard Paige's voice. "Just who the fuck d'you think you are, creeping back into town like this? You slithering, sneaking snake. You're an inch away from being fired."

"Jeepers," Paige said, "there's so much noise here I can't hear a word you're saying. Is that LaFleche? LaFleche the city editor?"

"You know damn well it's me," LaFleche said. "You're up to your old tricks, Paige, but they're worn out. I've got your number. Now get your ass into the office."

"It's no good. I can't hear a thing from your end. These goddamned lunchtime drinkers. They don't know how to talk in a quiet, civilized fashion. Maybe I should go straight over to Savage. He wanted to talk to me. I've got some good stuff on the Sutton Place kidnap."

"Listen good, Paige. I shall remember this. You won't always have Savage's ass to kiss. And when he's gone, you're mine."

"What's that you say?"

"Okay, Paige. I'm gonna switch you to rewrite. Unload it and then get in here." Paige could hear LaFleche shouting across to the editorial switchboard and then Liberty came on the line.

"What you got?" he said through a mouthful of food. Paige began a rundown of the facts he had gathered. Liberty kept saying, "Yeah, we got that." It was part of his act. You could never tell him anything; he already knew it. But he had to ask for the spelling of the victim's names.

"How come," Paige said, "that you need me to spell it out for you if you already have it?"

"Gotta freakin' check it, man. Always check it."

"How about the door, then?"

"The door? Oh, sure, got that from one of my contacts. Still, better give it to me, make sure."

"One of your contacts? You haven't been on the street for twenty years."

"Gimme the stuff about the door and I'll make sure you get a byline. LaFleche owes me."

"The door's on the south side of the park and it leads down to the FDR Drive. Some sort of escape or exit if there's a problem in the tunnel."

"I had that. How many steps?"

"Twenty."

"Not thirty-nine?"

"Twenty."

"Thirty-nine would have been better. Like the old movie. Who was it . . . Robert Donat? Better go back and count 'em again."

"Correction," Paige said. "The door's on the north side. Funny your contacts made the same mistake I did."

"North side, right. That's what I had."

Paige sighed and passed on the rest of the story.

When he had unloaded it all, he said, "Switch me over to Savage."

"Savage? What d'you want with Savage?"

"Ask your contacts. They're sure to know."

After talking to Savage, Paige called the unemployed actress again, but there was still no reply.

7 ◀

The noon editorial conference—the twelve o'clock follies—was held in Savage's office. Clutching their news schedules, the editors leaned against walls or sat on couches and chairs, preparing to describe the stories of the day and how they would cover them. In the Skipper's time, Savage thought, there had been fresh ideas and jokes and arguments and hard swearing, and the Skipper had orchestrated it all like a genial Tartar. But, then, it was his paper. He founded it and he ran it. Once, the city editor of that time and the features editor had swapped punches over the handling of an investigative piece and the Skipper had enjoyed every minute of it. No more. The Skipper was two years in his grave.

Now the editors took themselves so damned seriously and the conference was as bland as a lawyer's smile, and, too often, the result was a boring paper. It was partly his fault, letting Shannon set the tone. Savage had been with the paper for nearly fifteen years, and now ran the day-to-day operation, but sometimes he felt like an outsider. He glanced at the city desk schedule. The Sutton Place kidnapping for the splash. Two jumpers within three hours from the same high-rise on Madison. A political scandal in Brooklyn. Mob violence at JFK.

That goddamned Paige. With his hair all over the place, he was like a shambling, unkempt sheepdog, but he was a terrier of a reporter, wasted on Long Island. LaFleche kept staring reproachfully at him for letting Paige come back into the city. Everybody else was in shirtsleeves, but LaFleche always wore his jacket in the office as if to demonstrate that he was ready at a moment's notice to move into an executive suite.

"Trouble in the Mideast," the foreign editor, Bryant, said. "The Israelis and the Syrians. I don't like the look of—" He stopped as Shannon slipped into the office.

"Don't let me interrupt," the editor said. "Go right ahead. I'll just listen and learn."

Bryant's voice grew more portentous as he skipped around from Jerusalem to London to Paris and South Africa. When he had finished, he looked up at Shannon as if for approval. Shannon smiled at him.

"Perhaps I will interrupt after all," he said. "I bring good news." He walked forward until he was in the middle of the office so that now he was in the center of the gathering, in command. He was tall, broad-shouldered, graying. He wore his suits with flair. He could pose, Savage thought, for an idealized portrait of the Corporate Editor. Responsible. Concerned.

Skilled at his profession. He dined with the governor, the mayor, and the city's powerful. He lived not in the city but in suburban Connecticut. Savage didn't underestimate the man. Shannon could be a charmer. His voice was low, melodious, and he used it like a musical instrument to seduce, lull, excite. He could tell stories of defeats and of victories like a twentieth-century Scheherazade. He could offer visions of glory.

"First," he said, "I'm happy to tell you all that the Fallon Foundation has agreed to cosponsor with the paper a weekend seminar on 'The Media and The Government.'" There was a murmur of appreciation. "Great," somebody said. It sounded to Savage like LaFleche.

"We'll start with a dinner on the Friday night," Shannon went on. "We'll have panel discussions led by specially selected speakers on Saturday and Sunday mornings. And the governor has agreed to address us Sunday afternoon. The thrust of the seminar will be cooperation between newspapers and the government for the public good. Interface." Again the rustle of approval.

"We should try to make it an annual event," Savage said. Scenting irony, Shannon shot him a look.

"Yeah, expand it over time, perhaps," LaFleche said. "The Media and Medicine. The Media and Industry."

"How about the Media and the Mob?" It was Sue Chandler, the veteran copydesk chief. In her severely old-fashioned blouse and calf-length skirt, she was sitting on a window ledge holding a Styrofoam cup of coffee. "Maybe we could get the bosses of the five families to speak, tell us what's the favorite means of disposal these days." She looked poker-faced at Savage and he winked at her.

"Yeah," he said. "Get them to give us their views on federal prosecutors and the RICO statute, the latest word on Gotti. Is he spending his hard time earning a high school diploma?"

"That's ridiculous," Bryant said. "It would be like the paper giving them our stamp of approval." Shannon went on as if he hadn't heard the exchange.

"This could become an important event," he said. "Publicity, TV coverage, that sort of thing. All good for the paper."

"Where will it be and when?"

"The St. Regis, first weekend in September. Any of you living out of town will be put up there for two nights."

"How much will it cost?" Savage said.

"That hasn't been computed yet. But I know it'll be worth every cent."

"The news budget wouldn't let us send a reporter down to Miami on the Cuban refugee story last week," Savage said. "We couldn't afford to cover the Bickford trial in Denver." Even as he spoke, Savage knew it was useless. Money was always available for this sort of bullshit, not for gathering news.

"This is an entirely different situation," Shannon said smoothly. "The potential of this is tremendous. It's not just a story."

"Just a story. I thought we were in business to get stories."

Shannon ignored the thrust, turned from him, and Savage shrugged. The Skipper would have . . . Hell, the Skipper's time was gone. The Skipper had lived on Grammercy Square, not in Connecticut. He went to the fights, to saloons, to ballgames, and he stayed away from the powerbrokers, mostly, he said, because he didn't much like them. Anyway, he used to say, it was a newspaperman's job to stay away from them.

He had loved the movies. Sometimes he dropped into saloons to hoist one with ordinary New Yorkers, his readers, and so he knew what was on their minds. He had liked his drink, the Skipper. There was a story that on his way into the office every morning, the Skipper always stopped at a saloon where they had two shots of bourbon awaiting him on the bar and, barely breaking step, he drank them and, thus fortified, walked into the office ready to conquer.

He probably had drunk too much if the truth were known, but by God, he had enjoyed himself. And he had been human.

Savage looked across at Sue Chandler. Her hair was touched with gray and she was stoop-shouldered from decades crouched over a desk. Sometimes they went across the street for a drink and talked about the Skipper and his times. Savage had heard rumors that she had a long-running affair with the Skipper. Maybe Sue Chandler and he were both out of touch. Still, a familiar anger rose in him. They kept changing things and they were so sure they were right, but as the paper changed, people stopped buying it. Perhaps the people hadn't changed, weren't keeping up with Shannon's expectations of them.

Shannon said, "Okay, I'll let you guys get on with the important thing, getting out a superb paper. Savage's right on that. It's our most important task. But that doesn't mean we can't support those efforts with adventurous, even daring, thrusts into the future."

Moving gracefully to the door, he said, "I'll get out of your way, then." Before he left, he turned and looked at Savage. "Let's have a chat later," he said.

Savage nodded. He was thinking again about Paige and what to do with him. Paige was a drinker, a womanizer, liked poker and good times too much. What did he think he'd been placed on earth for, to enjoy himself?

8 ◄

The townhouse was on the south side of Fifty-ninth Street, in the middle of the block between First Avenue and Sutton Place. Dr. Duncan Campbell, now neatly filed away in a refrigerated cabinet in the morgue, had lived on the third floor of the converted brownstone. Paige, sweating heavily, pressed the button below his name. He then pressed the five other buttons ranged beside the front door.

A buzzer sounded. Paige opened the door and stepped inside. It was almost as hot in the small hallway as on the street where the temperature had gone over the ninety-degree mark. Up the flight of stairs ahead of him, a door opened and a woman said, "Who is it?" The voice was old and tremulous.

Before Paige could reply, the head and shoulders of a man appeared at the top of the stairs leading down to the basement. His dark hair was artfully styled into a casual tousle, a sprinkling of gray at the temples. His handsome face was defined by a thrusting jaw and high cheekbones.

"Have you come to beg for my autograph, or is it the mad doctor who brings you here?" he said. "Go back inside, madam, and close the door before a bestial rapist grabs you and has his way with you." This last was addressed to the woman upstairs. Paige heard a mutter of outrage and the sound of a slammed door.

"It's the doctor," Paige said. The man looking up at him sighed. He was almost as tall as Paige, but his close-fitting sports shirt and faded blue jeans showed a more sculpted figure, muscular and narrow-hipped. His feet were bare.

"Come on down and pursue your inquiries," he said. "You're not a police officer, I take it. They've been here already. So has the *Times*. A very belligerent young woman, hardly what one would expect."

"I'm a nonbelligerent," Paige said, showing his press card, "just looking for a couple of facts. You own the building?"

"The deed is in my name," the man said as Paige advanced down the stairs, "which is Chuckie Romping. But the deed means nothing. This is New York, and that means the tenants own the place. I am merely their servant, their lackey, dealing with their garbage, their incessant complaints, and if I'm very, very good, they deign to pay me a miserly amount of rent, usually about two months late. Come in."

Paige followed his host down a corridor lined with glossy photographs of actors into a living room with large windows giving on to shrubs and rose bushes in a patch of garden. A little brown dog lying

on a couch looked briefly at Paige, gave a perfunc-
tory bark, then ignored him. In a corner, a TV set was
on, tuned to an afternoon soap opera. The room
reeked of marijuana and Paige saw that Romford
held a brown cigarette between his fingers. But an air
conditioner was going at full blast and, after the
street, the room felt blessedly cool.

Paige settled into a canvas director's chair with
DONALD DUCK inscribed on the back and stared at one
of the characters in the drama unfolding on the TV
screen, then at his host.

"Yes, that's me," Romping said, sucking at his
joint. "I like to watch myself and study how the pro-
ducers are sabotaging my best work. I play Ham-
mond. I'm screwing my best friend's wife and my
best friend's screwing my sister. And that, of course,
is not everything that's going on. You want a hit? A
drink?"

"Better not."

"A dedicated young man." Romping took a seat
on the couch and, keeping his eyes on the screen,
tickled his dog's ears.

"I'm interested right now in your tenant, Duncan
Campbell. Did you know him well?"

"As well as I wanted to, thank you very much.
Nasty old geezer."

"Nasty?"

"He was a tenant," Romping said as if that were
explanation enough. "Still, he's gone, which is a
plus."

"He was a physician, right?"

"So he said, so he said."

"Did he practice in New York?"

"New York state, according to him. Somewhere up in the Adirondacks toward the Canadian border." Romping waved dismissively as if anywhere outside New York City was of no consequence. "Then he retired and came here to live with his son up on the third floor. That must have been a year or more ago."

"His son's on the third floor? I thought Campbell lived alone."

"So he did. The son moved out; probably had enough of the old man, if you ask me. He went to Illinois or Chicago or somewhere like that, and left me with the dear doctor."

"You called him the mad doctor. Was he crazy?"

"Probably. Most people in New York are, aren't they? But that wasn't it. He told me once that he had treated psychiatric patients, the demented, that sort. He'd spent years with the nuts. You call a physician who cares for feet a foot doctor. So I call a physician who cares for the mad a mad doctor. Logical, yes?" The fumes were starting to get to Paige. Still, for some reason, Savage wanted the story, so he pressed on.

"What was he doing in the park this morning?"

"Went there every day. He liked to sit there and watch the revolting children and their horrid moms. He'd go in the morning, come home for lunch, go back in the afternoon, in the summer anyway. Sometimes, he'd go in the winter, too. Probably nothing else to do."

"What was he like? Apart from being a tenant, I mean."

"I always thought he had a sinister aura. I'm very sensitive to that sort of thing. But he was just an old dodderer. The streets around here are full of them, people who haven't taken care of their bodies, never stepped inside a health club, and now wonder why they're falling apart in their seventies. Sure you don't want a puff? Very relaxing." Paige shook his head, wondering if the man had invited the visiting homicide dicks to share a joint.

"Did he ever say just where he'd worked before he retired—private practice, a hospital?" Without much hope, Paige was seeking something that might illuminate the senseless, random death of an old man in a park.

"Let me think. He did give me the name once. I think it was when he took over the lease from his son. A government hospital, he said. Can't remember the name right now although, for some reason, it brings to mind a duel."

"Did he have any friends, anybody who came to visit him?"

"If he did, I never saw them, not that I'd want to. Aren't you going to take notes? I thought reporters always took notes."

"I've got a good memory. How about the other tenants? Did he talk to them?"

"I shouldn't think so. They're a surly bunch. No joi de vivre, know what I mean?"

"He sounds like a hermit."

"New York is a city of hermits, all moldering away in their little high-rise caves. Quite barbaric."

"What about his son? D'you have an address for him?"

"You could try Chicago. His name was Alistair and he was some sort of doctor, like his pa. Alistair Campbell, too, too Scottish."

Paige was ready to give up. Campbell was a side issue, anyway, to the main kidnapping story.

"And you still can't remember the name of the hospital where he worked?"

"Sorry."

"You have a phone I can use?" Romping sighed at this further demand on his good nature, but said, "In the kitchen. Not long distance, I hope."

"Chicago. I'll pay you."

The Chicago operator said there were three physicians called Alistair Campbell in the city. Paige found his man at the second number, but the woman who took his call said Campbell was out shopping in readiness for a trip to New York.

"His father was killed," she said cheerfully. "He has to catch an early flight." Paige said he would try later.

He left $10 on the kitchen table and returned to the living room. In the chilled air, his creased, sweat-soaked suit had begun to dry out, but the fumes now swirling throughout the apartment were making him light-headed and he yearned for the frowsy air of the street.

The doorbell rang and Romping said, "Ah, that

must be one of my pupils. I give acting lessons to help support my pathetic lifestyle." He went to press a button by the door, then walked lithely toward the windows, where he pressed another button. Immediately water began to gush from a tiny fountain set in the crazy paving of the garden. Part of the decor for students, Paige thought, not for nosy reporters.

A moment later, a long-legged young woman in white shorts and a yellow T-shirt over meager breasts, her pelvis thrust forward, walked in. She looked to Paige like a fashion model dutifully obeying the decree that she should avoid food at any cost.

Romping drew her into an embrace and kissed her full on the mouth. "God, Jenny," he said, "I lust for you more every time I see you. Guess what, I've got some great Peruvian pure. I'll be right with you. This gentleman is leaving." Jenny had her arms around his neck and was kissing him with darting pecks. Romping's hands had slipped down her back to grip her buttocks, his fingertips sliding under her shorts.

"What about Campbell's apartment?" Paige said. "Can I see it?"

"Afraid not," Romping said over her shoulder. "A rude police officer took the keys and sealed it. Doubtless that means I'll lose even more rent."

As Paige left, Romping said, "I won't complain if you use my name in your little article. Hold on, I'll get you one of my publicity stills. Brighten up the crime page."

9 ◄

The unmarked, unremarkable, brown van with Connecticut plates was first spotted by two fifteen-year-olds, a boy and a girl, cycling on the cobbles beneath the West Side Highway. They were discussing a plan to run off together, maybe to California to meet film stars, in particular John Travolta because he was so cool, thus escaping the unreasonable discipline of their parents who ruled that they must be home by midnight on Saturdays. Their immediate problem was that their total resources amounted to $39.50.

Noticing that the rear of the van protruded four feet into the roadway, forcing southbound cars to swerve, they approached and saw that the sliding front doors were open. The front seats were empty. The radio, tuned to an all-news station, was on, but above the insistent voice of the newscaster, they could hear noises in the back. It sounded, they thought, like a child weeping. They tried to open the rear doors, but both were locked. They discussed climbing inside from the front seats but, instead, cycled to the boy's home on Jane Street in the Village, where they told his mother about the van and the noises coming from it.

At first, busy with her word processor, she took little notice, but then she remembered the commotion on the radio about the kidnapping at Sutton Place. She called the local precinct. By that time, two officers in a patrol car had come across the abandoned van. They climbed into the rear compartment via the front seats and, there, they found the children.

One was crying, but the other was contentedly gorging on Twix bars. Scattered around the interior, testifying to the feast, were dozens of candy wrappers. By then, the fingerprints of the two fifteen-year-olds, the children, and the officers were all over the van, but the fingerprint unit was called to the scene anyway.

Heralded by a blaring siren, the children, both now crying, were taken to St. Vincent's Hospital, where a preliminary examination indicated they had not been harmed, although the candy enthusiast was showing signs that he was preparing to vomit. He said his name was Bobby. The other child was too young to identify himself, but the Sixth Precinct cops, smug already, had no doubt who they were and happily anticipated triumphant appearances before the cameras for the evening news.

Assistant Chief of Detectives Burt Pillsbury, mentally preparing a statement for the press in which he would take a prominent role, arrived in the conference room at One Police Plaza with the commissioner and the mayor, both of whom had their own ideas about the role of leading man. They were in full agreement, however, on the need for a swift news conference before the FBI could try to muscle in.

The detective chief was introduced by the commissioner. In the course of his statement, Pillsbury said, "The kidnappers panicked, pure and simple. They suddenly realized, even as they fled, that they couldn't get away with it, not with thousands of alert officers hunting them, all responding to highly intelligent and dedicated leadership."

While he gave the details of the recovery of the children, the parents of the Cardiff boy, who had been waiting by their telephone at home for a ransom demand, arrived at St. Vincent's to claim their son in a tearful scene happily recorded by TV cameramen. Bobby Webster, pale from throwing up, was driven in a patrol car directly to New York Hospital, where his mother was recovering from the flesh wound in her upper right arm. The press was not allowed into the ward for the reunion, which caused some bad feeling and much abuse directed at the hospital's public relations director until he retired into his office and locked the door.

The van was swiftly traced to a Stamford antiques dealer, who, to avoid the cost of a parking garage, had left it overnight at the curb on Sixth Avenue while he settled in at the Hilton. When he emerged in the morning to start his buying expedition, he reported to the precinct, the van had disappeared.

A number of witnesses had come forward to describe a disabled brown van that had impeded traffic under the Sutton Place park at around 10 A.M. Two motorists claimed they had seen men carrying bundles into the van through the back door, but they could give no useful description of the men because they had been too distracted trying to filter into the moving lane. No, the men had not been wearing ski masks.

Ballistics had offered a preliminary summary of their findings. The bullets that had been sprayed around the park and into Charlotte Webster and the unfortunate bystander, Duncan Campbell, appeared to be 7.62 mm from one or more automatic rifles. Dusting of the park area and of the van had turned up no useful latent fingerprints.

The autopsy on Campbell disclosed that he had been killed by bullets in his throat and lungs. Also, bullets had penetrated his right thigh and stomach. Police were already in touch with his next of kin, a son living in Chicago.

In other circumstances, the sudden and violent death of Campbell might have received greater prominence, but against the background of the kidnapping and rescue, his death became merely a facet of the whole. Beyond that, the swift return of the children induced a feeling of disillusion in newsrooms around the city. What could have been a splendid running story, a circulation-builder for days, had turned into a one-day wonder.

The mayor, who was facing an election, said, "The important thing is the recovery of the children. Of course, we shall spare no effort to catch and prosecute the perpetrators and they will pay the penalty. But the safe return of the children to their agonized parents, that dwarfs everything else. Once again, the Finest, reorganized under my administration, have demonstrated their superb abilities in the continuing battle against crime."

Lieutenant Sarah vanAllen, however, had a number of questions about the episode. As a result, she viewed the whole matter a bit differently.

10 ◀

The first edition was rolling through the presses seven stories below and most of the dayside had gone, but Paige sidled into the newsroom and hovered at the back by the water fountain until he was sure that LaFleche had left.

The city editor's night relief, Purgavie, lanky and lugubrious, was staring into his terminal like a pessimistic fortune teller. At the copy desk, Sue Chandler was doing the *Times* crossword puzzle while two late-duty copyreaders were arguing languidly about Proust and Racine. The newsroom had the exhausted, scruffy look of a betting parlor at the end of the ninth race. Paige caught a glimpse of a front page proof on Purgavie's desk: BOYS RES-CUED—KIDNAP FAILS. There was a picture of Thor Cardiff in the arms of his weeping mother.

The paper's education correspondent, "He'll Pay" Bourke, was leaning over his terminal at the reporters' desks, complaining on the phone about his car. Paige had awarded him the nickname after noting Bourke's habit of pointing at somebody else while leaving a bar and saying, "He'll pay."

"The fucking springs are coming through the so-called leather," Bourke said. "It's like sitting on a wire brush." When he put down the phone, he headed past Paige toward the john. "May I help you, sir?" he said. "Unless they have business in the newsroom, visitors are not allowed."

"Up your academic ass," Paige said. Because of his education beat, and in spite of his wildly unconventional prose, Bourke strutted around as if he were an Ivy League professor.

"Tut, tut," Bourke said. "I suppose it's working in the potato fields of Long Island that encourages such earthy language."

Paige ignored him. He opened the paper bag he had brought in and took out a tired-looking cheeseburger and a can of beer.

"Hey, Paige." He looked around. It was the woman who ran the editorial switchboard at night. She seemed to suffer from a permanent cold and the floor around her was always littered with discarded tissues.

"Savage is looking for you," she said. "Wants to see you in his office. You look terrible."

When Paige walked into Savage's office, the managing editor looked up from the page proofs on his desk. "I gave you a byline," he said. "LaFleche was not pleased. You look terrible. Can't you get a decent suit, for God's sake?" Under the heat and sweat and pressure of the day's events, Paige's lightweight beige suit, a bargain at $70.50 from Goodwill Industries, had wilted like wet paper. He felt aggrieved. His suit had suffered for the sake of the paper.

"LaFleche doesn't want you," Savage said. "Says you have a personality problem. You're insolent and won't accept discipline, and apart from that, you say bad things about him that he can hear."

"It's because I won't buy drinks for him and his claque. One drink puts you on his right side. Two drinks gives you a good assignment. Three drinks, he loves you. Creepy bastard."

"Yes, well, wherever the truth lies, you have a personality clash which leaves me with a problem. What are we going to do with you? Send you back out to Suffolk County?"

"What about Rio? I have great contacts there."

"No, I think perhaps I'd better keep a close eye on you for a while, Paige. I'm going to detach you from the city desk and you'll work under my direction. That way, I'll be able to analyze your troubled personality. Perhaps I can save you from yourself."

"Suits me." By craning his neck, Paige could see a photograph of a boy on Savage's cluttered desk.

"Your kid?"

"Yes," Savage said shortly. "Okay, you can forget the kidnapping. It's pretty well wrapped up unless they catch the perps. In the meantime, I want you to pull a printout from the city desk file of a story slugged 'Ray.' It's about a little, old ex-convict. AP had a brief interview with him outside court, but most of it was chopped because of the kidnap splash. Interesting story."

It didn't sound interesting to Paige. "What about the women involved in the kidnap?" he said. "Find them and I've got a great story."

"LaFleche has other people on that. Right now, I want you to focus on the convict. I'm curious about a few things. Call it a preliminary test of your abilities. Of course, if you prefer, I can send you back to work for LaFleche."

"No need for that," Paige said hastily. "What d'you want, another interview?"

"An interview, some digging, the Paige touch. Find the old man, charm him, get his history, check it out, poke around. Then report back to me. Wrap it up by tomorrow night."

"What's it all about?"

"Pull up the story and you'll see. Get cracking."

Paige went back to the reporters' desks. He picked up the cold cheeseburger and saw that somebody had taken a big bite from it. He glared at Bourke's desk, but "He'll Pay" had gone. Paige tossed the hamburger remains into a trashcan, took a slug of beer, and dialed the Campbell number in Chicago.

Campbell was surly, said he had talked to the NYPD and Paige could get his information from them.

"You must be upset and I'm sorry to bother you at a time like this, but just a couple of questions," Paige said, putting on his charm. "He was a widower?"

"Right."

"How long had he been retired?"

"A bit more than a year. That's two questions."

"And he specialized in psychiatric patients?"

"Yes."

"Where did he practice?" There was a silence and Paige waited for the phone to be hung up on the other end.

"Upstate," Campbell said finally. "A place called Hamillton. Two l's. The hospital for the criminally insane. Now I've got to go. Please don't call again." This time the phone was hung up.

Complete waste of time. Two nuggets of information and neither of them worth offering to the copy desk at this time of night.

Paige called up the story Savage wanted him to chase, got a printout, then started on his expenses. Would they scream if he charged for a cab from the Hamptons? Fuck it, Savage had told him to drop everything and get in fast. Then he remembered, son of a bitch, he didn't have a bed for the night.

There was still no answer at the home of the unemployed actress. He hunted through his pockets until he found the number Lady Jane had given him. She was willing to give him shelter.

She lived in a small brownstone on East Sixty-third Street. Whether she had a title or not, she had money.

Lady Jane answered the door. She was in a loose-fitting ankle-length black robe and slippers. She wore a musky perfume.

"You're late," she said. "Never mind, we'll make up for it." She led the way into a wood-paneled room decorated in chintz and damask. It was cool enough to wear a jacket. Leather-bound books on fitted shelves lined one wall on each side of a black marble fireplace. A wet bar stood under a softly-lit picture of Lady Jane in a jeweled mask and a low-cut evening gown at a party.

"Let's have a drinkie, first," she said. "You look as though you need it. You're a mess."

"Been working all day. Got any food?"

"You can have a snack. Smoked salmon, toast, no butter. We'll get your weight down." He was allowed a glass of Scotch with it.

"I don't suppose you have any men's clothes," he said after she produced the food. He hadn't eaten since his triple-egg breakfast.

"You're not going to need clothes."

"I will tomorrow."

"I'll see what I can find. Finish that up. We'll have another drinkie, then we'll go to bed. It's late and I have to go shopping tomorrow."

They took their drinks up the stairs to a room with a canopied, four-poster bed. It had little steps on both sides for easy access. It was even cooler here, central air-conditioning, Paige supposed. There was indirect lighting and lamps on tables on both sides of the bed, an enormous wardrobe, and a chaise lounge in front of a bay window. Across the room was a photograph of a beefy, florid-faced man in a red jacket and riding britches, holding the bridle of a horse.

Alongside him was Lady Jane, also in riding clothes. She looked, maybe twenty-four, but her stare was just as arrogant and go-to-hell as it was now, at least ten years later.

"Who's that?"

"My late husband. He had the title, I had the trust funds. He broke his neck in a steeplechase in Somerset. I haven't ridden since—didn't like it much, anyway."

"You had the money?"

"My family did. Now I do, and the title."

"You should have a maid, staff, to look after you."

"They're on holiday."

"Why don't you live in England?"

"I do, darling, some of the time."

"This my room?" he said.

"Yes, and mine." She vanished into a small side room and he began to get undressed. He was exhausted.

He had stripped and climbed up the steps when the toilet flushed and Lady Jane reemerged, letting her robe fall to the floor as she advanced. He reached out to turn off the lamp on his side of the bed.

"Leave it on, darling," she said. "I like to see what I'm doing." She climbed into the billowy bed and said, "All right, now you can make up for last night."

11 ◄

She said she would be at a bar in Chelsea, Nipsy's on Twenty-third Street. Leaving the office, Savage found a cab on Lexington and headed downtown.

It was a joint. The tavern smelled of old beer, stale ashtrays, and the sort of disinfectant used in morgues. In the corner by the window, a TV set was tuned to a Yankee's game with the sound off. Two men in working clothes were sitting separately at the bar, shoulders hunched over, heads down above their glasses, staring into memories.

Down the left side of the room, across from the bar, were booths with red plastic seats that had been ripped and repaired with duct tape. There was a big calendar on the wall showing a beach in Portugal with two girls in old-fashioned, full-length swimsuits throwing a ball to each other. They seemed to be having a fine time. Overhead, a large fan turned slowly, spreading the smells evenly through the bar.

She was sitting facing the door in one of the booths, talking to a young black woman with a gold ring in her nose. VanAllen was in a gold-buttoned blue blazer and a gray skirt, its hemline flirting with her knees. Her companion was in dirty white dungarees over a black T-shirt. VanAllen was sipping soda water. The black woman was drinking beer and shots, every so often shaking a salt cellar into the beer. When Savage walked in, vanAllen's eyes went to him, but she didn't acknowledge him.

"What's this," he said to the bartender, "happy hour?" The bartender stared at him coldly but said nothing. Savage took a seat at the bar between the two customers and ordered a beer. Behind the bartender, a heavyset character with short hair and Popeye forearms, advertisements for Budweiser and Coors flashed distractingly on and off.

In the mirror, between bottles of Cutty Sark and Gordon's gin, Savage could see vanAllen listening to the black woman, who kept giggling. Savage wondered if she was high. Once, vanAllen looked up and winked at him before returning her attention to the woman.

Waiting, drinking his beer, Savage thought unhappily about Kit and the miserable journey back to New York.

That morning, the school quadrangle had been full of excited youngsters. On the grass under the old elms, boys and girls whooped and laughed, said good-bye to each other with high-fives, swore they would keep in touch, before walking off with their parents. Exams were over. Summer stretched endlessly ahead, promising bliss.

Savage watched for a moment, grinning at the exuberance, but couldn't spot Kit. He headed for the dormitory overlooking the southeast corner of the quad. Kit was still a junior, but there was talk of Harvard for him. He was bright enough, a straight A student except in math and a stalwart on the water polo and cross country teams. Next year, he would captain the polo squad. On the blackboard just inside the front door, somebody had scrawled in chalk, HAVE A GREAT SUMMER! Savage ran up the steps to the second floor of Hudson House and went down the deserted corridor to the last door. It was ajar and he went in.

In the bleak, sparsely-furnished room, Kit was stretched facedown on his iron bed. He looked as though he had grown another three inches. Everywhere on the walls were posters of rock groups, pro football players leaping and running, and bounteously endowed women spilling out of their clothes. Shirts, pants, socks, and athletic gear littered the floor. The closed windows imprisoned a faint smell of sweat in the room. It was like a barracks without a sergeant to enforce discipline. There was no sign of Kit's roommate, Post.

"Hey, Kit," Savage said, reaching down to shake his son's shoulder. The boy would rather sleep than eat. "Come on, it's time to get out of here."

Kit twisted on his back and looked at Savage. His face was stricken, his eyes wounded. Almost immediately, he looked away.

"I have to see the dean," he said. "They're gonna boot me out of here."

Savage stared at the boy. Kit liked to pull hoaxes, but his expression was too desolate for it to be a practical joke. Savage sat down on the side of the bed.

"What the hell happened?"

"Everything's fallen apart. I'm out."

"You'd better tell me."

"It was last night. I pulled an all-nighter for the last exams. Somebody brought some beer in and, Post and I, we had a couple of cans, more actually . . . he's out, too." He struggled with his emotions. "Everything was fine at first. I sat for English this morning, and then old Hampton said he could smell alcohol on my breath. I stalled, but eventually I had to say I'd had a drink. They came around here and found some empty cans. That was it. I'm history."

"Jesus, Kit."

"I know, Dad. I'm a complete jerk. It was just three weeks ago . . ." It was just three weeks earlier that Kit and Post had been put on the warning list for drinking beer. One more infraction, they said. And here it was.

"Couldn't you have a disciplinary committee hearing? Throw yourself on their mercy?"

"There's no way they're gonna let this pass, Dad. Post has already packed and gone."

Savage stood up and began to pace. "You a boozer, an alcoholic, Kit?"

"No, Dad. I like beer, but that's all. The first time it was the night we beat Hotchkiss, a celebration.

Last night, well, I wasn't thinking straight. It was hot and I was thirsty . . ."

"Does your mother know?"

"The school called her, must have been while you were on the road. They put me on the phone with her."

"You talked to her? What did she say?"

"She's pretty upset. Christ, I'm so sorry, Dad. I've let everybody down, you, Mom, everybody."

"What happens when you see the dean?"

"I guess he makes it official. I told him you were coming up and he wants to see you, too. Christ, what a mess."

"Who brought the beer in?"

"A guy, a senior."

"Who?"

"It doesn't do any good going after him. It was my fault."

"No snitching, is that it?"

"No snitching." With the weariness of an invalid, Kit got to his feet and went to the sink to throw cold water on his face. As usual, he needed a haircut.

They walked along the flagstones below the granite arches to the dean's office. "Let's go out with style," Savage said. "Head up, look the bastard straight in the eye."

The quadrangle was quieter now, but outside the office a dozen youngsters, boys and girls, noisily milled about. When they saw Kit, they fell silent and opened a passage for him to reach the dean's office. A girl called out, "Good luck, Kit," and a boy wearing his baseball cap backwards so that he looked like a World War I pilot said more softly, "Fuck 'em, sanctimonious pricks. You're better off out of here, Kit." But the rest just stared as if seeing themselves in his predicament. It was a juvenile version of dead man walking.

The secretary, a motherly-looking woman with an incongruous black patch over her right eye, waved them straight into the dean's empty office. "He'll be back in a moment," she said, and closed the door behind them. Kit sat stiffly in an upright chair while Savage went to stare through the window at the river where the crews raced in the spring. Now the water was low and so motionless that it looked like a narrow lake.

"Sorry to keep you waiting." The dean was suddenly with them like a genie out of a bottle. He always affected a distracted air as if his thoughts were of more important things than the matter at hand. He settled into a chair behind the paper-strewn desk.

"Kit told you?" he said. "Okay. This is very painful, but I've been talking to the headmaster and we agreed that there's no way that Kit can remain at the school. To break the same rule three weeks after a violation is too much." He sighed.

"How's this going to affect his college ambitions?"

"Well, it won't help. But colleges don't take drinking as seriously as we have to."

"And there's no appeal?"

"No appeal. I truly sympathize, but we can't make exceptions to rules that are very clear. It would be unfair to be rest of the school." The dean was expressionless, his fingers steepled below his chin.

Savage held back his bitter response. Go out with style. He and everybody else connected with the school knew there were exceptions, especially if the parents of a guilty youngster were wealthy enough to fund a new dormitory, new tennis courts, scholarships. At public functions, there was much talk from the headmaster of idealism, spiritual growth, the nurturing of young souls. But it was the same headmaster who had accepted millions from a Wall Street shark who had put an army of downsized workers on the street. A new complex of buildings was named after the benefactor. The head invited him to address a graduating class. The speech was full of inspiration and appeals for the graduates to search for the higher meaning of life.

"Come on, Kit," Savage said. "Time to go." The dean put out his hand and Savage took it. Go out with style. Outside, the youngsters turned to look at them.

"How did it go, Kit?" He gave them a thumbs-down and kept walking. A woman teacher that Savage liked was approaching down the hall. She saw his grim face and paused.

"I'm so sorry," she said. "We shall miss Kit. It's a shame. I've been thinking, maybe Holden Caulfield was right." Savage thought she was going to reach out to embrace the boy, but after a slight hesitation, she nodded at them and walked on.

In Maggie's BMW, Kit's belongings packed into the backseat and trunk, Savage said, "How's Christiane? Does she know?" He wasn't sure if there was a romance, but the two were good friends.

"She didn't have any exams today," the boy said. "She left last night, probably back in Paris now. I'll call her when we get home."

"And Johnny-boy?" Johnny-boy was an Indian from a poverty-stricken family in Bowie, Texas, who had been given a scholarship. Kit had tried to help him struggle in an alien elitist culture.

"He's not coming back. He can't take it, the way some of the kids treat him because he's paying nothing. I was thinking of going down to Bowie to try to persuade him to come back in the fall but I guess I'm not a good advertisement for the school right now." After fifteen minutes, when they reached the interstate, Savage glanced at Kit. He had escaped his troubles in sleep.

As he grew older, the boy's hair was darkening. Savage thought of the time, before he split from Maggie, when they vacationed on Martha's Vine-yard, and the memory that came back was of Kit's sun-bleached hair and his tobacco-brown body gleaming as he ducked in an out of the water at Gay Head. Maggie had wanted to stay at an expensive hotel in Edgartown while Savage had opted for a simple bed and breakfast, the Farmhouse, in West Tisbury. For once, Savage won the argument and eventually Maggie admitted she had enjoyed it. Then he thought of the proud grin on Kit's face when he put his team ahead with a home run. He pushed the memories away.

Savage had never said anything to Kit, but he had not wanted him to go to boarding school. He couldn't see what was wrong with a public school. Now Maggie would look at him, searching for any hint of satisfaction at the debacle. She'd want to switch Kit to another prep school.

Kit woke up as they encountered the potholes of Manhattan. The doorman, Mike, at the building on Fifty-fifth Street, came to help them with their luggage. He was Puerto Rican, but he had grown up in New York and his accent was pure Bronx.

"Hey, man," he said to Kit, "you've grown. You wanna put on the gloves with me?" Mike had been a lightweight Golden Gloves champion, but never good enough to turn pro.

"Maybe," Kit said, managing a grin. "If I'm around for a while."

In the apartment, Maggie looked as though she had been crying. She put out her arms and hugged her son. He was much taller than she now.

"Don't you worry, Kit," she said. "That school's no damn good anyway. We'll find something better."

"The school was okay," he said. "I screwed up. Simple as that. Maybe I'll go out and get a job. Knock around a bit. Try to grow up."

She stood back and stared at Savage. "Is that your idea? Have him drop out? Forget Harvard?"

"It's nothing to do with Dad," the boy said. "In

the car, I was thinking. I could take a year off. Maybe Harvard isn't for me. . . ."

"You'll do no such thing. Will he, Jake?"

Savage shrugged. "There's no rush. We have to think this out. It's Kit's life and he's old enough to help make the decision." When his gear was stowed away, Kit vanished into his room. Savage knew he was returning to the limbo of sleep.

"Oh, Jake," she said, "what a disaster. That crappy school . . . Maybe you were right all along."

"It's not right or wrong, Maggie. Kit's got it straight. He screwed up. We might as well accept that." Now the tears came again. She put her arms around his waist, her face against his shoulder.

"We're all messed up, this family, aren't we?" she said. "You and me, we can't make a go of it. and now Kit . . ."

"Kit will get over it. So will we." He stroked her back as if calming the fretting of a pet. She was still slim and supple. She smelled of rose water. Sniffing and dabbing her eyes, she stepped back and said, "Maybe we need a drink."

He took his Scotch and went to the window with its view of the towers of midtown Manhattan. He was still fond of her, but they had too little in common. Compared to her, he came from the wrong side of the tracks, if there had been any tracks in the obscure little town where he grew up. She was a corporate lawyer, the daughter of a corporate lawyer. She was very successful. That was part of their problem. She was used to money and spending it. He wasn't. He was uncomfortable with her relatives and friends. The reverse was true for her. She liked the opera and Le Cirque. He liked the movies and the corner restaurant.

"I have to get down to the paper," he said. That was another problem: his hours, which sometimes did not end until after midnight. Too many times, she had waited for him so they could go to a dinner party, to the theater, and too many times a story had broken and she had felt abandoned. Over the years, they had moved apart.

"I'm seeing somebody," she said."

"Oh?"

"A lawyer, a good one."

"Is it serious?"

"It could be. He makes me laugh, like you used to. We did have some good times, didn't we?" He put his drink down half finished. Giving her the car keys, he said, "I have to go."

"I know," she said.

In Nipsy's, Savage saw vanAllen slide a bill across the table. The black took it, came out of the booth and headed for the door. She was looking at Savage and then at the pile of change from a $20 bill that he had left on the bar. She stopped behind him.

"Give me the five," she said. She had a Spanish accent: *geeve me*. Savage picked up the five-dollar bill and let it stick up from his fingers. Her hand flashed out almost too fast to see and the bill was gone.

"Hey," the bartender said. "Get the fuck out on the street where you belong. We don't want your sort in here."

She looked at him and said, "Well, excuse me. What's your problem, Señor Asshole? Can't get it up no more?" and walked out. For a moment it looked as though the bartender was going after her, but he stayed where he was.

"You shouldn't encourage them," he said to Savage. "You wanna make a deal with her, go outside. She's a whore, always bothering my customers."

The man on Savage's left, stubble like grime on his chin, rheumy eyes, a flat cap on his head, said, "Fuckin' colored. Should stay where they belong, not come around spreading their diseases." He looked at Savage. "Keep your money in your pocket, mister."

"I didn't realize," Savage said, "that I'd hired you gentlemen as my financial consultants. When did that happen?" The other customer didn't look up from his glass.

"Buy you a drink?" vanAllen said, coming up behind Savage. "What did you give her?"

"A five."

"Big night for Ramona. Twenty from me, five from you, and she hasn't even dressed for the street yet."

"Don't bring her in here again," the bartender said. "This is a respectable bar. In fact, you can stay the hell away as well."

VanAllen stared at him. "I see a lot of violations

in here," she said. "First, it's boring. Second, you're suffering a shortage of manners. Third, your customers are unhygienic. Altogether, there's enough to bring in the State Liquor Authority, maybe close you down." The bartender's heavy-jowled face reddened.

Savage scooped up his change. "Get a shower, you smell like Fidel Castro's jockstrap," he told the man in the flat cap. Then to vanAllen, "Let's go. They're assholes and nothing we say will change that."

The bartender reached under the bar but kept whatever he had under there out of sight. They went out, leaving him muttering as he wiped the counter and took away Savage's half-empty beer glass.

Walking south toward her place on Jane Street in the Village, they looked at each other and laughed. VanAllen said, "What were you trying to do, take over my snitch? Ramona will just give it all to her dude, Alberto."

"You didn't flash your badge at that prick of a bartender."

"He'd probably have flashed his back."

"He's a cop?"

"I'm pretty sure he's on the job. You can usually tell. A good thing you're not a cop, having to prove how macho you are. There would have been blood on the floor. You know how many cops shoot each other in bars?"

"Your girlfriend come up with anything of value?"

"Maybe. Sometimes you can't tell until later."

"She's one of your snitches?"

"Yeah, a registered C.I. First met her a long time ago when I was undercover for Narcotics. Informants, it's the name of the game, as you well know. All great police work comes down to who has the best snitches. Damn, I forgot . . ."

"What?"

"My mom's in town, staying at my place. We can't go there."

"That's okay, we'll go to mine." Her mother lived in Philadelphia. She hated it that vanAllen was a cop, wanted her to marry, have kids, move out of the city.

Enjoying the cool of the evening, they stood for a moment looking for a cab.

"I saw Todd Paige today," she said. "He thinks you're a straight shooter. For an editor."

"Just the guy I need for a recommendation."

"He still doesn't know about us."

"None of Paige's business."

"He thinks everything's his business." They had met at the police academy just as his divorce was coming through. He was giving an award to the cop of the month. She was counseling female cadets. She was soon back on the street, but by then they had made the connection.

A taxi was cruising toward them. "You like a drink, wash the taste of Nipsy's away?"

"No," she said. "I'd like to go to bed."

In the cab, the driver had a Latino station going on his radio so loud that they could hardly hear each other talk. That was okay with Savage. Her hand was tight on his thigh and he was watching the lights on the street outline her profile, her cheekbones and full lips.

"It's been too long," she said. She had to lean over to make herself heard over the radio and he felt her breath on his ear.

He nodded. Two, more like three, weeks. He didn't think it was going anywhere. He was a man who guarded his privacy, but she was even more careful about revealing herself. When he asked why she had never married, she made a joke and steered away from the subject. She never talked about her childhood. There was mystery there, a remote, unattainable quality to her; maybe it made her more attractive to him.

They really didn't know each other, except what the intimacy of bed revealed. They were simply using each other on the few occasions when their free time coincided but, hell, what was wrong with that? In or out of the sheets, he liked her and knew she liked him. He was happy to help her, make sure she looked good in the crime stories the paper ran. He just wished she could find the time so that they could do ordinary things, go to the park, the movies, the beach. He didn't allow himself to think about what might be.

In his apartment with its view of the windows of another sixth-floor apartment, they faced each other and he touched her face with his fingertips, smoothing the tiny lines at the corners of her eyes. It was June, but she was winter-pale.

"They won't go away," she said.

"You need a good night's sleep."

"Later." They moved into each other's arms. She whispered about what she wanted him to do to her. Her mouth was warm and open, her tongue insistent.

She took off her jacket and shoes. She didn't, thanks be, say anything about the state of the apartment. It was a mess, had been since he moved in and took up the bachelor life again. At least he had made the bed, even if not to a nurse's satisfaction. Occasionally, he blitzed the place with a mop and vacuum cleaner, especially for the few occasions she visited, then for too long let the dust and the mess regroup. He opened a bottle of Australian wine.

"That Ramona," he said, filling their glasses. "There have to be easier ways to make a living."

"Tell me about it," she said, sinking on to the couch and tucking her stockinged feet beneath her. "Did I mention the first assignment I was given, straight out of the academy? Catching johns. I had to dress in skirts up to my crotch and practically let my breasts fall out. I was in my early twenties, after a convent school for God's sake, and college in Boston. Every night, I had to hang around the Lincoln Tunnel, waiting for horny motorists to proposition me. It could be below freezing with wind straight from the Arctic trying to mug me, and there I'd be giving the come-on to guys who weren't exactly auditioning for the role of boy next door."

"You resented it?"

"Of course I did. Still do. That's not police work. What business is it of the police if a man and a woman want to make a private, commercial arrangement?"

"The johns give you any trouble?"

"A couple of times. But I developed a technique, mainly to get out of the cold. I'd hop in the guy's car and, after the price had been agreed, tell him I had a nice warm room. I'd direct him straight to the precinct and lock him up. My backup team loved me. Most of the time, especially in the winter, they just waited in the warmth at the precinct until I brought in the johns and they took the collar."

"You have balls."

"No, I don't." They both laughed. She didn't usually talk about her work, any more than she did about her emotions, her thoughts, her background. Neither did he. He knew she had a father, a lawyer in Philadelphia, and a mother who occasionally came to visit and wanted her to find other work, but beyond that nothing. Their meetings were time-outs. Leaning back against him on the couch, she took his hands and steered them to her small, round breasts. Her blouse was so sheer it felt slippery. She twisted to kiss him. She smelled of lilac and tasted of wine.

When half the wine was gone, he drew her to her feet and said, "Let's go to bed."

The wine had given them a glow. They took the bottle and the glasses with them and sipped as they undressed. It amused and excited him that she always hid delicate, skimpy underwear beneath her anonymous street clothes. It was as though she concealed the sensuous, voracious truth from everybody but him. Everybody knew tough, ambitious Detective Lieutenant Sarah vanAllen. Only he knew the softer version. Now she had on abbreviated, silky underclothes that gleamed ivory in the diffused light from the living room. Her body was lithe and smooth-muscled like a swimmer's.

Their clothes ended in two heaps on each side of the bed. They met in the center of the sheets and her hand curled gently around his penis. In bed, she became a different person, pliant and tender and sometimes bawdy, as if escaping thankfully from the daily discipline of her work. In bed, she laughed a lot, giggled like a teenager at the things they did.

"Hello, Mr. Impudence," she said, squeezing him.

"Treat him nicely. He's the strong, silent type." His thigh was pressing into the tiny marsh between her legs, his hands stroking, then kneading, her smooth buttocks.

"He's amazing," she said. "Always lurking there invisible beneath your clothes and always ready to surge into attack mode at the right touch."

"He means well."

"Yeah? Well, I think I'm ready to settle his hash."

At first, as Savage began, she purred like a lazy cat. But then her breath quickened and she whimpered and, staring up at him with a frankly lubricious twist to her lips, urged him on and the sweat came from both of them until their bodies moved together slick as baby seals.

When it was over, she still gripped him with her arms and legs and said, "I felt that. Paige was right. You're a straight shooter." Her smeared lipstick and mascara, smudged like soot on her cheeks, had given her the face of a pretty clown. He went on to his back and she put her head on his chest, listening to the thumping of his heart. Stroking her hair, he stared at the ceiling.

"You're good for me," she said.

"And you for me."

Later, when they had cooled, he said, "Turn over." She smiled as if at a shared secret and shifted until her face was almost buried in the pillow. Her back was long and sleek and white, punctuated by the jutting salient of her rump. Naked, for all her slenderness, there was a lushness to her flesh. Savage straddled her, his buttocks pressing into hers, and he began to flex his fingers in the softness of her shoulders and neck.

She sighed and whispered, "You have all the skills."

"My pleasure," he said, and meant it. His hands moved down to stroke the sides of her breasts and then down to the narrow waist and the swell of the hips. From his forehead, a drop of sweat fell and was collected in the pretty little hollow at the base of her spine.

"When was your first time?" she said, her voice muffled by the pillow.

"I was seventeen. It was in a haystack, of all places, and it was fine. Don't believe that stuff about the straws sticking into you. If they did, I didn't notice it."

"Your high school sweetheart?"

"No. It was a woman, probably mid-twenties, but to me she seemed pretty old, very sophisticated. I met her at a dance."

"Did she know it was your first time?"

"Oh, yeah. She was very sweet and kind."

She reached blindly behind her to grasp and play with him. "Oh, la, la, Mr. Impudence is back," she said.

Afterwards, he was starting to drift off into sleep, but he stirred as she kissed his chest and left him.

"Now that I've had my way with you," she said, "I'm going to take a shower."

"What for? You're not staying?"

"I have to go look for somebody," she said.

"Look tomorrow. Jesus, you're working yourself into a nervous breakdown." She shrugged and padded naked into the bathroom. When she came back, she had a towel wrapped around her hips. Lying in the tumble of damp sheets, he put out a hand to her and she sat on the bed beside him.

"How's your boy doing?" she said. At first, he didn't answer. Occasionally, they talked about their families, but the unspoken deal was that they didn't ask, didn't tell.

"He has his problems," Savage said finally, "like all teenagers. I think time is the only thing that solves them." He didn't want to talk about Kit just then. His hand traced the curves of her breasts, teasing the nipples. He wanted more time with her but sensed that already she was thinking of other things.

"Except that you're a fine, lusty woman, I know practically nothing about you," he said. Then, "We're on the same track but heading for different stations."

"Maybe. But we can enjoy the ride."

She dressed while he lay there and watched her slip back into the role she played for others.

VanAllen went to the Sutton Place park after midnight and found Mickey Finn by using the bottle that lay in her purse. She had bought it at a liquor store on Third Avenue after leaving Savage. The lovemaking had made her feel loose, relaxed, yet not at all sleepy.

Officer Faso had been interrogated intensively, first about the kidnapping he had witnessed and then about the incident of the door being opened. From that emerged the story of the wino who had seen the surreptitious unlocking episode, but during the daytime there was no sign of Finn.

Walking down the ramp, vanAllen pulled out the pint bottle of Scotch. At the bottom, she tapped it gently with her lieutenant's shield so that it rang out musically.

"Cocktail time," she called out. "Come and get it." At first there was no response. She stood staring into the darkness. Beyond the park, a motor yacht decorated with yellow lights was pushing its way up the East River. From the deck and across the water came loud voices and laughter. Even this late, it was sultry, the air heavy with the threat of a storm.

"Out!" she called. "Last chance for a nightcap." She tapped the bottle again.

Finn's head poked up from the bushes. In one hand he held an almost empty bottle of Sneaky Pete, the second of two which had interrupted his plan to go shrimp fishing from City Island. The next day, he had decided, would be more convenient all around. VanAllen turned on the slim flashlight she had been holding ready, got a look at Mickey Finn, then turned it off.

"Come on down," she said. "We'll put our heads together, have a chat." He stared at this midnight intruder in a well-cut blazer and skirt.

"You one of the mothers?" he said, bewildered. Using her flashlight, she showed him her badge, then she showed him the bottle. He studied the shield, but then his eyes went to the bottle.

"You really a cop? They're improving the breed." Finn clambered down and reached back for his plastic bag. "Okay, okay," he said. "I'll go. I ain't hurting anybody here. Just getting a bit of sleep."

"Anybody else around?" vanAllen said, staring into the shadowed recesses of the park.

"Just me," Finn said. "And I ain't doing no harm. I'm always out by the time the kids come." His voice was thick with liquor and weariness.

"You were here last night?"

"Who said so?" Finn's voice came clearer now, touched with the anger of a citizen falsely accused.

"The officer who kicked you out in the morning. Want me to call him down? Or I can take you to the stationhouse, lock you up, give you somewhere to sleep."

"I was here," Finn said, defeated. "I helped the flatfoot with information and this is the thanks I get."

"Try this," she said, handing him the bottle. "Don't gulp it. Savor the smoky bouquet."

Finn put it to his lips, then told a rambling story about a man opening the door, leaving it ajar. Obviously, he knew nothing of the kidnapping that briefly had shaken and enthralled the city and nothing of the significance of the unlocked door.

"Describe the man," vanAllen said without much hope. Descriptions were always distorted or too sketchy to be of use. She knew two hit men, executioners for a Brooklyn family, who were walking around laughing and free because the published descriptions from witnesses had not fitted them.

"Fat," Finn said. "Piggy eyes, fat face. About five feet nine inches, gold watch on left wrist. He was in brown pants and a yellow shirt, no, make that orange. No tie. Middle-aged, maybe fifty-five. Nasty-looking bastard." Not bad, vanAllen thought.

"Can I go now?"

VanAllen looked thoughtfully at Finn, who was clutching the pint of Scotch like an actor with an Oscar. She could lock him up, hold him as a material witness, but it might be weeks, months, before she felt the collar of a suspect. There might be another way.

"What's your name?"

"James Finn. Call me Mickey."

"Okay, Mickey. You've got yourself a date. I want you to come with me and look at some pictures. You hungry? We'll get you a sandwich, a pizza, whatever you want. Leave your bag here. I'll make sure nobody bothers you in the bushes tonight or any other night. In fact, I want you to sleep here from now on. Consider it your home."

"You mean it?" Finn could hardly believe it. Cops didn't act like this.

"That guy, the guy who opened the door," he said. "I wouldn't be surprised if he was in the joint. He had the shuffle of a lifer. Check it out." Finn didn't know why everybody was so interested in a simple case of lock-picking, but he could sense the umbrella of official sanction opening above his rumpled head and he wanted to keep it there.

"You've done time?" vanAllen said.

"A little," he admitted coyly.

"What for?"

"It was an argument."

"You won an argument and they hit you with an assault charge?"

"Nah, I lost. The jury said the prosecutor won the argument. What's your name?"

"VanAllen. Sarah vanAllen."

"Well, listen, Sarah, I'll come look at your mug shots, but I ain't leaving my things here. This is a tough city. They'll take the buckle off your belt. You mean it, Sarah, about letting me sleep here from now on?" He sounded like a tenant awarded a reprieve from a rapacious landlord.

Alarmed at the familiarity emerging from Finn, vanAllen said, "I'm a detective lieutenant. You can call me lieutenant."

Finn picked up his bag, took a swig from the bottle, and followed vanAllen up the ramp out of the park. City Island and the shrimp could wait.

12 ◀

A t the same time that vanAllen was escorting her grimy, unshaven prize from the park, a few blocks away Dan Mahoney was leaving a restaurant with Watson and Lopez. They stood on the sidewalk for a moment, chatting and enjoying the softness of the summer night. Manhattan, for all its brutality and ruthlessness, sometimes could be as tender and languorous as a South Seas village. Behind them, the door opened and closed, letting out, then cutting off, the subdued roar from the busy bar.

"Need a ride, Dan?" Lopez said. "I have the car around the corner." When Mahoney was in office, Watson and Lopez called him Governor in private and in public but now they were just old friends, all on a first-name basis. Lopez, once Mahoney's chief of staff, was doing very well in real estate. Watson, no longer Mahoney's counsel, was back at the white-shoe law firm he had left for four years in Albany. Almost every Tuesday night, they met at Eamonn Doran's on Second Avenue to talk about old triumphs

and defeats—and future possibilities. Eamonn Doran's
was where they had started to plot the coup which had
given Mahoney the party leadership and the governor's mansion. Now, six months after the failed
reelection effort, they were on different paths, but
Tuesday night at Doran's had become a tradition.
"Think I'll walk," Mahoney said. "Clear my head
and my lungs. You two should give up your cigars
and I shouldn't drink wine on top of vodka. Anyway,
you guys are heading for the West Side. See you next
week." He gave them a wave that was half salute and
started down Second Avenue while the rear lights of
the traffic shot ahead of him like scarlet tracer bullets.

Mahoney was waiting for the light to change at
Fifty-first Street when he heard the soft toot of a car
horn. Looking around, he saw a black Lincoln town
car with dark-tinted windows pulling up alongside
him. The driver had his window down. He wore a
chauffeur's cap.

"Thought it was you, Governor," the man said.
"Let me give you a ride. No charge."

Mahoney smiled and shook his head. "Thanks,
but I'm enjoying the walk. Do I know you?"

"It can be dangerous walking around here at
night," the driver said. "Jump in and I'll get you
home safely. It's Forty-fifth Street isn't it?" Mahoney
wondered how the chauffeur knew where he lived
and again shook his head.

But then the car slid forward and the rear door
swung open. A hand reached out to grip his elbow. At
the same moment, he heard hurried steps behind him

and somebody laid a heavy arm on his shoulders and pushed his head down while the man in the car pulled him in. Mahoney was a big man, but he was off-balance and went into the car as if diving into shallow water.

At first he was too astonished to speak, but then, as he was jerked down into the backseat, he spluttered, "What the fuck . . ." The door closed and the car was moving, joining the swift parade of downtown traffic. Mahoney felt a jab in his side, and looking down saw a black revolver in the hand of the man on his left. All the windows were up. He heard the click of the door locks.

There were three men in the back with him, one on a jump seat staring back through the rear window. The glass partition behind the driver's seat was down and the chauffeur was watching Mahoney in his rearview mirror. There was a St. Christopher statuette on the dashboard.

"Want another drink, Governor, a nightcap?" one of the men said. He had a Southern accent. He had a rawboned face as if every time he shaved he took off the outer layer of skin. Mahoney could imagine him guarding a still in the backwoods of Tennessee. "Scotch, gin, vodka. Whatever's your pleasure." There was no bar in the car.

"This isn't funny," Mahoney said. "You dumb fucks. I'll have you all in front of a judge."

"Yeah, you like the courts, don't you, Mahoney? You like to use them to screw people. How's it look behind, Jackie? See anything?"

"All clear so far. There was a big old Buick hovering around, but it's turned off."

"Okay, Ferret," the gunman said. "Keep on down Second, the take a right on Thirty-third. Let's make sure."

"Hey, I got a question for you, Governor," the man with the Southern accent said. He had liquor on his breath. "They call the president Mr. President. Why don't they call a governor Mr. Governor?"

Mahoney said nothing. He was jammed between two of the men, unable to move let alone make a grab for a door. He wished he hadn't drunk so much, that he could channel his racing thoughts.

"All right, assholes," he said. "You want to tell me what the fuck this is all about?" His voice was steady, but the shock of being taken off the street was replaced by a knot of fear building in his belly. The men, all wearing dark, anonymous clothing, were too focused, too tense, for this to be anything but deadly serious. The air-conditioning was on and the air inside the car was icy. Mahoney felt as though he was shrinking, his suit suddenly too large for him.

"It's too long a story for tonight," said the man with the revolver. He had an arid voice and his face was gaunt. "Let's just say it's payback time. Once you had the power to right a wrong. You did nothing. Fact, you did your damnedest to keep the wrong in place. Now we have the power and it's payback time." The speaker fell silent, brooding out of the window. They were swinging off Thirty-third Street and moving uptown on Third.

"I don't know what the hell you're talking about," Mahoney said. "Tell me what it's all about, then maybe something can be done about it. Is it money? I can get you money."

The gunman was silent for a moment, then he said, "Must feel pretty good, Mahoney, giving speeches, having people admire you, lots of applause, eating at the best places, plenty of money in the bank. Sleep in silk sheets, I bet. Lap of luxury. We've been reading all about you."

"What's that got to do with you bastards?"

"Few months back, when you were still in Albany, you remember a guy tried to sue . . . ?"

The chauffeur, Ferret, cut in. He sounded nervous. "This can still go wrong," he said. "Let's cut the talk. He's seen our faces. We talk too much and things go bad, it could bring the heat down on top of us . . . Jesus!" Suddenly there was a police car behind and its roof lights were flashing and its siren was beginning to moan. The men next to Mahoney turned to stare back, their faces lit by the revolving light.

"You make a sound, a move, and you're dead," the gunman said. The revolver was pressing hard into Mahoney's side. Their heads swiveled to watch the cruiser. It went past and, gathering speed, shot up Third Avenue.

"Probably time for dinner," Ferret said. "Assholes. In a hurry to get their pizzas."

"Where are we going? I can get money," Mahoney said again, watching the flashing lights receding up the avenue. "I work at a bank. I can get money any time." It was true. He worked at a bank, in the board room when he felt like showing up.

"Take a right on Forty-second." The car slid past the lights of the *Daily News* building, caught the green, and turned down Second.

"How does it look behind?"

"Okay. We're clean." Now they turned left and climbed up to the Tudor City complex. The car stopped on the bridge above Forty-second Street and its headlights went off. For a moment they sat there, all of them staring out at the quiet residential street. A man was walking his dog, but he turned off under a canopy and vanished through a front door. Nobody else was on the street. There were no lights coming from the windows overlooking them.

"Okay, let's do it," said the one with the gun. But then he said, "Shit! Hold it."

A young couple, both in evening dress, were strolling hand in hand toward them on their side of the street. They seemed to have all the time in the world.

"Make a sound and I'll blow out your guts," the gunman said. All of them sat silently while the youngsters wandered toward them. The pair stared at the parked town car, then turned to lean on the parapet of the bridge. In front of them, the brilliant citadels of midtown Manhattan reared up into the darkness and, below, the east-bound traffic streamed by, carrying late-night travelers toward First Avenue and the FDR Drive.

The boy, blond hair slicked back, wearing a

white dinner jacket, put his arm around the girl's shoulders and drew her closer. He said something and she giggled. They both turned to stare at the car as if trying to see if anybody was inside. Mahoney wondered if they could see the watching men in spite of the tinted windows.

"This is no fucking good," the gunman said. "You left the sidelights on? They've noticed the car, might have spotted the license number."

"It was a crazy idea," the driver said. "I told you it was crazy."

"Fuck you," the Southerner said. "You're a pussy. Where are your balls? We can blow both of them away and still do what we have to do."

"You're out of your mind, man." It was the driver again. "We gotta give it up, go back to the flip side."

"Right," the gunman said. "That's it, let's go." The driver put the car in gear, turned on his headlights, and they moved off. The couple at the parapet turned to watch them go.

"Looks like your lucky night, Governor," said the man with the gun. It was still jabbing into Mahoney's side. "We're gonna let you off the hook, take you home. But first, you better let us have your money and your wallet. Your watch, too."

Mahoney shrugged. He handed them over. He had no doubt these were killers but he felt his confidence trickling back. "Now tell me what the fuck this is all about," he said. "You snatch me off the street, take me for a joyride and then take me home."

"Shut the fuck up," the Southerner said. He sounded angry, and Mahoney wondered why. What the hell did it mean, the ride, the stop above Forty-second Street? The whole thing couldn't have taken more than half an hour. They were all silent as the car moved around the blocks to Forty-fifth Street and his brownstone. How the hell did they know where he lived? The locks clicked open. They sat for a moment looking up and down the dark street. There was nobody in sight. There were doormen on the block, but at this hour they were probably snoozing in the lobbies.

The man on his left swung the door open and said, "Get out." Mahoney followed him out of the Lincoln. He didn't look back, but was conscious of footsteps behind him. He reached for his house keys. First he was going to call the cops, and then he was going to call Watson and Lopez, tell them what had happened.

"Hey, Mahoney." It was the Southerner. Mahoney turned. The man was right behind him. The knife came up and into his belly. When the Southerner pulled it out, a thin spout of blood followed it. As Mahoney groaned and sank toward the ground, the Southerner deftly twisted him around by his hair. Bending from behind, he pulled the head back and to the left before using the knife again. He sliced through Mahoney's carotid artery.

The others were already back in the Lincoln, but the killer paused to wipe his knife on the clothes of the slumped body before, with a glance up and down the street, he joined them and the car moved smoothly off.

◀   ◀   ◀

When the word came in, vanAllen told Mickey Finn she'd be back and left him flicking through mug shots of prisoners recently released from maximum security. She took a cab back to midtown.

The entire block of Forty-fifth Street, a mix of brownstones and tall apartment buildings with canopied entrances, was cordoned off at both ends with yellow police tape. Death was making it pulse with life as it never did during its busiest daytime hours. Cruisers and unmarked cars were all over the place, some with their rooflights flashing and their doors still open. Two-way radios were hissing out words in an unceasing monotone. Slewed across the street in the middle of the block was an ambulance. A noisy generator had been brought in to power the high-intensity lights that showed a knot of men in civilian clothes gathered in a wide circle around the body. Other men were kneeling, holding up the red blanket that covered the torso. A photographer had finished his work and was stowing his equipment in a leather bag.

At the tape, vanAllen showed her badge to a patrolman who was turning away a pizza delivery man. She looked at her watch. Jesus, who ordered pizza at three A.M.? Aiming over the tape, TV camera crews were shooting the scene.

In the crowd around the body, she saw the commissioner, as dapper as if he'd just stepped out of his office, the mayor with his public relations woman, the assistant chief of detectives sucking up to the mayor, his deputy, a couple of inspectors, and what looked like half the homicide division. Up and down the floodlit block, other detectives were questioning doormen, most of whom seemed to be shaking their heads. From the windows above, people stared down.

"Hey, Lou, how they hanging? Still riding to the sound of the guns?" It was Jimmy James, a first grade from the 17th Precinct who fancied himself a lady's man in spite of a wife and four kids. James was carrying the crime scene log. He had been on her backup team when she was undercover for narcotics, sometimes buying her meals after a good bust. He had made a pass at her once and never showed any resentment at her rebuff; he just switched his attention to easier targets, such as rookies just out of the academy.

"What have we got, Jimmy?" The hovering tiredness was seeping into her now, numbing her thoughts, and she still had to go back to Mickey Finn. She wasn't going to be of any use here in this circus.

"It's Mahoney all right, the ex-guv. Had his throat slit. Right outside his house. His wife's upstairs having a fit."

"He was going in or coming out?"

"In. Spent the evening boozing at Eamonn Doran's."

"The techs getting anything?"

"Not so far. No weapon, no prints they can find. No witnesses. Nothing."

"What's it look like?" Two men were bringing a body bag from the ambulance.

"You ask me, it was a mugging that went bad. Ran off with his watch, wallet, money. He took one in the belly as well as the throat."

"Sounds like overkill," she said. He snickered.

"Yeah, well, you got that right. It's gotta be a crackhead and they're not exactly brain surgeons, if you know what I mean. Thought he'd do the job right."

"Even so, why stick him twice?"

He shrugged. "You wanna make it a crime of passion, some jealous husband? A political enemy? I don't think so. You want my opinion, they won't look too deep. Let it go as just another terrible street crime. Nobody's safe."

She stared around at the posthomicide ritual. First the kidnapping and now Mahoney. The tabloids would be having orgasms. She found herself thinking of Savage, snug in bed. She dismissed the idea of calling Paige. He still owed her for the kidnapping tip and this was already old news.

"You want me to put you in the crime scene log?" James said.

She shook her head. "Not much point. I'm not going to be any use in this carnival."

"You look good in skirts," James said. "You got classy gams, should show 'em more."

Gams? She was going to let him have it when she realized he was paying a clumsily sincere compliment and, anyway, she was too tired to climb on her high horse.

"Thanks, Jimmy," she said.

13 ◀

When Paige came out of the subway at Foley Square, he walked into a scrim of water. The stifling heat had finally been broken by the storm that the forecasters had been predicting for the last twenty-four hours and the front was flushing the dead air out of the city. Marching through the explosive deluge to the courthouse, Paige was wearing the same suit as the day before. It couldn't be damaged much more; he looked as though he had spent two nights on a Greyhound bus. Anyway, the rest of his clothes were still in the motel on Long Island.

He had managed no more than five hours sleep after Lady Jane finally let him alone. She left the bed first and astonished him by running a bath for him and bringing a cup of coffee to him in the marble tub. The soap was richly scented, the towels thick and luxurious. This was the way he was meant to live. She found him a man's razor and a clean pair of men's socks. They were purple but better than nothing. He didn't ask about their original owner.

Floating around in a lacy, high-necked peignoir, talking idly about the decadence of her friends, she even cooked him a soft-boiled egg, together with a piece of toast, no butter. But when he pushed the envelope with a hint that she might be kind enough to press his suit, her unblinking blue eyes became glacial, and she said, "Just because you've been of small service to me doesn't make me Mrs. Jeeves." She emphasized the word *small*.

However, when he patted his pockets with a worried frown, she disappeared and returned with $100. "I can't think of it as real money, like sterling," she said.

"I'll have my expenses in a day or so."

"Quite," she said. Perhaps she had forgotten about the $300 she'd handed over the day before.

"See you tonight," she said as he left. It was an order. "And you'll have to show a little more stamina or you'll be in trouble." She was like some goddamned cannibal complaining about the feast just devoured.

On the subway, Paige reread the printout of the story about Savage's ex-con, Ray Bliss. It was confusingly written and didn't give Bliss's address. As best Paige could understand it, Bliss claimed that, although perfectly sane, he had been transferred from a prison to an institution for the criminally insane merely because he had caused problems in the penitentiary. It was a neat way of dealing with an agitator.

Call him mad and put him away. Certified as insane, he could be held as long as the authorities wished, never mind parole or release dates.

Nonetheless, Bliss somehow had managed to bring his case before a panel of federal judges who had ordered his immediate release. Once out, he had launched an attempt to sidestep the Eleventh Amendment, which ruled that a plaintiff born in one state could not sue a different state in a federal court. The three appeals judges turned him down.

In the courthouse, Paige found the law clerks' office and asked for anybody familiar with the Bliss case. They knew all about it. During Bliss's long struggle to appear before the federal judges, he had become something of a pet of the young clerks and they had helped him.

"He'd have made a damn good attorney, better than some I've worked with," one of the clerks said. "He spent years hitting the books, and beyond that, he has natural ability."

Paige, dripping rainwater on to the carpet, was not much impressed. He didn't think there was any such thing as a good lawyer.

"What was the rap on him?"

"Killed his wife," another clerk said. Blond and chubby-cheeked, ripe with good health, she looked as though she should be sucking up a milkshake in Minnesota instead of looking after thousands of dreary legal files and writing judges' opinions in New York City. "But he's a sweetie. He was locked up so long that he's like a man from Mars, an ET.

He's not plugged into the modern world, videos, the Internet, computers. You should get into some dry clothes. You're sopping. You'll catch pneumonia. Hang on, I'll find a towel for you." She bustled off.

"Why didn't he sue in the state courts?" Paige said. "He wouldn't have come up against the Eleventh Amendment that way."

"A matter of principle," the other clerk said. "He argues the state is the guilty party because it kidnapped him from the prison and held him illegally for all those years. You can't quote me, but in my view, he could walk into a New York court and get a chunk of money with no problem. But he's not after the money. He wants to expose the people who did it to him which, he believed, meant federal court. All down the drain now. It's astonishing he got as far as the court of appeals, a little old jailbird straight out of a time machine. A real character."

The girl returned with a ragged towel and, clucking disapproval at Paige's soggy state, mopped him as best she could. When he left, he had her phone number as well as Ray Bliss's address. Well, she would have been upset if he hadn't asked for it.

Outside, the rain had stopped and the sidewalks were already drying. It was cooler, but the sun was out and Paige could feel the heat beginning to build again. He went back into the subway and headed for Harlem.

Savage's convict lived on the top floor of a grubby, decaying building on West One-hundred-thirty-sixth Street, three blocks from the Hudson.

Puffing and sweating, Paige climbed five flights of stairs until he stood on the top landing. The place smelled of urine, mildew, and long-ago cooking. His breath was laboring and he fretted that his heart was about to rebel. His shoes crunched crack vials on the floor. Across the landing from Bliss's apartment, there was a steel door of the sort favored by drug dealers. This was no place to suffer cardiac arrest. Vowing to cut down on the booze and get more exercise, he knocked on the ex-con's door.

Ray Bliss was a little chipmunk of a man with a friar's fringe of white hair and bright, inquisitive eyes behind cheap, metal-rimmed spectacles. He wore tattered sneakers with no laces and a blue track suit two sizes too large. When Paige introduced himself, Bliss nodded impatiently as if he expected the reporter, and said, "Come in, come in. I'll tell you all about it."

The spacious, high-ceilinged room built in more gracious days was like an oversized cell. The wall plaster was peeling, and rusty pipes emerged and vanished through ragged holes in the floor and ceiling, which was rimmed with friezes. Brown linoleum on the floor was worn through in areas of heavy foot traffic. In one corner, a yellow bowl half full of water stood beneath a damp patch on the ceiling. Yet the room was clean and aggressively neat. The worn sheets and ratty blankets on the truckle bed were folded as if for inspection. Papers, pens, and pencils on a sagging desk that looked as if it had been reclaimed from a town dump were aligned as if with a slide rule. There was no telephone, no TV, just a small radio softly playing jazz. Fading photographs, evidently of Bliss in his glory days on Broadway, were taped with perfect symmetry to the flaking wall above his bed. Ray Bliss was no longer under discipline, but after decades of enforced, institutional obedience, he still lived as if he were.

The scene, though, was not entirely grim. Big windows, the glass clean, although one pane was cracked, were open to the sunshine which drenched the dingy room in an almost Mediterranean light. Paige, his breath slowing, settled cautiously into a battered armchair while Bliss boiled hot water on a gas ring for coffee.

"They call me the Forgotten Man," Bliss said proudly. For all his years in prison, he spoke formally without prison jargon and he used old-fashioned locutions. "That's right. New York buried me for a lifetime. But I beat them in the end." He paused, then said wistfully, "Or, I almost did. Those judges yesterday, they just couldn't find the courage to give me justice if it meant confronting the Constitution. You know what I told them? I said, 'The Eleventh Amendment immunity which says a citizen cannot sue a state in federal court tends to invest a state with the despotic and, hence, unconstitutional power to perpetrate major federal felonies against a citizen of this nation.'" He beamed at Paige, pleased with himself.

"Nice turn of phrase," Paige said. "Very good." He took a cup of coffee from the old man and wondered how much trouble he was going to have keeping Bliss on track. It looked as though it would take all of his considerable talents.

"Tell me about it, from the beginning," he said. "Why did you kill your wife?"

"Oh, that," Bliss said dismissively, "that had nothing to do with my case. The important thing is the wicked kidnapping by the state of New York and the years of rotten treatment that resulted." Paige sighed.

"If I'm going to tell your story properly, then I must have everything," he said. "From the beginning." Bliss, he suspected,was a rigid man with tunnel vision. That, probably, was why he had outlasted the ordeal and finally won his freedom, if living in a cell-like room in the ghetto was freedom.

"My wife," Bliss said, "was an adulteress and a thief. After we split, she got a hold of a shyster lawyer and they put the bite on me for alimony. I was very young and making swell money. They planned to bankrupt me, no doubt about it." He had grown somber and angry.

"You don't regret killing her?"

"Why should I? She deserved to die." He looked at Paige as if the question was puerile, the answer obvious.

"And what was your line of work?"

"I was a dancer, a tap dancer, and a good one. I was on the verge of becoming a Broadway star. I could have gone to Hollywood, like Cagney, made movies. And they were gonna ruin my life, that woman and her crooked lawyer. So I got a gun and went down to meet them in the lawyer's office, and I shot her dead and I wounded him. I wish I'd killed him, too. I was gonna turn the gun on myself, but it jammed and the cops came and locked me up."

"What did you get?"

"It was second-degree murder. They gave me twenty-five years to life. Disgraceful."

"Well, killing your wife is going a bit far." Bliss didn't hear him.

"They sent me to Sing Sing, and I soon found out what was going on there. It was a racket from top to bottom. There were gangsters doing time and the warden let them run the place. They had liquor, swell food, sometimes women, and they lorded it over the rest of us."

"When were you eligible for parole?"

"If I kept my nose clean, I could have gone before the board in 1954."

"You didn't keep your nose clean."

"I tried to get word out about what was going on. They got sore. I became known as a 'difficult' prisoner. They transferred me to Attica. It was the same there."

"You tried to do something about it."

"You bet. So they moved me to Hamillton."

"The Wilderness?" The Hamillton penitentiary, in the Adirondacks southwest of maximum-security Dannemora, was notorious for its harsh discipline and security. Nobody ever escaped from Hamillton.

Paige stared at the little man. Was it just a weird coincidence? Campbell had been a doctor in Hamillton, at some insane asylum.

"Yes, the Wilderness. It was as corrupt as the other prisons. I wrote to a relative, telling her that the warden was stealing funds intended for inmate necessities. The screws read my letter, passed it on to the warden who destroyed it."

"Go on," Paige said. He was taking notes on a pad that was almost falling apart from sitting so long in his hip pocket.

"I tried to take legal action, a deposition to the American Bar Association. That did it. They gave me a sanity hearing. Less than twenty-four hours later, I was transferred next door to the Hamillton State Hospital for the Criminally Insane. I was trying to get the truth out, so they said I was mad."

It was extraordinary, coincidence or not. One day the story was Campbell, the next it was Bliss, and both were tied to the same insane asylum. Was Savage playing some game with him?

Bliss showed Paige a copy of the Certificate of Lunacy that he had secured after his release. The diagnosis was paranoid schizophrenia. "Patient states the penitentiary was full of official corruption," it said, "and in his letters has shown the paranoid idea that members of the staff are against him. He was circumstantial in his conversations, paranoid, and suspicious."

Bliss started to put the document in the desk drawer, but then handed it to Paige. "I have more copies," he said. "You can keep it." Paige folded it and stuffed it in his pocket.

"Did you know a doctor called Campbell?"

"You kidding? He was the guy who signed that certificate. He was a piece of scum with a medical degree."

"You know he was killed here in Manhattan yesterday?"

"It was on the radio. I wondered if it was the Campbell from the Wilderness. Got what he deserved. But he wasn't the only one. We had guys in the hospital from prisons all over the state. Hamillton was the coffin, the place where the system buried its problems. There was nobody to complain to. We were all mad, signed, sealed, and delivered. There was so much frustration and hatred in that place, it turned the air sour."

"Worse than the joint?"

"Much worse. Sing Sing, Attica, even the Wilderness, they were rest homes compared with the hospital. A few of the guys were insane when they came in, but others went over the edge because of the way they were treated."

"What was so terrible?"

Bliss, his hands and feet shackled, was taken out of the Wilderness by three hacks in the middle of a heavy snowstorm. He shuffled up the street alongside the prison wall with its guard towers until they turned in to the hospital grounds. The walls around the hospital were just as high.

Inside, shaking the snow off his head and shoulders, he thought, at least it's warm in here, warm and quiet after the constant racket of the pen. The first thing Bliss noticed about Ward 2 was the high gloss on the wooden floor. Then the chairs. They were like thrones lining the walls of the room, thick armrests, hard flat seats, and high straight backs. There were about forty chairs in that room and most were occupied. He and Baum, who had been transferred a few days earlier, were assigned to chairs at different ends of the room. He sat and looked around. This wasn't so bad, he thought. Then he realized that nobody was talking, except the blue-uniformed attendants clustered at the doorway. They gossiped or read newspapers or smoked. The men in the chairs were allowed to do nothing but sit.

There was a clock on the wall, a clock with a pendulum. Bliss found himself watching the swing of the pendulum, letting the tick of the clock lull him. He found he was becoming hypnotized and he forced himself to look away. Across the room he saw a black man. The man was sitting stiffly in his chair, clutching its arms with straining fingers. Bliss stared and saw that the man was paralyzed with fear. Like an infection, the fear spread to Bliss. He wanted to shout his rage, throw himself at the door, but fear held him back. Three days later, the black man was found dead in a bathroom. He had been stabbed. Nobody was accused. It was as if it never happened.

Whenever the attendants looked at the prisoners it was with contempt. An attendant was of lower status in the town of Hamillton, paid less than a prison guard. Contempt was one way to redress the balance, contempt and brutality, because these were madmen who could never complain. Outside, the attendant was inferior. Here, he ruled.

Sitting on his throne that first day as the minutes and hours passed in motionless silence, a terrible understanding came to Bliss. Dear God. This was all there was.

The men sat on their thrones all day long, all week long, all month long, all year long. The horror of the desert that lay ahead engulfed Bliss. Some of the prisoners were slumped in their chairs, their faces lax, their eyes glazed. That's what it did to you, he thought, more fear slithering into his mind like a poisonous snake.

Paige said, "You stayed there all day?"

"Except for meals and a couple of hours in the yard if it wasn't raining. Every morning, we had to polish the floor of the room. There was a big block of wood covered with cloth. We had to put thick wax on the bottom and drag it up and down with cords. One man stood on the block like a charioteer to give it extra weight. It was called walking the wax. Sometimes they brought in another block and made us race while they made bets. If you lost, you spent time in a straightjacket. If you left your seat, they put a jacket on you. That's how they treated insanity."

He never saw a doctor, never received therapy. Occasionally, nurses would appear, but they kept their distance. Along with the others, Bliss suffered beatings by attendants who looked on such violence as a pastime that relieved the tedium of their duty hours. In one beating, Bliss suffered a ruptured eardrum. He saw a Mohawk Indian choked to death by an attendant with a towel. And the rapes . . . that Billy Waddell.

Attendants, enjoying the irony, threatened they would drive Bliss crazy. One broke the arches of his shoes when he saw Bliss, the Broadway dancer, try to take a few dance steps in the yard. They wouldn't let him have a pencil or paper. He did calculus in his head, made up short stories.

Maimings, killings, humiliation, and endless misery. There was nobody to step in. These were not only criminals, but insane criminals.

And then, with the help of a nurse on temporary duty at the hospital, he smuggled out letters and fought his way into the courts, and finally, he walked through the doors of the Hamillton State Hospital for the Criminally Insane and was free.

"Even at the end," Bliss said, "when the federal judges ordered us freed, the state tried to block it. The judges gave them hell, called it an American Gulag."

Getting it all down, Paige felt a growing sense of excitement. He had a story and it sharpened his senses like the first taste of alcohol. But he couldn't understand how it had been missed until now.

Bliss flourished a copy of the judges' order. "You know what happened?" he said. "That insane asylum was closed down because most of the prisoners were sane. The commissioners and their henchmen must have known it was a dumping ground for people like me who wouldn't go along with their vicious and corrupt prison system. I ended the whole iniquitous policy.

"The whole town was guilty, too. They all knew about it and nobody raised a finger to help. I'll tell you why. We were their bread and butter. So that they could have jobs, they let us rot."

Paige eased his aching fingers. "Was anything done about those responsible, the prison wardens, the commissioners, the attendants?"

Bliss shrugged. "I don't know and I don't care. The ones who put me in there must be retired or dead. They'll get their justice in hell. There must be a special hell for men who do that while walking tall, proud, and respected."

He was an old man, tired now by his long recital, but the bitterness lingered like gangrene. Paige grunted with satisfaction. When LaFleche saw it all spread out below Paige's fat byline, he would go ape. Oily bastard. It had everything: one man against the system, cruelties and injustice, decades of corruption reaching, perhaps, to the upper levels of state government. And, finally, vindication for the little man sitting in a room in Harlem.

Checking the dates, Paige knew now why the story of the judges' anger, the closing of the hospital, had never been published in New York City. The federal chief judge, Cohen, had issued his angry order during the last newspaper strike, the guild disaster. Paige had been supported through the strike by an instructress from a health club. He winced as he remembered how she had made him labor around the Central Park reservoir with all the health nuts, fed him salads and weighed and measured him every morning. After that, even the loathsome LaFleche had been a relief.

Paige struggled out of his chair. "You're a tough old bird," he said. "We'll need pictures. I'll send a photographer around." Heading for the door, he thought he'd have to check some facts, dates, talk to people. There was this weird coincidence of the doctor, Campbell. It was getting hot again.

Making his way down the dark stairwell, Paige began to compose the opening paragraphs of the story that would drive LaFleche into a long-term depression. It would be tough to make Bliss, a wife killer, into a sympathetic figure, but that hardly mattered. It was the enormity of the long-term conspiracy by the state that would blow readers' minds. He was so deep in thought that the sound of feet climbing the stairs did not register at first. But then, halfway down the first flight, he saw shadowy figures moving up.

He was alone on a stairway in a slum building in the middle of Harlem, probably a drug dealer's haven. At least two, maybe three, men were climbing toward him, almost certainly heavily armed. He was trapped, at the unlikely mercy of hardened killers who didn't think a day had been well-spent without a bloody brutal murder or two. Mustn't panic.

Paige thought of racing back up to Bliss's door,

but it was too late. They were too close and coming fast. They would have him before Bliss could open the door.

"Yo," one of them said. "The fuck are you?"

There were four of them, ranged two in front and two behind. All white from what he could make out in the gloom.

"I'm leaving," he said. "I was just visiting a friend, that's all." There was no room to slide past them.

"The fuck you're leaving," the man said. "Who you been having a little visit with, pal? You don't belong here."

"The tenant on the top floor, name of Bliss. An old friend."

"Yeah? We're old friends of his, too. He never said anything about you. Now, who the fuck are you and what are you doing here?" It was absurd, Paige thought, having to introduce himself as if he had just stepped into a cocktail party in midtown.

"Todd Paige, a reporter," he said. "I'm helping Bliss. In the news business, we like to help people whenever we can."

"You been talking to Ray? What about?"

"Oh, the difficult times he's had, that sort of thing."

"Prison?"

"Well, yes."

"The hospital?"

"Yes, a very inspiring story, the sort of story that will arouse a lot of public interest in what happened all those years, the evil that men do, that sort of thing. A very significant story, one brave man against the system and so on." Paige realized he was babbling.

They said nothing. They just stared at him. One of the pair on the lower level was smoking a cigarette, blowing the acrid smoke up at him. Paige couldn't make out the problem if they were Bliss's friends. They were still, as if frozen in place.

"Let's see some identification," the leader said. The man at his side put his hand in his pocket and suddenly there was a knife in his right fist. He held it so that the tip pointed at Paige. He started up the two steps to Paige's level, his left hand beckoning Paige toward him, a lupine smile on his raw-boned face.

There was a noise behind Paige. The four on the stairs were looking past him now. He twisted and saw that the steel door across from Ray Bliss's place had opened.

Out of it came two men, both black. They stopped when they saw the group on the stairs. One wore an Italian-styled blue pinstripe suit, a shirt so brilliantly white it seemed to glow, a red tie, with brown-and-white shoes and a cream straw hat set just so on his coffee-colored head. A pink handkerchief peeped delicately out of his breast pocket. The other was in an army fatigue jacket with military insignia on the shoulders. He had dreadlocks and a vicious half-moon of a scar across his cheek. Both were wearing black sunglasses with silver frames.

The two groups, black and white, stared at each

other while Paige shifted uneasily between them. He saw that the knife had disappeared.

"What we got here?" said the black in the suit. He pulled his jacket open so they could see a pearl-handled handgun stuck in his belt. His voice was lazy, almost sleepy. "Annual national convention of snitches and narcs?"

"Shit, it's showboat time, a superfly," said the man who had pulled the knife.

"You be here on business or to integrate the neighborhood, whitey?" The glasses hid the black's eyes so that his expression came only from his mouth. He was grinning, but there was not much humor in his voice. Paige put his back against the wall so that he could see them all without twisting his neck. They were like two wolf packs running into each other. He felt like a bone.

"None of your motherfucking business."

"You poh-lice? Here to serve and protect?"

"You can take your questions and stick 'em up your ass, see if there are any answers in there."

"Shut up, Billy." It was the leader of the four. The black in the fatigue jacket lifted an arm and pointed at the knife-man. "You done time? Upstate?" he said.

"So?"

"Billy . . . something. You in the Wilderness a while back. I see you in the yard." He leaned over and whispered to the man in the hat.

"A'right. You not here to buy? Here to see Ray Bliss?" The tension was draining away but the jacket was still open, a hand near the weapon. "We got no quarrel with you and no time for this shit, got business to take care of. How's about you gen'lemen stepping aside and letting the brothers through?"

The man in the fatigue jacket turned back and locked the steel door. The four whites stood where they were for a moment, but then at a nod from the leader pulled back against the wall.

Superfly went first, his jacket still open, his head turning first one way, then the other, as he passed the first two men below. He took his time. As if choreographed, Paige moved, slotting himself behind Superfly, and went down the stairs and past the next two men. They watched him but made no move to stop him. Paige felt like a merchant ship picking up its escort. As he went by them, he said, "Have a nice day."

He was sweating hard, only partly because of the heat in the stairwell.

He was still on the heels of Superfly when they reached the second landing. The black in the suit stopped and turned.

"What you want, ofay?"

"Out of here."

"You in trouble?"

"I was. Not now."

"You sure? Check him out."

Scarface ran his hands expertly up and down Paige's body.

"He's cool."

"You sure know how to wear a hat," Paige said.

"You reckon?" The black showed his teeth and ran his fingers around the brim, tugging it down a fraction over his right eye.

On the street, the man in the suit said, "You a big fucker, ain't you, Slick?"

"Big enough."

Superfly gently slapped Paige's cheek. "You take care now, you hear?" he said. The next moment he and Scarface, both employing a modified pimp roll, were heading for a white Volvo parked at a fire hydrant and Paige was walking toward the subway. He was moving fast, trying to get the shakes out of his legs.

Bliss heard the voices outside his door but took no notice. There was a lot of traffic around the steel door across the landing.

A few minutes after they died out, he heard a knock. He had no fear of neighborhood punks. He had spread the word that he had nothing but the miserly supplementary social security that Washington had awarded him. There was no spyhole in the door, so that when he opened it, wondering if Paige had come back for something, his surprise was complete.

14◄

Standing there were Billy Waddell and the Teacher. Behind them were Jackie Baum and Ferret.

"Hello, Ray," the Teacher said, and they walked in. In the middle of the room, Jackie put his hands on his fat hips and looked around. "Not the Ritz, Ray, but not too bad all the same," he said. "Looks as though you're doing okay." Jackie sounded uneasy. He wouldn't make eye contact with Bliss.

The Teacher went to the window and stared down at the street. Billy Waddell didn't speak to Bliss. He poked his head into the tiny bathroom, stared at the photographs above the bed. Just as silent, Ferret closed the door to the stairs and stood with his back against it. He looked haggard, skin and bones, his muscles wasted.

"You had a visitor a little while back, Ray," the Teacher said, turning from the window. "Big guy, sloppy dresser, hair all over the place. Friend of yours?" Bliss wondered how they knew the reporter had been to see him. If they saw him coming out of the building, how did they know he'd been with Bliss? Had they been watching the building, scouting him out?

"He's a newsman," he said. "He's interested in what happened to us up in the Wilderness, going to put a story in his paper. You guys want some coffee? How did you find me?"

"We asked around," the Teacher said. "You're quite famous, Ray. Getting into the appeals court again, all that. We caught it on the radio and you got some ink in the blats, too. Pity you didn't make it with the judges. You might have cleaned up."

"Yeah, how did you find me?"

"Jackie did that. He called your niece in Arkansas, the one who came to see you just before they let us out. In a couple of weeks, during her vacation time, she's coming to see you here, check you out. Sends her best." She was the only relative he had left. He had written her, told her where he was.

"It's good to see you, Ray," Jackie said. Bliss wondered why he looked so uncomfortable standing there. Jackie was an old friend. They'd known each other for nearly thirty years, watched each other's backs, suffered and struggled together. Yet he kept avoiding Bliss's eyes. Billy Waddell had given up his examination of the room. Coltrane was on the radio. Billy turned it off, went into the bathroom and, leaving the door open, relieved himself noisily. Bliss thought he was like an animal marking his territory. When he came back, zipping up his pants, all of them faced Bliss in a wide circle as if standing at the four points of the compass.

"Those niggers across the hall," Billy Waddell said. "You know 'em? They dealing?"

Bliss shrugged. "I mind my own business," he said. "They don't bother me none."

"Fuckin' jungle bunnies. Strutting around like they used to in the joint, as though they own the world. Don't know how you can live up here, nothing but niggers." Billy Waddell was as full of hate as he had been in the Wilderness.

"What are you guys doing?" Bliss said. "Where are you living?"

"In the city," the Teacher said. "We rent rooms on Eighth Avenue, down by the tunnel."

"You working?"

Billy Waddell gave a snort of laughter. "Yeah, man, we're working," he said. "Taking care of business."

"I got some money from my folks," the Teacher said. "We're making out. We pick up some work, here and there."

"You're all living together?"

"Yeah, just like the Wilderness. The money goes farther that way. We're like a unit, aren't we, Jackie?"

"Sure, we stick together. I don't have to tell you, Ray, it's not easy out there. When I came out after all those years, I felt like I was on some different planet, Mars or something. I still don't believe the way women dress and talk and act nowadays." The Teacher was staring at Bliss. He looked more confident and commanding, Bliss thought, than he had in the hospital, but there was still that strange, distant look in his cold blue eyes.

"You tell the reporter about us, Ray?" he said softly.

"He wouldn't have done that," Jackie said.

"I'm asking Ray."

"Hell, no, I didn't tell him about that stuff," Bliss said. "He wanted to know what it was like in the hospital, how I managed to get into court. That's all."

"We wanted you in with us," the Teacher said. "It's not too late. You're invited." Bliss knew why they wanted him. It was because of Jackie. They wanted Jackie because of his skill at boosting cars, picking locks, cracking safes. And they wanted Bliss because he was Jackie's pal and Jackie had told him about it.

"Did you guys hit Campbell?"

"D'you care?"

"Not much. He should be dead after what he did."

Billy Waddell said, "How did you know about Campbell?"

"It was on the radio, in the papers, the kidnap in the park. One paper had a picture of Campbell, looked like it was taken when he was up at the Wilderness."

"The reporter ask about him, Ray?"

"He mentioned him."

"You tell him about Campbell?"

"Just that he'd signed the papers, nothing else."

"So you told him that Campbell was responsible for what happened to us. You tell the reporter Campbell was on the list?"

"No. That's nothing to do with me."

"He's lying." It was Billy Waddell. "He always talked too much."

"Ray's no liar," Jackie said. "Just because he heard about Campbell doesn't mean—"

"Bet he didn't hear about that bastard, Crain," Billy Waddell said. "We got him last fall, up in the woods. I was gonna throw the cocksucking governor, Mahoney, off a bridge, toss him down in front of a bus, see if he bounced, but it didn't work out."

"Shut up," the Teacher said. "I'll do the talking here. Are you with us, Ray? You know better than anybody, it has to be done. You tried the courts for justice and that didn't work. We're the only court you've got left."

"You kidnapped the kids to cover the hit on Campbell?"

"Not a bad idea, Ray," Billy Waddell said. "But it wasn't like that. We grabbed the kids when the cop showed up just as we were gonna take care of Campbell. We got him anyway. It worked like a dream, like it worked with Crain in the mountains, like it worked with Mahoney, like it'll work with—"

The Teacher said, "Be quiet, Billy."

"What does it matter now?" Billy said rebelliously. "Whether Ray's in or out, it don't make no difference if he knows."

"Something could have gone wrong," Bliss said. "Suppose something happened to the kids."

"Nothing went wrong, except they got sick on the candy we picked up to keep them quiet," the Teacher said. "We plan, we reconnoiter, we don't go off half-cocked. You know something, we all went back to Hamillton, separately, and we walked around looking in the faces of those good citizens, good Americans, those smug bastards who helped bury us alive. Every one of them deserves to be hit, and when we've finished what we have to do, we'll let 'em know what happened, one way or another. Bet on it."

Ferret was silent, like he always was. Ferret wasn't stupid, and Bliss often wondered what went on in his head.

Billy said, "I went to the funeral of one of the screws. Remember Tiny Waldron, liked to beat up on Jackie? Died of a heart attack. When people asked why I had come, I said I was very fond of Tiny and, Jesus, were they were impressed, those straw-sucking hicks. Wow, I'd come up for his burial? Even brought flowers. I could hardly stop from laughing out loud. And while I was playing the sad mourner, I talked to them and I found out where the worst of the douche-bags were, what they were doing. Cock-suckers."

"You hear?" the Teacher said. "We use our brains, take our time."

"What happened to Crain?"

"We followed him in the woods when he went hunting," Billy Waddell said. "We blew his lying

head off. Right, Teach? When they found him a
week later they reckoned it had to be an accident.
Dumb bastards." His Alabama accent was as strong
as ever; he seemed to delight in recalling the
killings. Bliss didn't condemn them for what they
had done, what they still planned to do. He could
understand the depth of their hatred for men who
condemned them—and him—to hell as casually as
ordering a cup of coffee.

Bliss had killed, too, when the emotion seized
him. Yet this was not for Bliss, these coldly calculated executions, this justice outside the law. He
wanted nothing to do with Billy Waddell. Billy had a
sick mind, loaded like a weapon with hatred—probably should never have been released.

So what did they want with him? He looked at
them, at worried Jackie, at the silent Ferret, at Billy
Waddell, and at the stony-faced man they called the
Teacher. Every man in the room was a loser, except
Bliss knew it. If he had ever known the Teacher's real
name, Bliss had forgotten it long ago. The Teacher
was a cold man.

Bliss could feel the tension building now in this
decaying room in Harlem.

"He's not with us and that means he's agin us,"
Billy Waddell said. "We couldn't get him to join up
when we were in the Wilderness. We argued for
hours, you remember, in the yard. It's still the same.
And we had a vote."

"You can't do it," Jackie said. "You can't, not to
Ray . . ."

"We can't trust him," Billy Waddell said. His voice was excited. "Let him alone and he'll go blabbing to the cops. We had a vote and it was three to one."

"But it was Ray that got us out," Jackie said. "Without him, we'd still be walking the wax, sitting on the thrones. I want the others dead, but not Ray." He moved to Bliss's side and turned to stare defiantly at the Teacher. A police car went by outside, its siren whining.

"He could blow the whole fucking thing," Billy Waddell said. "Ray has to go." He was loving it, and there was fear now in Bliss as there had never been in the Wilderness in the worst times. Billy Waddell wanted him dead because of what had happened in the Wilderness and the Teacher needed Billy. Jackie, even if he stood with him, was an old man, and Bliss was older still. Two worn-out hulks heading for the breaker's yard.

"We'll have a little test," the Teacher said. "A test of Jackie's loyalty to the compact. Jackie, you're a friend of Ray's. You do what has to be done. Prove you're not pussy like Billy says you are."

Billy Waddell giggled and said, "Christ, Teach, you're a pistol."

"No." Jackie's voice was thin and anguished. "I can't and you can't."

He was shaking. "When we left the hospital," the Teacher said, "we set out to do a job of work. We became men of justice. Ferret's illness held us up for a while, but it didn't stop us. We chose our targets and now there are two left. I don't care what happens to me after they're dealt with, but I'm going to see the task is finished. It's all planned. Ray's no more important than we are. It's the job that's important." His bony, haunted face was expressionless.

"If Jackie won't do it, we'll have to. Sorry, Jackie, you lost the vote." He was pulling a knife from his pocket. Billy Waddell already had his out.

15 ◀

From Harlem, Paige went straight to a bar, Farley's on Fifty-seventh Street. At night, it was a favorite of aging gamblers as well as divorcees and widows who spent their mornings with the *Wall Street Journal* studying the market before mercilessly harrying their brokers. Now it was quiet, almost empty.

He ordered a J&B on ice and tried to sort out what he had learned. First, Campbell had been killed by the kidnappers in the park. Campbell was a doctor retired from the Wilderness. Bliss was a prisoner delivered to the insane asylum by Campbell. The four men in his stairwell were friends of Bliss, probably ex-prisoners. Could they be the kidnappers? Could Bliss be in cahoots with them? Was it a weird coincidence? What did Savage know about it all?

He ordered another J&B from the white-aproned bartender. Bliss didn't seem the type to involve himself in that sort of caper. He was too inflexible, self-righteous.

"You look like my ex-husband." It was a woman two seats up the bar. She was expensively dressed in a black linen number above chubby knees, frosted-haired, at least forty but well preserved as if she'd been quick-frozen. Probably a beauty when she was young. She was drinking a martini.

"Is that a compliment?"

"Not really. He was a bastard. Most men are. You married?"

"Nobody will have me."

"I'm sure that's not true." She moved down to sit beside him. "How old are you?"

"Nearly thirty-five."

"I'm thirty-two." Right, if she had lost ten years somewhere. "I'm thirty-two, the prime of life, and I'm bored rigid. My life is so uneventful, usually I don't know what day of the week it is. The one way I could tell was the *Times* had a sports section on Mondays, science, very boring, on Tuesdays, a living section, whatever the hell that means, on Wednesdays. Now they've changed that, mixed everything up, so I don't know where I am."

Paige reckoned it wasn't her first martini of the day. She had a full mouth with a discontented droop at the corners. Her ears and fingers were heavy with jewelry. She was stirring her drink with a red-tipped forefinger and then sucking it.

"Your suit needs a good press," she said.

"I know. Been very busy."

"You know the only thing that makes me feel as

though I'm alive is a good fuck." Paige looked at the bartender. He was imperturbable as a butler, ignoring them, reading a newspaper.

"One of the joys of life," Paige said agreeably.

"You like to fuck?"

"When I'm in the mood." Paige was staring at the paper in the bartender's hands. The headline was about the stabbing of the former governor, Mahoney. He frowned. Something was stirring in the back of his mind, but he couldn't hold it still to examine it.

"You sure you're not gay? There are a lot of gays in this neighborhood. Often, you can't tell, which doesn't seem fair, wastes your time."

"You live around here?" Paige said.

"Park Avenue in the sixties. Why? You want to take me home, do some fucking?"

"Can't right now. Maybe later?" She gave him a look, then produced a silver pencil and scribbled a phone number on a plain white card she took from her purse.

"What's your name?" he asked.

"Chloe."

He wrote it alongside her number.

Paige finished his drink, tossed some of Lady Jane's money on the bar, and said, "Forgive me. I have to go."

"If I'm not home," she said, "you can leave a message."

"I'll do that." Well, he might need her if Lady Jane became too insufferable. Sometimes Paige felt ashamed of himself, but not often.

In the newsroom, Paige waited until LaFleche was busy talking to the picture editor, then slipped along to Savage's office. The managing editor was on the phone. He beckoned Paige in and after a few moments put the phone down. It took about fifteen minutes for Paige to describe the events of the morning.

At the end, Paige pulled out a transcript of the federal judge's order releasing Bliss and the other inmates from the hospital, together with Bliss's certificate of lunacy. He put them on Savage's desk.

"All that in one morning, even faster than you ordered," he said. "It was damn hard going and extremely dangerous, but I don't mind hard work and risking my life if it's for the good of the paper and helps satisfy the people's historic and constitutional right to know."

"Yes, admirable," Brand said sardonically. "Which bar have you been in? You smell like a distillery."

"I was under great pressure. I needed a drink."

"Jesus, you really are a buffoon, Paige. You never know when to stop, do you? You dress like a wino and you get up people's nostrils and cause trouble all around. If you would only . . ." He fell silent, passing a metal ruler from one hand to the other in mesmerizing sequence.

"Sorry," he said abruptly. "Things have been getting on top of me lately. Forget it."

"That's all right. I know how it is, the constant pressure to be topnotch."

"For Chrissake, Paige . . . oh, hell, where's Bliss?"

"Up in Harlem. Why?"

"I'd like to talk to him."

"You're not satisfied with my report?"

"Your work, as usual, is superb. Nonetheless, I'd like to talk to him myself. I have a reason. Bring him down to the office."

Only when he was back in the newsroom did Paige remember he hadn't asked Savage about his interest in Bliss. He was walking back to the reporters' desks when somebody shouted at him. It was the photographer, Silver, who had been sent up to get some shots of Bliss. Silver usually covered baseball, thought anything else was beneath him.

"Where are the prints?" Paige said.

"What d'you mean, prints? The guy wasn't there. You send me all the way up to One-hundred-thirty-sixth Street in this flaming heat and there's nobody fucking home. I nearly got mugged, too."

"You nearly got . . . You sure you went to the right address?"

"Course I'm sure, Paige. I hammered on his door and there was no fucking answer. I hung around, tried again, then I called in and they told me to come back. I wasted the whole afternoon on your shit." He turned and stalked off.

It took Paige half an hour to reach Bliss's apartment. When his hammering heart had recovered from the climb up the stairs, he stood for a moment, admiring his courage in returning to the scene of his deadly encounter. He knocked and knocked again. Nothing.

He had to go down the stairs, find the superintendent who looked like Mike Tyson on a bad day,
argue with him, hand over ten dollars for the key,
and then struggle back up. He opened the door and
stepped inside. It was dark now, and only a glimmer
of light came into the apartment from the street
lamps. The wall light switch just inside the door
didn't work and Paige had to fumble around until he
found a table lamp.

Bliss and another man were lying on the floor in
the middle of the room. Paige realized that in his
search for the table lamp he had nearly stepped on
them.

There was blood on their clothes, on the linoleum, and splattered on the bedsheets. In the right
hand of each man was a knife. Chairs and tables had
been upended. Papers, pens, and pencils were scattered throughout the room. The end of the bed had
collapsed. Part of a sheet was wrapped around the
unknown man like a hastily-arranged shroud. Ray
Bliss's apartment no longer looked like a prison cell.

The ambulance men arrived at the same time as two
cops in a patrol car. None of them had bothered to
switch on their flashing lights and sirens. Paige took
them up to the room. The superintendent didn't go
up. He'd seen bodies in the building before. In the
apartment, Paige, who was feeling queasy, waved at
the bodies like a stage manager telling the actors to
get on with it and went to suck in some air at the

open window. It was the fourth time he had climbed the stairs and his chief emotion was relief that he would never have to do it again. One of the cops joined him at the window.

"Who the fuck are you?" he said. After showing his press card, Paige was explaining his role when, behind them, one of the paramedics said casually, "That one's gone, but there's still a spark in the other." Bliss was still alive, if only just. The medics didn't try to work on him. They nudged the knife from his hand and put him on a folding stretcher. One of the cops touched something on the floor with the toe of his shoe. "His false teeth, uppers," he said. "Better take 'em, case he makes it." The medics took Bliss and his teeth away. The body of the other man remained. The eyes were wide as if he were examining the cracked ceiling.

"Looks like they had a little disagreement," the cop said. "Who are they?" His partner, kneeling, was going through the dead man's pockets.

"I don't know who he is," Paige said. "The live one's Ray Bliss, an ex-con who was helping the rag on a story. He lived here. I saw him this morning and then I came back tonight and there they were."

"No ID, but there's a letter to somebody called Jackie Baum," the partner said, getting to his feet. "It's a ConEd bill." He was counting money. "Thirty-five dollars and change. A handkerchief and a pen and a key. That's it. He traveled light." He put the money in his pocket, saying, "I'd better look after this."

"Where have they taken Bliss?" Page asked.

"Columbia-Presbyterian, probably," one of the cops said. "He looked like a goner to me, though. Can you imagine, two old farts killing each other like that?"

They had to wait more than half an hour before two detectives arrived, complaining bitterly about the stairs. "It's always the top apartment," one of them said. "They can't kill themselves on the ground floor or, better yet, out on the street." He was wearing a Hawaiian shirt, decorated with purple flowers and fizzing champagne glasses, hanging outside his pants as if he had just come off the beach. "He's white? Makes a change. Where's the other late lamented? I thought there were supposed to be two stiffs."

The uniforms explained the situation, and the other detective, who had been disdainfully prowling the room, said, "Best for all concerned if he croaks. Wrap it up nicely. Any cash on them?" The patrol car cops became interested in Bliss's show business pictures.

While they stayed to wait for the ME and the morgue wagon, Paige went with the detectives to the 26th Precinct to sign a statement. He was trying to make some sense out of it all. The men on the stairs must have had something to do with it all. He told the detectives about the episode on the stairs, but they weren't impressed. "Lot of nuts in New York," Hawaiian shirt said. He was chewing Tums like candy. From the stationhouse, they gave Paige a ride to Columbia-Presbyterian, and he waited in the reception area until they came down half an hour later.

"He's still alive," Hawaiian shirt said without enthusiasm. "They've got him in surgery and the docs say he has a small chance of making it."

"Did you talk to him?"

"You kidding? He's not exactly making speeches up there. He's more dead than alive. No rush. He's not going anywhere for a while. The precinct is putting a cop on his door."

Lady Jane had given Paige a key to the brownstone. The lights downstairs were out, but there was a glimmer at the top of the stairs. He went into the kitchen and found some cold chicken in the refrigerator. He washed it down with a glass of milk.

She must be asleep. He thought of stretching out on a couch in the living room where he could rest in peace but finally climbed the stairs. He was undressing, trying to be silent, when she said, "Hello, darling. You're late again. Better hang up that dreadful suit." Christ, she sounded like a long-suffering wife.

"I bought you a toothbrush and a few clothes when I was shopping. You'll find them in the bathroom." She sounded sleepy and didn't lift her head from the pillow.

"Any pajamas?"

"Pajamas just get in the way." When he slid

between the sheets, she rolled over against him, a hand reaching down between his legs. "I've decided I quite like you," she said. "At least you show willing." But a moment later, her hand relaxed and she began a gentle snore.

16 ◀

Lady Jane had bought him three pairs of khakis from Calvin Klein which fitted okay, socks, underclothes, and a half dozen sports shirts with rabbits embroidered on the chest.

She woke him at nine o'clock and immediately wanted what she called a frolic, but at least he had managed a full night's sleep. Was it wishful thinking, or had she become softer, more amenable? She gave him cereal, skim milk, and scrambled some eggs for him. Then, sipping coffee, she watched him while he ate.

"I'm having a dinner party," she said, "introduce you to a few friends, maybe Mary the man-eater and that hot new novelist, Mickey McGovern. You could discuss literature, postmodernism, biographies, and scribbling like that."

"When?"

"In a day or so."

"Going to be very busy."

"I'm sure you can spare me a little time. In fact,

I know you can." The imperious note was back in her voice and Paige wondered if it was time for another declaration of independence from British domination. But he said, "Sure," and called Columbia-Presbyterian. Bliss was in grave condition, no visitors, but there was a slim chance he might recover.

He called Savage and told him about Bliss's plight.

"When can we talk to him?"

"They don't know yet. He's still comatose."

"Be there when he comes around."

"If he does. Listen, I was wondering about your interest in Bliss. I think I'm missing something." But Savage had hung up.

Paige considered buying a white coat and a stethoscope, better still, renting them, but instead went to the hospital and told the girl at the reception desk he was a detective from the 26th Precinct with new orders for the patrolman guarding Raymond Bliss.

He was directed to the third floor where, along the corridor, he saw a uniformed man on a chair morosely staring at a NO SMOKING sign.

Paige walked briskly, authoritatively, along the corridor and, when he reached the cop, said, "DA's office. Open up. I have to take a statement from Bliss." The cop remained slouched in his chair and looked at Paige with soft, spaniel eyes.

"Yeah," he said, "go right in, sir. Of course, if you do, I'll have to arrest you for impersonating an officer of the court, along with a few other things I'll think of on the way to the stationhouse."

"Officer," Paige said, "it's very important that I talk to Mr. Bliss, so important that I'm prepared to make it well worth your while."

"Press, huh? Maybe I'll do you for attempted bribery as well. It'd get me away from this lousy post."

"I meant, of course, that I might be able to help your career. A word in the right place . . ."

"Gee, thanks. However, my career is on a roll since my sister started dating the commissioner."

"You don't understand. This Ray Bliss is a friend of mine. I spent all yesterday morning with him and I was able to help the police with vital information after he was found." The door alongside the cop opened and vanAllen came out, followed by a white-coated doctor.

"Paige," she said, "what are you doing here?" She was in one of her dark pants suits.

"Pursuing certain inquiries."

"He was trying to get in, lieutenant," the cop said. "Tried to bribe me." He was still slumped in his chair.

"Paige always uses checks for his bribes," vanAllen said, "and they always bounce so it doesn't count. And whatever you do, officer, don't try to look smart while you're on duty here. The way you lounge around in that chair gives the place a homey atmosphere." The cop nodded.

"Thanks, lieutenant," he said. VanAllen seemed on the point of saying more, but instead, rolled her eyes at the doctor and said, "You want a cup of coffee, doc?" He looked at his watch and said, "Okay, a quick one." They walked down the corridor with Paige trailing behind.

"How's Bliss doing?" Paige said.

"Remarkably well," the doctor replied. "A tough old guy, that one." The doctor was Chinese, with a round, smiling face. His smooth cheeks glowed as if he had an electric light lodged in his mouth.

"The knife just missed his aorta which carries blood from the left ventricle of the heart. Another fraction of an inch and he would have been done for. As it was, the blade penetrated his lung and collapsed it."

"You don't have to talk to Paige, doctor," van-Allen said.

"You know, I was the one who found Bliss," Paige said. "Probably saved his life. Not that I'll get any thanks around here."

"Thanks," vanAllen said. "Of course, the doctors here may have had something to do with it as well." In the cafeteria, Paige was allowed to buy the coffee and they took a table in the corner.

"Is Bliss talking?" Paige said. The coffee tasted weird.

"Not to me," vanAllen said.

"He was talking to the nurses," the doctor said. "He was discussing some law case. They thought he was an attorney."

"Has he been charged yet?" Paige said.

"No, but he will be."

"What about the stiff? Has he been identified?"

"What's your interest in all this, Paige?"

"You show me yours and I'll show you mine."

"Okay, if that's the way you want it. The kidnappings in the park."

"The Wilderness."

"What do you know about the Wilderness?"

"Ray Bliss was up there in the hospital. I'm doing a story about him." The doctor, looking puzzled, softly excused himself, telling vanAllen to have him called if necessary.

Paige pushed away his coffee cup. "You didn't tip me about Mahoney," he said.

"Couldn't find you."

"Why are you interested in Bliss?"

"Mickey Finn."

"Let's not start up again. Who's Mickey Finn?"

"A wino in the Sutton Place park who saw the door being unlocked so the kidnappers could come up from the drive. I found him, and he spent a while eating pizza and looking at mug shots."

"He came up with somebody?"

"He came up with a hard-time con named Jackie Baum, released from the Wilderness about a year ago. Did time in the pen after being convicted of armed robbery and moved to the hospital next door when they decided he was insane. He left a young woman paralyzed for life and they threw the book at him. Pal of Ray Bliss. This coffee is terrible."

"You found this Jackie Baum?"

"I found him. In the morgue. Sheer luck that I made the connection. The stiff that Ray Bliss knifed, his old pal, was Jackie Baum."

"Jesus, why would Baum and Bliss start sticking knives into each other?"

"That's what I'm here to find out."

"What does Bliss say?"

"He won't say anything. He doesn't like cops."

"You should show him the warm and caring side of your nature."

"I'll show him the inside of a cell as soon as he's on his feet again." Paige hit the table with his fist.

"Hey," he said, "I've got a great idea."

"Yes, I thought you would have."

"I'll go talk to Bliss. He'll open up to me because I'm not a cop and because we already talked and he knows he can trust me." Paige was delighted with his inspiration. "You're very lucky I showed up, when you come to think about it. Let's go." Paige started to get up from the table, but vanAllen remained where she was.

"Wait a minute, Speedy Gonzalez," she said. "Bliss is under arrest and I'm not having a civilian like you talking to him." She paused and added, "Unless I'm present. Even then it's highly irregular, but circumstances might warrant it." Paige sat down again.

"What are you gonna do?" he said. "Crawl into the room and hide under the bed? He won't talk, even to me, if you're hanging around, and you know it. Anyway, you'd have to give him his rights. Let me just have a chat with him and then—remember, I'm a trained observer—I'll tell you what he has to say. Okay?"

"I have to be there."

"Look, what have you got to lose? Without me, you're getting nothing. With me, at least you'll get something. I tell you, he knows me. We spent hours together before he was hit and he talked his head off about the hospital."

"There's still the matter of reading him his rights."

"Oh, come on. You don't have to use what he says, not in court. You don't need it with all the other evidence you've got. The thing is, Bliss could lead you to the kidnappers. Maybe he's one of them. Let's go." This time, vanAllen stood up.

"Okay," she said. "But I'll have to get the doc's permission."

Bliss was lying on his back, his arms straight down his sides outside the sheet. Tubes and wires snaked from his body to various bottles and machines. Alongside the bed were an oxygen tank, a suction machine, and a defibrillator. Intranasal cannulas were clamped to his nose. The room was dimmed by half-closed blinds, but Paige could see that Bliss's eyes were closed.

"Ray," he said softly, approaching the bed. The doctor had said he could stay for no more than ten minutes. Bliss opened his eyes and stared up at the ceiling. Paige moved to stand where the old man could see him.

"How're you doing, Ray?" he said. Bliss's eyes focused on him.

"It's you," he said. His voice was weak but clear. His teeth were back in place.

"I found you in the apartment, Ray. Got you to the hospital just in time."

"Where's the cop?"

"She's gone."

"Don't like cops, male or female."

"I don't blame you. What happened, Ray? You had a fight?"

"Is it true Jackie's dead?"

"He's in the morgue. What happened?"

"Poor Jackie. He couldn't go along with it, not when we were pals."

"Go along with what?"

"Nothing."

"Look, Ray, you're in serious trouble. They're gonna hit you with a homicide charge when you get out of here, maybe while you're still in that bed."

"I didn't kill Jackie. It was a setup."

"If they convict you, Ray, you'll go back inside. Maybe back to the Wilderness. They'll say they were right about you all the time." A bleakness settled on Bliss's gray and wasted features. Wherever he was sent, after closing the hospital, after humiliating the system, the guards would be waiting for him. He hadn't many years left, anyway. He would die in prison. Still, he stayed stubbornly silent and if there was despair in him he wouldn't let it show.

"Who killed Jackie, Ray?"

"They shouldn't have killed Jackie and they

shouldn't have tried to kill me. The old PK as well. They got him."

"Who got him, Ray? The four guys I met on your stairs?"

"God, maybe he is crazy."

"Who's crazy?" Paige could feel rising irritation, and he had to struggle to keep his temper. He felt certain that the answers to all the questions bedeviling him were in the little man lying there, but they might as well have been locked in a safe.

"I'm not saying any more. I suppose the cop's waiting outside, waiting for you. Or have they got the room bugged?"

"You'll go back to the Wilderness, Jackie. They'd love to send you back." Bliss flinched, but then his mouth set in the old obstinate line.

"In all the time I spent in Sing Sing and Attica and the Wilderness, the hospital, I never once snitched. Once, in Attica, I got put in the hole because I wouldn't play the canary. I'm not gonna start now and that's it."

His gaze went from Paige to the ceiling. If there had been pride in his record of never informing, now there was sadness in his lined face.

"It's not snitching to save lives. They may be planning to kill more people. You could save them, Ray." Paige paused and added, "Like I saved you." It did no good. Bliss would say no more. He lay there staring up and Paige knew it was over.

"I'm sorry, Ray," he said. "I'll do what I can for you, but they've got you by the short hairs. Maybe I

can at least help keep you out of the Wilderness."
There was no sign that Bliss had heard the words. He
studied the ceiling as if he were alone.

VanAllen was unimpressed with Paige's effort at
interrogation. "If it was a setup, why doesn't he tell
us who arranged it?"

"When I came out from his apartment, there
were four men on the stairs, all menacing as hell.
Maybe they were the ones who set it up. Maybe they
were the kidnappers."

"What did they look like?"

"It was too dark to see them properly. All white,
but I'd hardly recognize them if they walked down
this corridor."

"Some reporter." It was the uniformed man, still
slouching in his chair.

"Maybe they were just guys living in the building."

"They said they were friends of Bliss. Got any
more on the kidnapping?"

"Bits and pieces."

"What about the woman who was shot? She
available now? Make a nice feature."

"She's up in Connecticut, recuperating with a
friend who was in the park when it happened.
Melissa Fox." She gave Paige an address. "This has
all been a waste of time," vanAllen said.

"That's where you're wrong. In an interview, an
experienced man, a trained observer, knows that the
atmosphere, together with what is not said, is just as
important as what is said—" Paige broke off.
VanAllen was stalking away down the corridor.

"Anyway," Paige called after her, "at least he talked to me."

He looked at the lounging cop and said, "Better stay alert, officer. Otherwise, Bliss might rip out all the tubes, jump out of bed, and take off at high speed."

17 ◀

Instead of exposing himself to LaFleche's malice at the office, Paige took a cab back to Lady Jane's brownstone. She was watching a TV talk show on which three strippers in skimpy dressing gowns were arguing that by taking off their clothes they were championing free speech.

"What 'straordinary creatures," Lady Jane said. "That one with the orange hair, she looks like my sister, the one who's always whining about Daddy leaving me his money. She called me Daddy's favorite. God, I was everybody's favorite."

Paige retreated to the kitchen, where he called Savage and reported his lack of progress with Bliss. The managing editor mystified and pissed him off by telling him to delay his Ray Bliss story until later.

"Look," Paige said, "I wanted to ask you something. I can't help wondering why you're so interested in Bliss."

"Try not to wonder," Savage said. He gave Paige the go-ahead to find the woman who had been wounded in the park. The phone at the Connecticut address was unlisted.

"Have to go up to Connecticut," he said to Lady Jane who had given up on the strippers. "You doing anything?"

"I was thinking of going to Brooklyn."

"Nobody goes to Brooklyn."

"Quite. But there's supposed to be a darling little restaurant on the river with marvelous views of Manhattan. You can come if you like, have lunchipoo."

"How about an afternoon in the country?"

She sighed. "You need a chauffeuse again, I suppose. I should get a cap with a shiny peak. Sure you're not trying to use me for your fantasy?"

But she agreed to take him, this time in a green Range Rover that looked as though dirt had never been allowed to touch its wheels, let alone its exterior. It carried a vanity plate: LADYJ 3. She must have a goddamned fleet of autos in her garage. "More suitable for the country," she said. "They'd probably be overawed if they saw a Mercedes."

All the way up, Lady Jane played a Beatles disk, frequently singing along with them in a tuneless but utterly confident voice. After half an hour of cruising past secluded estates west of Stamford, they finally found the Fox place. The acreage was surrounded by high wooden fencing, but the tall iron gates were open and they drove in alongside expansive lawns which gave way to a sprawling mock-Jacobean mansion. Off to the left was an ivy-covered guest cottage. A dark blue, late-model Mercedes and a Grand

Cherokee stood on the gravel by the front door of the main house.

"A Mercedes salesman must have strayed into wildest Connecticut," Paige said. The establishment, he thought, screamed of money.

To their right, they saw the sun-splashed glitter of a swimming pool. There were tables and chairs and gaily-colored umbrellas to the side, and somebody was doing a lazily-expert crawl through the shimmering water. The free-form, granite-sided pool was dressed up with an artificial waterfall which tumbled into one end through artfully-arranged ferns and flowers.

A woman was sitting under one of the umbrellas alongside a little trolley bearing an ice bucket, bottles, and glasses. She wore a summery dress, her right arm was in a sling, and Paige knew he had found what he was looking for. Followed by Lady Jane, he ambled over to her and said, "Mrs. Webster? Charlotte Webster?"

She looked at him nervously. She was plump, with a pleasant, round face.

"Nothing to worry about, Mrs. Webster," he said, showing the palms of his hands as if to prove he had no weapon. "Todd Paige, from one of the New York rags."

"Press?"

The swimmer had come to the side of the pool and was gracefully climbing out. Paige gave her an approving nod. She was tall and tanned and lissome, and she wore a sleek black tank suit. Standing there, the water streaming down her body, she looked at Lady Jane and said, "Who are you, his auntie?"

Lady Jane smiled sweetly and said, "Darling, you really should find your glasses now that you're out of the water. Vanity can be so dangerous—I had a friend who broke her ankle because she wouldn't wear her glasses."

The swimmer—it had to be Melissa Fox— looked at Lady Jane's off-white Isaac Mizrahi silk dress. "Attention, Kmart shoppers," she said.

"What I find 'straordinary about America," Lady Jane said, "is the way people from belowstairs are allowed to come up and mix with their betters." Paige stared, first at Lady Jane, then at the woman in the swimsuit. They had hardly met and they were going at each other like a snake and a mongoose. Funny, really, because they were so similar, aggressive, blond, blue eyes, okay looks, about thirty-five.

"I just want a couple of minutes with Mrs. Webster," he said.

"Let's throw them out," Melissa Fox said. "I'll go get the horsewhip." Instead, she went to the trolley and picked up a glass. The ice tinkled seductively and Paige looked at it wistfully.

"D'you have a press card?" Charlotte Webster said. Paige fumbled in his pockets and produced his police card, which said he could pass police and fire lines if officers were feeling in a generous mood. She examined it, handed it back. "It's all over, thank God," she said. "There's nothing more to say."

"Is Bobby all right?"

"He's fine, thank you. The kids are taking a nap."

Melissa Fox put down her glass and said, "We

could have them both frog-marched down to the road, toss 'em out. That would be satisfactory."

Lady Jane suddenly said, "Dinner at the Schrafts, the Dakota, three weeks ago. You were in a black number, practically falling off you, and wearing far too much jewelry. Your husband kept putting his hand on my knee."

"Ah, yes," Melissa Fox said, "now I remember. You had at least one too many drinks, as I recall. Quite embarrassing all around. I'd offer you a drink now, only you'd probably do a repeat."

"Oh, Melissa," Charlotte said, "let's not be beastly to them. I feel so good, so grateful, for everything today."

"You're very kind, especially after your ordeal," Paige said. "I had just a couple of questions. About what happened in the park. And about Campbell."

"The man who was killed? God, that was so terrible, on top of everything else that day. Poor Dr. Campbell. Melissa, couldn't we offer them a drink? It's so hot." Melissa shrugged assent, and Paige, with a muttered word of gratitude, helped himself to a glass, ice, and vodka. It went down beautifully. Lady Jane slipped off her shoes and sat at the side of the pool, dangling her feet in the water.

"What d'you want to know?"

"Campbell. Did you know him?"

"Not really. I just talked to him occasionally, chatting, nothing more. He said he was a retired physician." Page sank into a garden chair.

"Nice guy?"

"He was pleasant enough, I suppose. A little shy, I think. He was just terribly unlucky, being there when those men started shooting. I can't help wondering if it was partly my fault that he was killed. If I hadn't lost my mind when they snatched Bobby and rushed at them, they might not have fired at all."

Melissa Fox had been staring at Lady Jane as if making an inventory of her flaws. Now, she dove back into the pool, making sure to splash Lady Jane's silk dress.

"Tell me what happened."

As Charlotte talked about that day in the park, Paige scribbled in his notebook, getting up once for more vodka.

By the time she finished her account, Melissa had come to the side of the pool. She was supporting herself with her arms in front of her on the edge while her feet lazily kicked in the water.

"I don't think it was just by chance that the doctor was hit," she said slowly. "I don't think it was stray bullets."

"Oh, Melissa, it was an accident," Charlotte said. "I mean, they meant to fire, but they didn't mean to kill him in particular. They were kidnappers. The stray bullets just happened to hit him."

Melissa shook her head. "Maybe the first burst was wild, when they hit you," she said. "But when he fired the second time, I got a glimpse of him. He wasn't simply spraying bullets. He was aiming directly at the bench where Campbell was sitting. The more I think about it, the surer I am. The papers said there were two other people on that bench and neither of them got a scratch, just Campbell."

"Didn't you tell the police?" Lady Jane said. Melissa flexed her arms and came out of the water. There was a white sunpad on the tiles, and she stretched out on it on her belly, drops of water rolling from her tanned back and legs.

"Look," she said to Paige, "if you insist on bothering us, you can at least make yourself useful. Get hold of that suntan oil and go to work. Just the back of my legs, I think. And bring my drink over here."

He took her drink over to the pad and opened the bottle of suntan oil.

"Did you tell the detectives?" he said. Lady Jane was standing up and slipping her shoes back on.

"No. Well, I tried to, but they weren't interested. All they wanted to know was, would I recognize the kidnappers? Joke. Their heads were completely covered."

"Why would a bunch of kidnappers want to kill a bystander not even related to the kids?"

"Beats me. But I reckon he was aiming at the doctor, not just anybody. Now get to work with that oil, you hear." Paige was about to kneel alongside the sunpad when Lady Jane said, "I don't think there will be time for slapping suntan oil on her cellulite, darling. I've just remembered I have to be back in town." She gave Melissa Fox an icy smile but didn't get one back.

"I still have a couple of questions," Paige said.

"Well, I have to go. Perhaps you can find another way of getting back." Paige put down the oil.

"How are you feeling now, Mrs. Webster?" he said. Lady Jane was walking back toward the Range Rover.

"A little uncomfortable still. It throbs. But I was very lucky, it was just a flesh wound. They say there won't even be much of a mark. The doctors kept me in the ward overnight for observation and then let me come up here so long as I promised to take it easy. Melissa has been wonderful and my husband is taking the train up to see me this evening."

"Better go and catch up with your keeper," Melissa Fox said.

In the Range Rover, Lady Jane gave him a look and said, "That woman. Her husband tried to get his hands on me and she tried to get her hands on you."

"Actually," Paige said, "she tried to get my hands on her."

"Darling," Lady Jane said, "you have to understand something. She wasn't interested in you. In her pathetic way, she was trying to upset me. . . ." Paige was thinking, son of a bitch, suppose Melissa Fox was right and Campbell was the target all along—it put everything in a different light.

"However, at the moment, while you're enjoying my bed and board, you will focus your attention only on me. When I've finished with you, you can mess about with anybody you like, including raddled creatures in Connecticut, but that moment has not yet arrived."

Paige was silent. He thought he was developing a headache.

18 ◄

It was after midnight when Morgan arrived back at his summer place. The $200-a-plate dinner in Albany had been the usual goddamned nonsense: too much whisky, too many handshakes, too many bad jokes and too many politicians. For once, the food at the hotel down the hill from the Capitol had been tolerable and he had overeaten. The ice cream cake, followed by the brandy at the bar, had been a mistake. Morgan disliked these affairs; he would rather have sent a check and been done with it. Instead of listening to the ramblings of the senate majority leader he could have been relaxing with Sibelius. It was one reason he had left state government.

Still, in his business, the contacts made at fundraisers were vital. The truly successful attorney was not the silver-tongued orator but the man who was trusted and accepted as a peer by the right people and awarded a slice of the pie. If the truth were known, he reflected, the other guests probably were as bored by him as he was by them.

It was a beautiful night. Leaving the Continental in the driveway, he strolled down the flagstone path to the little beach at the edge of the lake. The glossy water threw back the glow of the moon and he was tempted to strip and take a plunge. Picking up a pebble and skimming it across the surface, he thought, Not with my full belly. He turned and looked across the lawn to the sprawl of the house. No lights except on the porch. Mary must have fallen asleep long ago. Perhaps he would wake her, play the ruthless ravager. Plumper now than on their wedding day, she was still a handsome woman who could arouse him with a sidelong smile.

In the summer months that they spent out here at the lake, she slept naked. After all these years, she still responded to him like an ardent girl and she wouldn't mind being woken. Perhaps not. He had an early appointment in the morning, and besides, his stomach was uncomfortably distended.

Morgan was in the kitchen drinking a glass of hot milk when the phone rang. He looked at the clock. For Pete's sake, it was nearly one o'clock in the morning. He lifted the receiver from the wall phone.

"Is that Morgan?" It was a man, maybe a Southern accent.

"Yeah, who the hell's this?"

"Davey Morgan?"

"No," he said. "You've got the wrong number, pal. Jesus, you know what time it is?" The man had hung up. There was an extension in the bedroom and

the call must have woken Mary. Oh, well, he thought,
fate wants her to be ravished and I must obey.
Turning off the kitchen light, he went upstairs in the
dark, taking off his jacket and tie as he went.

Morgan awoke with one arm still around her shoulders. Lying on her right side, she had her lax left hand
resting on his stomach. The moonlight had gone and
the room was dark. Twisting his head, Morgan saw
from the illuminated hands of the bedside clock that
it was 2:17. The wind must have come up; through
the open windows he could hear the steady slap of
water against the dock at the end of the beach. With a
little sigh, Mary pulled her hand from him and rolled
on to her other side. She was breathing steadily and
he was reluctant to move his arm and perhaps wake
her again. After welcoming his assault so eagerly, she
deserved the rest. Remembering her avidity, he
smiled into the darkness. In public, she was so deco-
rous, in bed such a wanton.

He wondered what had awoken him. There had
been a burglary at one of the houses across the lake,
at the Simpson's, but that had been a month ago and
two teenagers had been charged. Had he locked
the doors? No, usually they never bothered out at the
lake. Perhaps the raccoons had turned over the
garbage can again.

He was still drowsily debating with himself
whether to get up when the door swung open. The
beam of a flashlight dazzled, almost blinded him.

Behind it, he sensed rather than saw figures. The light hovered over the bed, then settled on him. Besides him, Mary was stirring, coming awake. Struggling into a sitting position, he threw up his arm to protect his eyes from the glare.

"What the hell?" he said. "Get the fuck out of here."

"My God," Mary whispered. As his eyes became accustomed to the light, he saw there were three of them. All wore ski masks and carried automatic rifles. Suddenly Morgan remembered the phone call. They had wanted to make sure he was at home. With dread moving in on him, he knew it was more than a burglary. The man with the flashlight was carrying his weapon by a sling over his shoulder, but the other two were pointing their rifles directly at Morgan.

"Joe," Mary said. He put his arm around her bare shoulders, pulled her towards him. His head was full of visions of the Manson gang, creeping and crawling into sleeping households, killing for no reason other than the delight of killing. All that blood, all that giggling horror. Or the Clutters in their lonely Kansas farmhouse, bound, knifed, shot.

"Morgan." It was the man with the flashlight. "Joe Morgan." The words were flat, a statement not a question.

"I'm Morgan," he said. He was astonished at the steadiness of his voice. "Who are you? What d'you want?"

"Anybody else in the house?" He shook his

head. Thank God, the kids were far away, Joe Jr. doing a summer course, Maureen working as a camp counselor in Michigan.

"We're alone. Who are you?"

"You don't know us, Morgan, but we know you very well. Draw the curtains." One of the men moved to the open windows and pulled the drapes across. Mary's hand was gripping his naked thigh with painful intensity. Really alone, he thought. The only house in sight of theirs was half a mile across the lake. The privacy had been one of the attractions when they bought it. Alone and naked to mine enemies. One of the invaders leaned forward and switched on the bedside light.

The warm glow that earlier had illuminated their pleasure now mocked. It showed a man at each side of the big bed, the third at the foot, all staring down at him through diamond-shaped eye-holes. Mary's breath was coming in jerky spasms and she was moaning softly with terror. The man with the flashlight turned it off, put it on the bedside table by the lamp, and took his weapon off his shoulder. Like the others, he was wearing gloves. The guns were black and lethally ugly, with magazines curving down in front of the trigger guards.

"Mrs. Morgan, get up," one of the men said. His voice was cold, without inflection. "We want to talk to your husband. Alone." Now she clung to Morgan with both hands, pressing her face into his chest and away from the nightmare around her. Her breath was coming so fast that he thought she was hyperventilating.

"You won't hurt her?" he said.

"If she does as she's told, gives us no trouble. It's you we want to talk to." The man at the foot of the bed turned and went into the bathroom that led directly off the bedroom. He switched on the light, looked in and said, "This'll do. There's no phone."

"Too close." It was the one who seemed to be their leader. "She'll hear. Go find some other place and make sure it has a lock. Check on the other bedrooms while you're at it." His voice was calm and controlled, as if he were ordering from a menu. The other man went out of the bedroom, but the two remaining guns remained unwaveringly on Morgan.

"Get up, Mrs. Morgan."

"She's got nothing on," Morgan said. "For God's sake, have some decency."

"I said, 'Get up, Mrs. Morgan.'"

"It's all right, Joe," she said. Her breathing had steadied and her grip on him loosened. "We have to do what they say. Then they'll go away." She pulled her head down and kissed him.

"Please do what they want, Joe," she said. "For my sake." Throwing back the sheet on her side of the bed, she put her feet on the floor and stood up. Standing there, her arms straight down her sides, she looked defiantly at the intruders.

The man on her side of the bed laughed softly and said, "Very nice, Mrs. Morgan. A little chubby, but very nice all the same." Morgan recognized the Southern accent.

"Damn you," he said. "Give her a robe." They

ignored him. The third man came back into the bedroom. He was smoking, flicking the ash onto the rug.

"I've found a place, Teach," he said, "another
bathroom down the corridor. No phone, one small
window that doesn't open, and it's got a lock and key.
There's nobody else around." He glanced at the
naked woman without interest.

The Southerner found one of Morgan's ties in
the closet. He went behind the woman, jerked her
arms until they met at her back, and tied her wrists
together. He looked down at her buttocks and said,
"She's got a little mole just above her crack. But I
expect you know all about that, Morgan."

"You hurt her," Morgan said, "and I swear . . ."

"You're in no position to make threats, Morgan,"
the leader said. "The days when you can hurt other
people are over. Stick her in the bathroom." The
Southerner took a grip on her dark hair where it fell
behind her shoulders and on her bound wrists. He
started to push her out of the room. At the door she
twisted her head toward her husband.

"I'll be all right, honestly, Joe," she said. There
were tears in her eyes. Tears for me, he thought. Her
captor shoved her forward, out of the room. Morgan
heard her say, "I love you, Joe." Then she was gone.

Morgan looked at the bedside clock and for a
moment thought it had stopped. It was less than ten
minutes ago that he had opened his eyes in the
friendly darkness. He heard the distant drone of a
plane and he thought wistfully of people reading,
quietly talking, sleeping, far above him, their only

concern the time of arrival. He heard a door slam, heard a key turn, and then the third man returned. "All secure," he said. "Neat little bush she's got."

Morgan sat straighter in the prison of his bed, his arms and hands outside the sheet that draped him from the waist down. At least Mary was out of whatever was to come.

"Can I put some clothes on?" he said without hope. It was as if he hadn't spoken.

"Morgan." It was the leader. "You're a thief and worse."

"What? What have I stolen?" He had stolen nothing from these men who said he didn't know them. It had to be some terrible mistake.

"You stole time. You stole the prime of our lives." A glimmer of understanding crept into the back of his mind.

"You're felons," he said. "You must be mad." At the words, a snort of laughter came from the man at the end of the bed.

"Morgan, you remember when you were the State Commissioner of Correction?" Of course he remembered. He had served the state for three years and not enjoyed any of them very much. When the administration changed, he had been glad to go back to his private practice and forget any absurd dreams of high office. He wasn't cut out for that stuff.

"You were convicts when I was commissioner?"

"We were more than that, Morgan." He stared at them and for a moment bewilderment displaced his fear.

"Can I have a drink?" he said.

"Get him some water, Billy," the man at his side said, and the fear flushed back into Morgan. Until then, they had been careful to use no names. Now they didn't care that he knew the first name of one of them, maybe didn't care if he knew all their names. With his wife gone, it didn't matter. He knew they meant to kill him. Terror froze his limbs.

Billy came back from the bathroom with a glass of water and put it on the bedside table. It was filled to the brim and some of the water slopped over. Morgan couldn't bring himself to try to pick up the glass. He knew his hands would be shaking so much and he was ashamed. He had to dig his fingers into the sheet to keep them still.

"You know the Wilderness." Again, it was a flat statement.

"Hamillton? I was there a few times. Introduced some reforms, visiting privileges, and so on." It was pathetic, the attempt to ingratiate himself.

"You remember the hospital next door to the prison?"

"The hospital for the insane? You were all in there? My God, is that what this is all about? You were in there . . . madmen? And they let you out, those crazy judges."

"After years and years, long after our sentences should have ended, Morgan. You and the rest stole twelve years of my life. And even at the end you tried to keep us in. You wanted to keep us in that stinking hole forever."

"For God's sake," he said, desperation strengthening his voice, "I had nothing to do with that. I didn't decide who went into the hospital. That was up to experts. And when the inmates brought suit, the state had to contest it. That's the way the system works, don't you see that? The judges hear the testimony from both sides and they make their decision. And you were released. You won."

"Oh, is that right? You remember getting any letters from me, from Billy Waddell?" It was the Southerner. Morgan shook his head; he was so petrified he could hardly remember his own name. Then he realized, this Billy had given his full name. Oh, God.

"I know you got them, you scumbag," Billy said, "because I got people outside the hospital to mail them. Six times I wrote to you, Morgan. I told you what they were doing in the Wilderness, how they were calling prisoners insane and putting them in the hospital. Burying them alive."

"I wasn't responsible . . ."

"Didn't matter who actually did it. It was your responsibility because you were commissioner. Now, a slick lawyer like you might claim that, even so, you knew nothing about it because they kept it from you. But you can't because I wrote and told you what was going down." Morgan was frantically trying to discipline his thoughts, but all he could think was: Jesus, they're gonna kill me and I won't even see their faces, know who they are. Except for this awful Billy Waddell.

"I never saw the letters," he said. Of course he didn't. Letters like that, they were routed to the appropriate department and handled there. "A commissioner can't read all the mail that comes in," he said. "Don't you see that? Don't you?" How could they? They knew nothing of the bureaucracy that protected the upper levels of government from intrusion by the public, from prisoners and their relatives. There was no time for that sort of communication. Commissioners deal with matters of policy. They gave speeches, attended conferences, approved budgets, looked to the future. When the suit by the inmates of the hospital reached the courts, the lawyers of the department had said, Leave it to us and we'll deal with it. No problem. And he had left it to them, and now these madmen with guns were arrayed around his bed in the middle of the night.

"Our attorneys handled the suit," he said. "That's their job. I had nothing to do with it. Nothing, I tell you."

"We're wasting time." It was the man at the end of the bed. He was looking around for an ashtray, finally dropped his butt on the rug and ground it out with his heel.

"If Billy wants to talk, let him," the leader said. "Billy feels real personal about Morgan. He's entitled."

"I'm just about finished," Billy said. "You never even replied to my letters, Morgan. Couldn't be bothered, right? Who cares about a bunch of losers up in the Wilderness? You're guilty, guilty like the rest of the fat-assed public officials who stick their snouts in the trough when it's their turn. You've been sentenced and now comes the time for it to be carried out."

"For God's sake, you gotta listen to me . . ."

"You ain't alone, Morgan. Old Crane, the PK who'd put a man in the hospital if he didn't like the color of his hair: he put Jackie and Ferret away. Campbell, the quack who certified we were mad. Mahoney, the governor . . . justice has caught up with all of them." He paused, staring down at Morgan.

"Next is you. We're putting things right. A righteous Department of Correction, you might say."

Crain? Campbell? Morgan had never heard of them. The muscles in his hands were aching from gripping the sheet, but he couldn't make them relax.

"An inquiry," Morgan said frantically. "I'll insist on an inquiry. We'll get the whole truth out, take action against those responsible. I'll get you compensation for the time you spent in there."

Billy Waddell seemed to have lost interest in him. He was taking off his gloves, loosening his belt. "Now, I do believe I'll steal something from you, Morgan," he said. "Part of the payback. Think I'll go and see your bitch, have a bit of fun. Give her something else to remember. She a screamer?"

"God damn you . . ."

"Maybe we'll take her with us. The three of us should be able to keep her happy." A moment later he had gone.

"For pity's sake," Morgan said, "you promised

she wouldn't be hurt. She hasn't done anything. Do what you like with me but . . ." Muttering, moaning, he started to get out of the bed. The leader reversed his rifle and smashed the butt against Morgan's head. Morgan groaned and slumped back into the sheets. Blood was seeping from his temple.

They waited silently, watching him recover. They wanted him awake, conscious. By the time he started to move, when he opened his eyes, the woman in the bathroom was wailing.

The two men looked at each other and nodded. Their guns came up. They straddled their legs. The thunder of small-arms fire overwhelmed the screams coming from the bathroom.

19 ◄

Brennan, shaggy-haired, horn-rimmed glasses, was a copyboy who had a hard-on for the paper, its editors, and reporters. He tolerated the photographers. He had graduated with honors from the Columbia School of Journalism, which, he believed, entitled him to a staff reporter's job. That was the minimum. Really he should be in charge of one of the foreign bureaus or the Washington office.

Instead, he spent his time listlessly fetching coffee and takeouts for the desk-bound editors and reporters, or carrying proofs around. During the football season, he handled bets. Free moments were devoted to any unused terminal. Brennan was an accomplished hacker. After breaking into the paper's confidential files, he knew how much everybody made and who had negative comments on their records.

Paige cornered him on the copyboys' bench and asked if he was busy. Brennan was cutting his fingernails.

"'Course I'm busy," Brennan said. "What d'you want, Paige?" He resented Paige like he resented every reporter who was holding a job that should be his.

"Can you get into the personnel files?"

"Is the Pope a Catholic?"

"Has to be, doesn't he?" Paige said absently. "Here's the deal. Get into one of those files for me and I'll put in a good word with LaFleche for you, maybe get you a reporter's slot."

"Gee, thanks, Paige. I could owe my future distinguished career to you. Except that LaFleche despises you. I shouldn't be seen even talking to you." Indeed, LaFleche, in his buttoned jacket, kept glaring at Paige from the city desk like a caged lion tantalized by a grazing wildebeest.

"You get into those files and I'll owe you. How's that sound?"

"Terrible. Twenty dollars sounds much better." They agreed on $15.

"Where's the cash?" Brennan said.

"You get it when I get the printout. And please aim your fingernails somewhere else than into my coffee."

"Jesus. Okay, whose file d'you want?"

"Savage. See if you can find out his background, any ex-wives, children, relatives, education, that sort of shit. As much detail as you can find. Good practice for being a reporter."

"Don't need practice. I'm ready. Thinking of changing my name to Lance Whitefeather, Native

American, and applying to the *Times*. Tell 'em I'm dyslexic to make sure."

"When you're into Savage, see if there's any reference anywhere to the Wilderness, a guy called Ray Bliss or any inmates."

"What are you up to, Paige?"

"Confidential at the moment. Tell you later. When can you produce?" Brennan said he would have to use a terminal in the library, and he couldn't leave the bench until after deadline. Paige would have to wait.

Paige went in to see Savage. The managing editor said, "Well?"

"It's coming together," Paige said. "It's like a maze, but I think I can see daylight."

"Get on with it."

"Campbell, the doctor shot in the park. It was a hit. I talked to Charlotte Webster, the woman wounded in the kidnapping. She was staying up in Connecticut with a friend, Melissa Fox."

"So?"

"Get this. Melissa told me that she saw one of the gunmen in the park firing directly at Duncan Campbell. She insists it was not random firing to keep heads down but deliberately aimed shots intended solely for Campbell. And, when you think about it all, it fits."

"Go on."

"That kidnapping made no sense. They go to all that trouble, planning it, finding automatic weapons, unlocking the door, coming up the steps, getting away, and then when they've got what they want and are in the clear, what do they do? No ransom demand. They abandon the kids and walk away, saying, 'Oops, sorry, let's forget the whole thing.'"

"What was it all about, then?"

"A cover. The whole object of the operation was to kill Campbell. They only grabbed the kids because the cop appeared in the middle of it all. They weren't the target. Campbell was."

Savage was staring at him, thinking it over.

"Next, you've got the killing of Jackie Baum, released from the Wilderness. Then there's Mahoney. He was probably governor while these guys were in the hospital. Who better to blame? And we don't know how many others might have been knocked off by these guys without attracting suspicion."

"We can't be sure they were all in the hospital."

"They know Bliss, they had to be up there. I tell you, what we've got is a bunch of ex-cons from the insane asylum at the Wilderness getting their revenge on the people who put them there. Helluva story."

"Very neat, Paige. So, why did Bliss and his pal cut each other up? I'm sure you have the answer to that, too."

Paige fell silent. Then he said, "Well, not immediately. Killers falling out, maybe. Life is complicated. It needs a bit more work." It was an aspect of editors he particularly disliked. They were always looking for holes in his stories.

"Here's what you do," Savage said. "Go back to Columbia-Presbyterian and talk to Bliss."

"He's under guard, a cop at the door."

"That's been taken care of. Lay it out on Bliss, see what happens."

There was a different cop sitting outside Bliss's room. He looked at Paige's press card and said, "You can go in." Paige was impressed. Savage must have pulled strings at Police Plaza.

Bliss looked a little better, more color in his cheeks. The cannulas were still attached to his nose, but most of the equipment that kept him alive had gone. He listened silently as Page described what had been discovered: Campbell, Mahoney, Baum.

"Fill in the holes," Paige said, "and you get yourself off the hook. That's a promise."

"You run the DA's office?" Bliss's voice was remarkably strong. The brightness was back in his eyes.

"The cops asked me to talk to you. You say you didn't kill Jackie Baum and I believe you. How can it hurt to tell what happened?"

"I'm not snitching."

"It's not snitching when we already know most of it."

It took nearly half an hour, but Paige knew he was getting through to the old man. Finally, Bliss said, "Okay, I'll tell you what happened. But it's not for me. It's for Jackie. The bastards."

At the end of it, Bliss said, "They claimed they whacked the old principal keeper, Crain, as well.

Up in the woods." Bliss didn't care about any of them, just Jackie and his loyalty and what it had cost him.

Paige frowned. "I still don't get it," he said. "Why did they want to kill you and Jackie? What had you done to them?"

"It was Billy Waddell. He hates me."

"Why?"

"He was always trying to make it with some of the young guys in the Wilderness. Jackie and I, we stopped him a couple of times. He never forgave us. He's a psychopath."

"Even so, why did the Teacher and the other guy go along with it?"

"I don't know." Bliss was looking tired, spent. "They probably didn't trust me to keep my mouth shut. Maybe they felt they had to go along with Billy Waddell, to keep him in the compact. I don't know. They're on a killing spree. What did one or two more matter?"

Outside the hospital room, vanAllen was looking through a window at the clouds banked up over midtown. The different shadings and edges made them look like old marble. She turned when Paige came out.

"Did he talk?"

"He talked. Did you arrange it, me going in?"

"Who else but your fairy godmother?"

"Savage fixed it with you?"

"Right. What did you get?"

"Christ, you know Savage?" Paige was staring at

her. He didn't like the feeling that something was going on and he knew nothing about it.

"Paige, I know all sorts of people. What did Bliss say?"

Paige told her.

When he had finished, she said, "It's all self-serving, getting him off the hook."

"Doesn't mean it isn't true."

"I gave up believing felons like Bliss a long time ago. Maybe it's true, maybe it's not. We'll see."

At the office, Brennan stuck his hand out.

"Twenty dollars," he said.

"Fifteen. Where is it?"

Brennan took the $15 and handed over a brown envelope.

"Don't read it out here," he said. "Too many inquiring minds wanting to know."

Paige took it to the john. Savage had worked on three papers before coming to the rag, where he started as a crime reporter in Brooklyn, worked Manhattan, moved to features, nominated for a Pulitzer for a series on the mob, then city editor, managing editor. Divorced. One child. College in Binghamton. Degree in history. Born and grew up in . . . son of a bitch . . . Hamillton.

20 ◄

On the telephone, Savage's father sounded vigorous and cheerful, glad to hear from his son. The dog was barking in the background.

"How's Jasper?" Savage said.

"His legs are bothering him. He's old, poor feller. I think, maybe, when he's gone, I'll get a spaniel. Easier to take for walks."

But when his father heard about Campbell's death, the tone of his voice darkened.

"He should have stayed here," he said. "I never understood why he wanted to go live in Manhattan, just because his son was there. It's dirty and dangerous, not like Hamillton."

People in Hamillton liked to say it was no different than any other small town and better than many. Sure, it was isolated, surrounded by the peaks of the Adirondacks, and most towns did not have 3,500 criminals penned up in their midst. But the children, they said, grew up there like any other children. They went to the central school on the outskirts and played baseball and football, in the winter skated on Duke's Pond, learned to hunt and fish. Some went off to college and some stayed to work in the town.

Other kids in other towns might think of the city hall or county offices as the center of their communities, but in Savage's hometown everything revolved around the maximum security prison, one of a dozen in the Adirondack region. It was the reason for living there. Nearly everybody, including Savage's father, worked within the walls or ministered to those who did.

It was a company town and the industry was the prison. Stores, offices, a dry cleaner's, a small cinema, lined one side of the main street. On the other was the wall, with gun towers at each end.

Outside the prison, the law-abiding were a minority, with a population of only 1,500. The census ignored the different reasons for living in Hamillton and reported the total population at 5,000. The town remained untouched by depressions and recessions, for whatever happened to economies elsewhere, it had a growth industry in its midst.

As an imaginative child, Savage thought of the twenty-foot, granite wall as a dam holding back the evil inside which would overwhelm his town should the barrier break and crumble. His father, eventually the principal keeper, went inside every day to make sure the dam held. That was how the young Savage had seen him, anyway.

By the time he was a teenager, he knew it was just another state prison, one that collected the hard cases. Still, the wall was oppressive. He liked it best when snow softened the harsh angularity of the wall. Sometimes, with other kids, he had climbed the hills to the north so that he could look down into the yard and see the prisoners at exercise. As he grew older, he hardly gave it a thought. It was just a part of the town. But, even so, he had been glad to leave for college and move among people who did not spend their lives penning in other people. During the years he had worked on small papers up and down the Hudson Valley, learning his trade, finally finding a home in New York City, he had gone back only occasionally. His wife didn't like the town or its people. She had never gotten on with Savage's father.

Savage remembered the madhouse, next door to the prison. It was a huge, red-brick Victorian gothic mansion that could have been used in a Hitchcock movie. Perhaps it was the knowledge of the insanity massed inside that had made it seem even more sinister, even more menacing than the prison.

When he had gone north in the fall to help bury his mother, his father, now retired from the prison service, told him that the building had been cleared of its inmates and turned into offices as an administration annex to the prison.

Savage knew now that, in fact, Hamillton was different than other small towns. People shied away from talking to strangers because of a "no fraternization" rule aimed at suppressing corrupting relationships between relatives of prisoners and guards outside the walls of the Wilderness. It worked against a friendly atmosphere. Beyond that, there was a rigid caste system, based, like the military, on rank which was observed by families in the day-to-day life of the town.

Guards and prison officials might try to sanitize their children from any contact with life behind the wall, but it was inevitable that sharp-eared youngsters would pick up references to rapes, brutality, knife fights, and suicides in the Wilderness. Savage's father never talked at home about his work, or the occasional turbulence in the prison, but that didn't mean the youngster didn't hear of them elsewhere.

His mother, a frail, gauzy woman, was the respectful satellite to his father's authoritative planet. Savage realized years later that her frequent retreats to her room had less to do with her recurring illnesses than with the bottles he occasionally saw, bottles that never went into the garbage for fear the collectors might spot them and talk. Looking back, Savage also realized that his father had been patient and protective with her.

Savage's father was proud that no prisoner had ever escaped for long from the penitentiary or the hospital next door, but sometimes the blast of a steam whistle signaled that an attempt had been made, and the townsfolk knew that the prisoners were being herded back for lockdown and searches were being launched. Every child in Hamillton knew what the whistle meant.

Whatever the abnormalities of Hamillton, Savage's father had chosen to remain in the town after his retirement. He lived alone now in the same white clapboard house with a big yard on a road running off the main street, where Savage had grown up. The road was named Rancie Street after a warden of the twenties. Inevitably the kids called it Rancid Street.

"What sort of guy was Campbell?" Savage asked.

"Tough but fair." It was the phrase that Savage remembered so well. In Hamillton, it was an accolade. It was the way his father had been described.

"Why does a doctor have to be tough?"

"To see through their medical scams. He didn't let them put anything over him. A good man. He helped set up the volunteer ambulance corps and supported it with donations."

"D'you remember Ray Bliss?"

"Bliss? Sure, I remember that bastard. Why?"

"Maybe it's a coincidence. The day after Campbell was killed, Bliss was found knifed in a tenement in Harlem, along with another man."

"Good riddance. Is he dead?"

"Not quite, although the other guy is."

"Another ex-con?"

"Yeah, a guy named Jackie Baum."

"Baum? Sure. Those guys stick together when they get out." Over the phone, Savage heard the pop of a beer can. While Savage's mother was alive, his father never drank. Now he allowed himself the occasional beer in the evening.

Savage could picture the big kitchen, the white-tiled counter that his father had made, the heavy wooden table that Savage had helped carry back from a barn sale, the dog's bowl by the back door.

"When I was up in the fall, you said they closed the hospital, made it an annex of the prison?"

"Right. That was Bliss's work. A real jailhouse lawyer, that one. Cunning as the devil, and the judges believed him against all the evidence. It was a disgrace, what they said about Hamillton. I think that was why Campbell left town, if the truth were known. He was heartbroken. And then this happens to him. You can blame Bliss for his death."

"Was Bliss insane?"

"He was a certified lunatic, like all the rest in the hospital. Campbell examined him and certified him. Then those judges turned them all loose. Incredible."

"If he was mad, how come he managed to get into court and persuade the federal judges, three of them, that he was right and the authorities were wrong?"

"Those judges, they weren't doctors, like Campbell. You can be paranoid and still be sly enough to persuade people you're okay. The paranoia drives you, makes you even more determined. I talked to Campbell about it and he explained it all." The older man's voice was angry and bitter now.

"Was Campbell a psychologist?"

"He had all the right qualifications for the job."

"You hear of anybody else connected with the Wilderness dying unexpectedly, maybe in suspicious circumstances?"

"What are you driving at?"

"I don't really know, Dad. But I have to tell you that there's a strong possibility that three or four guys, all from the Wilderness, are on the loose killing the people they blame for putting them in the hospital. You know the ex-governor, Mahoney, was killed on the street a while back. Campbell was hit, then almost immediately Bliss and another guy were found in a pool of blood. Maybe it's all coincidence, but maybe it's not."

"That's crazy. Nothing like that has happened up here. "There have been some deaths, naturally. People get old, they die." He paused, then went on thoughtfully, "The only funny one was old Crain, the PK before me."

"Crain died, right?"

"Last fall it was, after you were up here, he had a hunting accident. They found him up in the woods with his head blown off. They reckon he tripped and fell and his gun went off. I gave the eulogy at his funeral."

"What was funny about it?"

"Oh, nothing, really, I suppose. Except that Crain had been a hunter all his life and it struck me as odd that something like that would happen to him. I could see it with somebody from the city, running around making a fool of himself with a gun. But not Crain. He knew guns and how to use them without killing himself, that's all."

"Did you raise any questions about it?"

"No, why should I? The state police looked into it and they decided it was an accident. That was it."

"Still, you wondered?"

"I did a bit."

"You thought somebody might have killed him?"

"Good God, no. There was just the possibility that he took his own life, that was all. It didn't really matter much either way. An accident or a suicide. He was dead. And it was better for his family that it should be an accident."

"Could he have been killed, murdered?"

"Anything's possible but it was never suggested."

"I have to tell you, Dad, there's a strong possibility that Crain was one of the victims. Bliss says the gang claimed they killed him in the woods, made it look like an accident."

"They were smarter than the state police, fooled the investigators? You're talking about stupid punks. They don't have the smarts for something like that."

"Nobody else has died suspiciously?"

"Nobody."

"Who was responsible for transferring prison inmates into the hospital?"

"I told you, Campbell. The doctor examined the prisoners, and if he decided they were mad, they went next door." His voice had become testy, as if he couldn't be bothered with old history.

"But somebody had to bring the case to the attention of Campbell."

"Well, of course. It would go through the principal keeper's court. If the PK decided there was something peculiar about a prisoner, if he acted strangely, then the doctor would be called in to give an opinion."

"You know what this all means, Dad. I don't want to alarm you but if they blamed Crain, they could blame you, too. You could be a target."

"That's ridiculous." He sounded angry. Murder was natural in New York City, not in Hamillton.

"What about the warden? Did he have anything to do with transfers to the hospital?"

"He knew if a prisoner was transferred, he gave his okay, but it was up to Campbell to make the decision from his medical knowledge."

"I want you to be careful, Dad. It may all be nonsense, but you should be on your guard."

"Look, son, I'm tired. I'm gonna broil a steak and settle in." At the end, his voice was strained, and Savage wondered if it was simply tiredness or something else.

Hanging up the phone, Savage thought that none of it made much sense. Even supposing Campbell had been killed because of his work in the Wilderness, and even if Crain's death had a question mark over it, where did Bliss and the other man fit in? There might be no connection whatever. Just a couple of killings in Manhattan and a hunting accident in the mountains.

Except there was another killing in Manhattan, Mahoney, and that, too, could have a connection, if distant, with the Wilderness.

Only a few minutes after Savage put down the

phone, vanAllen came on the line. She spent no time on pleasantries.

"There's been another killing, this time upstate," she said.

"Who?"

"Joe Morgan, a lawyer. He was state commissioner of correction until last year. He was blown away at his summer place outside Albany last night and his wife was attacked."

"She survived?"

"Barely. They raped her. She's in Albany Medical Center under sedation. I'm going up to see her."

"Jesus. Can she identify them?"

"They all wore masks. But she says there were three of them. It's got to be our boys on a rampage. And they're moving fast."

21 ◀

Paige expected the tailor to be obsequious, but he was almost as imperious as Lady Jane. With his lacquered black hair, he looked like Rudolf Valentino equipped with a permanent sneer. Obviously he disapproved of Paige, his manner, his clothes, his haircut, his fingernails.

He referred to customers as *we*. "We have a problem with our arms," he told Paige, busy with the tape measure. "One of our arms is longer than the other."

Lady Jane was watching the activity from a Louis Quinze chair in the salon on Madison Avenue. Nobody was admitted without an appointment; strays who knocked on the unmarked oak door were ignored. The place looked like a drawing room, the only sign of its use some swatches of material on an antique table and a long mirror.

"How long will it take to run up a dinner jacket for him?" Lady Jane said. "We don't have a lot of time."

"Three or four weeks," the tailor said.

"Absurd. He'll need it in two or three days. He'll have to make do with a ready-made outfit."

"We don't provide that sort of service." He was bending and running a hand holding a tape measure deep into Paige's crotch.

"Expense is no object."

"In this establishment, it never is."

"But you can recommend some place where we can buy one."

"No, I can't."

"Well, I'm sure you can provide him with an appropriate shirt and tie, cummerbund, patent leather shoes, that sort of thing. Take your shirt off, darling."

Paige stripped off the rabbit-decorated sports shirt and tossed it to her. He sucked in his belly, but Lady Jane eyed him and said, "We still need to lose some weight." The tailor sighed, threw his tape measure on the table, and started looking through some boxes on shelves in an alcove.

"I'm going to ask Mary the man-eater," Lady Jane said, "and her so-called Italian count, Mickey McGovern, and his paramour and, perhaps, Claus if he's in town. His impression of Queen Victoria is quite amusing. Who's Chloe?"

Paige looked over and saw she had withdrawn the white card from his shirt pocket.

"Who?" he said, before remembering it was the creature in the bar, Farley's.

"Chloe," she said.

"Oh, that's my sister."

"You have trouble remembering the name of your sister?" Her tone was chilly.

"Didn't hear what you said."

"I see. Well, I must give her a call, have her around for something."

"She's away. Won't be back for months." Paige put on a pale blue shirt with ruffles down the front. He thought it looked pretty good.

"That's not white," Lady Jane said.

"It's this year's color," the tailor said.

"Find him a white one. And a black tie."

"Do we have a telephone we can use?" Paige asked. It was in the untidy work area that lay behind the elegant receiving room. Savage's secretary said the managing editor was busy.

Lady Jane wanted to lunch at the restaurant across the river in Brooklyn, but Paige insisted they go to the bar across the street from the rag. He would call Savage from there.

Savage was skimming through the story about Joe Morgan's murder from the AP bureau in Albany.

As far as investigators could tell, nothing had been stolen from the summer camp. "It was a carefully-planned execution, no doubt about it," said a state police spokesman. The body had been discovered by a mailman whose attention had been caught by water flowing under the front door and onto the steps. Morgan's wife, trapped in a bathroom, had managed to turn on the faucets and eventually the water had

spilled under the bathroom door and down the stairs
until the mailman noticed it. The killers had long
gone, leaving no trace except for the bullets that had
blown away Joe Morgan. From the wife's description of the weapons, they had used assault rifles. She
said the magazines on the weapons were banana-
shaped.

Savage put in a call to the state police and
reached the deputy superintendent at the headquarters in Albany. Yes, the New York police had contacted him and laid out the possibility of a hit team
roving the state. Yes, he knew about Duncan
Campbell and the former governor, and of course,
now Morgan.

"The BCI is handling it all," he said. "We're
assuming there's something to it. Ballistics reports
Morgan was killed with 7.62 mm slugs, maybe from
AK-47s. Like Campbell. So of course we're taking it
seriously."

"You realize that my father could be a target.
They were in New York, then Albany, which means
the bastards are moving north."

"Your father and a number of others, Mr.
Savage," the deputy said. His tone was friendly
enough, but Savage could tell the man believed
police work should be left to the police. "We could
put together a hit list, a potential hit list, as long as
your arm, starting with the governor, the corrections
commissioner, and going down through wardens,
deputies, and guards, anybody connected in any way
to the prison system. I can tell you—and this is off

the record, certainly not for publication—that we have increased security around the governor and other state officials, but there is only so much we can do in the way of protecting other people."

"Look, dammit, I have special reason to be concerned about my father—"

"I'm sure you have, Mr. Savage. It's very natural that you're worried, just as many other people might be. However, we're spread thin. The best I can do is have a trooper go around to your father's house, but I can't promise that he will remain there. We have other responsibilities."

Savage's lips tightened. He might be a power in New York City, but his writ did not run into the headquarters of the state police.

"You'll let me know of any developments?"

"Of course, Mr. Savage," he said blandly. "Rely on us. Now, I must go. It was nice talking to you."

At least the state police were alerted and taking action. It was true that there could be targets other than his father. Still, he could not dispel his alarm. Crain had been the principal keeper before his father took the post, and Crain probably was the first victim. His father had carried out the same duties that Crain had. He could have been responsible for one or more of the hit team going to the hospital.

Now there were questions in Savage's mind about his father's work as principal keeper, about his role in sending prisoners to the hospital for burial alive. He had read and reread the transcript of the judge's order releasing Bliss and the others, and if it was to be believed, there had been great wickedness in Hamillton and his father had been a part of it.

He told his secretary to find Todd Paige.

"He was trying to reach you earlier when you were busy," she said. "He's going to call back."

Paige was sitting with Lady Jane at the crowded bar of Costigan's across the street from the paper. He was drinking Scotch and wearing the tan tropical suit that she had bought him at Brooks Brothers while tracking down a dinner jacket. He thought he was looking pretty damn dapper.

"My expenses will be through any day now," he said.

"Quite."

"Pay you back as soon as I get them."

"That's nice. Listen, roly-poly, I thought we were going to have lunch."

"Don't fret. First the cocktail, then the feast. We can slip around to the Chinese place next door in a minute."

"Who are all these peculiar people?" she said, staring around at the lunchtime drinkers, most of them from the rag. "Friends of yours?"

"Not really. They're not our sort of people." In the mirror, Paige saw the somber figure of Purgavie, who had become tiresome with his insistence that Paige owed him $25. Purgavie was pushing his way toward them and shouting something.

"That man seems to want you," Lady Jane said. "That one who looks like a mortician."

"Paige," Purgavie called out, "you're wanted on the phone. Savage's secretary." Perhaps he had forgotten the $25 at last. "And I want a word with you afterward." Creep.

"I'll be right back," Paige said. "Have another glass of wine."

When he returned, he found that Brennan, the hacker, and another copyboy, equally shaggy-haired, were talking earnestly to Lady Jane while peering down her cleavage. Paige got rid of them by suggesting they buy drinks.

"What extraordinary young men," she said. "They were telling me about their work as foreign correspondents. They just got back from the Balkans. One of them was wounded in Bosnia."

"Oh, yes? And did they get around to the Pulitzer Prize they shared last year?" He could see Freddy the bartender flicking through the sheaf of tabs, his certainly among them. It was time to go.

"A Pulitzer?"

"Never mind. I've had enough slumming and there's no time to eat. I've got to haul ass for Albany."

"Haul what?"

"It's an expression."

"Where's Albany?"

"Upstate, it's the capital of New York."

"And how, pray, will you get there?"

"I don't know, rent a car, take a train." Purgavie was hovering, looking petulant.

"Let's take the train."

"You want to come?"

"I've never fornicated on a train."

"It's only two or three hours and I don't think they have sleepers."

"We'll manage something."

Justice is always violent to the party offending, for every man is innocent in his own eyes.

—Daniel Defoe
"Shortest Way with Dissenters"

22 ◀

Trooper Damien Vaughan was hungry, frustrated, and irritated. It was the third time in a month that he had been called to the Kowalik place to deal with a family dispute. It was a job for the deputies, but each time they said they were busy and asked for his help. Albany's policy was cooperation with the sheriffs, but like a speck of grit in the eye, the thought persisted that the deputies were dumping the Kowa-liks on him and laughing when they switched off their radios.

He tried to ignore the lurking suspicion that these country cops were mocking a homeboy from Brooklyn for intruding into their white-bread territory. Only a few years ago, the state police had been all-white, all-male. At the barracks, nobody said anything out of line but he knew there was resentment toward the blacks and women now being recruited in increasing numbers. On the radio he had heard references to "the new breed." Fuck it. There was no percentage in blaming every problem on the color of his skin or of theirs.

With Kowalik it was always the same. First he hit the bottle, then his wife. The infuriating thing was that she would never sign a complaint. Vaughan parked the blue-and-yellow cruiser half on the untrimmed grass verge, put on his campaign hat, and went along the path toward the sagging porch where the wife waited with red marks on her forehead and cheek.

"He says he's gonna stick a kitchen knife in me and then in himself unless I tell him where I've got the money," she said. Her voice was a flat monotone as if she were reporting the arrival of another bill. Her hair was in curlers and she wore an old blue pants suit and grimy sneakers. She might have been pretty once, but now her eyes were tired, her skin gray. Kowalik was sitting at the kitchen table, an empty glass and bottle at his elbow. A rusty knife lay on the other side of the table. His rumpled hair was down over his eyes. His feet were bare and dirty.

"She won't give me my money," he said with a failing attempt at indignation. "It's mine and she won't give it to me."

"It's the grocery money," she said. "He drinks and drinks and we starve."

Kowalik muttered something, staggered to his feet, and went to the battered refrigerator. The door was dotted with magnetic letters that formed the words, USA FOREVER. When he opened the refrigerator, the smell of rotting fish invaded the kitchen. In three years upstate, Vaughan had seen poverty among whites as bad, if not worse, than anything in Brownsville. Kowalik came back opening a can of beer. "Last one," he said, slopping beer into the glass.

"Here," he said, "have a drink, officer." He thrust the glass at the trooper and half of the beer spilled out on Vaughan's uniform pants. Jesus, family disputes. He'd rather have a shoot-out. It took Vaughan twenty minutes to sort it out. Kowalik put his head under the tap and, now subdued, promised he'd go to bed. The knife went back into the kitchen drawer, ready for the next time he got drunk. No, Mrs. Kowalik wouldn't sign a complaint, thank you. "He's my husband," she said. "I can't, can I?"

Vaughan advised them to go to the family counseling service, but he knew it was a waste of time. He, or better still a deputy, would be back when the next bottle appeared in Kowalik's hands. At least there were no children at home for them to screw up. Back in the cruiser, he called in to report the dispute settled. He could smell the beer on his pants.

Still irritated, he was back on Route 9 west of the Northway, heading north, when word of the Morgan murder came over the net. APB, three men believed armed with automatic rifles, ex-cons, killers, and rapists. There was more, but that was what it amounted to. No description either of the men or the vehicle they might be driving. If the killing happened more than six hours ago, he calculated, and they headed up the Northway, they could be across the border enjoying themselves in a bistro in Montreal by now. More likely they had gone south down the thruway to lose themselves in New York City. Right now, the hamburger he would eat at the Crossroads Diner was of more interest. He might have some of Jeannie's cheesecake, too.

The layby two miles south of the diner was empty except for a black Ford Taurus, barely visible through the tangled undergrowth that divided it from the road. Vaughan would have missed it except for the glint of sun on the coachwork. He braked, reversed, and cruised into the layby. Two men. Must have had a flat. As Vaughan pulled into the layby, he saw they were tossing a jack into the trunk, slamming it closed. He braked, reported the New York plate number and location to the dispatcher, and got out. The men were standing, one on each side of the car, waiting for him. Middle-aged, innocuous-looking.

"You guys need help?" he said.

"Just a flat. No problem. We changed it." One was in brown jeans and a white T-shirt, the other in an open-necked sports shirt and tan slacks. Nothing exceptional about them, except that suddenly Vaughan had a feeling. It was like somebody running something cold up his spine. He halted a few feet from the car. His hand touched his holstered .38.

"License and registration," he said. Neither of them moved. They just stared at him. Now he knew. Vaughan had been a trooper for three years, and he had never used his gun except at the range. But there it was, in his hand, and he hoped he wasn't making a fool of himself. Just that morning, Vaughan had scolded little Damien Junior for touching the gun as it hung in its holster on his chair. It was only to be handled in a crisis, he had said. Now he pointed the revolver first at one and then the other.

"Step to the back of the car," he said. "No sudden movements. My finger's itchy." The .38 felt strong and comforting in his hand. The men looked at each other and one of them shrugged. They walked until both were by the trunk. No traffic going by, and anyway they were largely hidden from the highway by trees and scrub.

"Turn and face the fucking car," Vaughan said. "Both of you, put your hands on the trunk, spread your legs." One obeyed, the other hesitated and then did as he was told. Vaughan considered searching them. The sports shirt, hanging outside the pants, could conceal a gun in the belt. Better not. One man he could handle. Two was different. Better get on the radio. Jesus, suppose he'd caught the guys everybody was looking for. He had to fight down the rising euphoria. If these were the Albany guys, where were their automatic rifles? He couldn't risk a look into the car, not with two of them. Better call in.

"Either of you mothers move, you get it," he said. On the highway, two cars went by, one overtaking the other, without any indication the drivers had noticed the scene in the layby. With his weapon covering them in two-handed combat position, Vaughan started to back slowly toward the cruiser. Both men turned their heads to watch him.

Just as he reached the car, he heard a sound

behind him and the thought flashed into his mind, Christ, there's supposed to be three of them. In that moment, as he was about to swing around, the side of his head exploded. Pain engulfed him.

The force of the blow was such that his upper body slumped to his left, but not before his .38 discharged, whether from reflex or intent he would never know. Dimly, before the blackness received him, Vaughan heard the roar of his weapon. The recoil spun it out of his hand as he toppled and man and gun crashed down together.

Still holding the wooden club he had swiftly fashioned from a fallen old branch among the trees where he had gone to relieve himself, the Teacher bent over Vaughan and lifted an eyelid. The trooper was out. Blood was trickling from the right side of his cranium and he was breathing with a rasping sound. His wide-brimmed hat was still on his head, but the blow had knocked it sideways so that Vaughan's left cheek was pressed into it as if into a cushion.

"Teach." The Teacher looked up. Billy Waddell was staring down at the collapsed figure of Ferret sprawled over the trunk. As they both watched, Ferret slowly slid down until he was kneeling as if in prayer, his body leaning against the back of the car. A moment later, he crumpled at the middle and gently tilted over on to the dirt. The Teacher moved swiftly to the body, turned it over. Ferret had been hit in the back by the trooper's random bullet and the exit wound, leaking intestines, was enormous, as if a steel fist had smashed through the torso.

"D'you believe that?" Billy Waddell kept saying over and over. "You believe that?" His astonishment was so great that, for the moment, he seemed unaware of their perilous position, the radio car that might draw the attention of any passing motorist, the dead man at their feet and the unconscious trooper.

"Get the belts," the Teacher said. "We'll tie the bastard up, toss him in the woods." His voice was cool, unexcited.

Billy Waddell stared at him. "That fucker whacked Ferret," he said. Anger had replaced shock. "That dirty nigger blew away Ferret."

"Get the belts," the Teacher said. He turned and strode to the radio car. The engine was still running. Sliding behind the wheel, he slammed the door and spun the wheel until the cruiser was heading toward the line of trees from which he had emerged a few moments earlier. The Teacher slammed down the accelerator and smashed through the brush. A maple sapling almost halted him, but he stepped down harder and the car, wheels churning, ran over it and went forward. Turning hard right and then left, the Teacher maneuvered the car twenty feet into the trees before bulky trunks barred further progress. He looked back. A jumble of brush would shield the car from anything but keen scrutiny.

With a hiss of static, the radio came to life. "Victor-three-oh, respond." It was a woman's voice. "Victor-three-oh, respond." The Teacher leaned forward and turned switches until it went dead. He was straightening saplings and undergrowth, trying to

cover the tracks of the cruiser, when the shot came
from the layby.

Billy Waddell was born and grew up in a two-room,
dirt-floor shack, no glass in the windows, on the outskirts of Sunflower, Alabama, not far from the Mississippi border.

He was eight before he put on a pair of shoes,
cracked sneakers donated by the Baptists. He never
knew his father and, early on, decided he didn't
want to.

He was the youngest of three boys, all with different fathers, born to Sarah Waddell, who sometimes worked at a crossroads gas station until her car
broke down for the last time and she couldn't get
there. After that, she didn't do much of anything
except entertain the occasional visitor and drink the
beer they brought.

Most of their neighbors were black and the
school the Waddell boys attended until they dropped
out was ninety percent black, like all the teachers.
With the casual cruelty of children, the black kids
laughed at the white kids who lived as badly as they
did. "Yo just po' white trash, lower 'n a snake's
belly. . . ." On the dusty patch of dirt that served as the
playground, Billy Waddell learned to fight with the
fury of anger and humiliation until finally they let
him alone except for the sneering words from bigger
blacks.

He was nearly ten when he realized what was

going on in his mother's room on so many nights. He would lie on the broken-backed couch sweating in the torrid darkness listening to the whispers and the creaking mattress and the groans. Sometimes, afterward, the visitor would slap his mother around. After getting a blow that sent him crashing to the floor, Billy learned not to try and stop it.

Some of the visitors tossed him a quarter, even a dollar a couple of times. Most of them were white, but some were black. He hated them all. When he found the courage to ask his mother why she slept with niggers, she first ignored him, then said, "They all bastards, don't matter, niggers or white." She treated Billy with indifference. He and his brothers were just another burden in her cheerless life.

He was just thirteen, a big kid for all the hunger that was his frequent companion, when the imperial wizard came over from Birmingham for a cross-burning. After a walk of more than two miles, Billy found the field. Cars and pickup trucks, rifles racked across the rear windows, lined the side roads, and in the flare of torches he could see the cross ready for burning, thirty feet high and surrounded by Klansmen in white robes and peaked hoods. Most of the crowd, though, were in ordinary clothes, some of them women, all slapping at the mosquitoes battening on their arms and faces, some drinking from beer cans. As he made his way toward the cross, there was a commotion in the darkness to his left. A group of men, some in robes, some in farm clothes, were

shouting at two men they had surrounded, one of
them carrying a camera.

"Fuckin' spies from up north, come to tell lies
about us," one of the men shouted.

"Nigger lovers!"

"Goddamn Yankees."

A hulking youngster in jeans and a white T-shirt
lunged forward and smashed his fist into the photographer's face. It was like a signal. The next moment
the mob surged and the two disappeared into a
whirling mass of arms and kicking feet. Fascinated,
Billy Waddell watched. He would have liked to join
in, kicking the two strangers, but he couldn't get
close enough.

It ended when the imperial wizard in full regalia,
a cross in a circle on his chest, strode up and ordered
his followers to stand back. One of the two was
sprawled unconscious, the other moaning and
writhing on the dusty ground.

The imperial wizard, John Booker, looked
around and beckoned to two uniformed deputies who
had stood back, watching the attack. The fat one had
taken Billy in when he lifted a watch from the
Woolworth's in Sunflower.

"They've had enough. Get 'em out of here,"
Booker said. He had a high-pitched voice that con-
trasted oddly with the mystery of his robes and
masked face.

"Lock 'em up? Disorderly conduct, maybe
assault, and trespassing?" The deputies reacted as if
Booker were their superior.

"No. I know these boys. They're with a Chicago paper, down here to cause trouble. Just drop them off in town. They've learned their lesson."

Somebody ground his foot into the camera, then pulled the tangled film out. Amid jeers, the two were lifted roughly and carried to the deputy's unmarked car.

Later, the cross was set ablaze. It was the most exciting moment in Billy Waddell's wretched life, better drama than any movie or baseball game. He stood on the fringe of the crowd as John Booker mounted a farm trailer and, with the flames lighting their faces, called on the crowd to fight for Aryan domination over the black savages who were taking control of the country with rape and murder and robbery.

They must reject the panty-waisted, pointy-headed, cookie-eating, bleeding-heart liberals in Washington who wanted to take their guns from them, who were ignoring state's rights, vote them out of office and send them back to the sewer from which they came. The crowd rumbled with approval.

When he had finished, when a collection had been held and the cross had crumbled into ashes, Billy was walking back over the tussocked grass when he felt a hand on his shoulder. It was the imperial wizard.

"I saw you listening, son," the man said. "You like what you heard?"

"Yes, sir."

"You here on your own?"

"Yes, sir. My ma's gone into town. She don't care what I do."

"You'd join the Klan, ride with us, fight for white people's rights?" Booker took off his hood. His red hair was receding from his sweaty forehead. He had a button-nose and underslung chin. Out of his hood, he wouldn't have drawn a second glance.

"I'd join in a damn minute," Billy said. It was the first time in his entire life that anybody had shown interest in him. And this was one of the leaders of the righteous white rebellion against the niggers.

The field was almost empty now, cars pulling away into the darkness, their headlights throwing splashes of light on hedges and trees.

"Let's talk," Booker said. "Tell me about yourself." Billy Waddell hesitated, and then it poured out of him as if from a breached dam: the misery, the loneliness, his mother's indifference to him, the days when there was no food in the house, the way the niggers looked down on him. It hadn't been so bad when his brothers were still at home, but they had long gone, just as he planned to go.

"You come with me, Billy," Booker said. "My wife will look after you. I'll take care nothing like that happens to you ever again." He stripped off his robe. Under it he wore a cheap, worn blue suit and a wrinkled white shirt, open at the neck. He led the way to his car, an old Pontiac rusting at the bottom of the door panels. It smelled of stale cigarette smoke.

"What about your ma?" he said.

"Fuck her," Billy said. "She don't care what happens to me."

"You sure?"

"When Jo-Jo left, she didn't say a thing. Same with Luke. Glad to be rid of them."

"You ever been to Birmingham?"

"No, sir. I'd sure like to see it." Before Birmingham, though, they stopped at a greasy spoon and Billy Waddell shoveled hash and pie into his mouth while Booker smoked and watched him.

"Tell you what," Booker said as Billy finished his pie and washed it all down with the last of his Dr. Pepper. "There's a motel next door. We can stay there and I'll get you home, introduce you to my wife, in the morning. Better than driving at this time of night." A question mark popped up in the back of Billy Waddell's mind, but he ignored it. He was in the middle of an adventure that would take him away from Sunflower.

In the motel room, there was a black-and-white TV set and, after relieving himself in the mildewed bathroom, Billy sat cross-legged in front of it, switching between the two channels. There was no TV set, no radio, in his home. Here there was even a laboring air conditioner. When he looked around, Booker had gotten into the bed. He was wearing a T-shirt with sweat marks in the armpits.

"Better get some rest, Billy," Booker said.

"Where am I gonna sleep?"

"Why, right here."

"With you?"

"Nothing wrong with that," Booker said. He

moved a few inches over to one side. "Plenty of room for both of us."

Watching Ed Sullivan, Billy said, "I'll sleep in the chair."

Booker's voice hardened. "You come on over here, Billy."

"I'll be fine in the chair."

"You gotta learn to do what you're told. Come here." Billy didn't move. He knew he was in trouble. The next moment, Booker was on his feet, dragging him back to the bed. He wore nothing below his T-shirt. Billy fought him.

"You little bastard, you playin' hard to get?" Their struggle ended on the bed. Booker was sitting on his legs and he had Billy's left arm pinned down but the right one was free. Booker's breath was foul. Billy Waddell reached out and got a grip on a heavy drinking glass on the bedside table. He smashed it into Booker's forehead.

The imperial wizard snorted and a thin line of blood trickled down his face. "You murderous little viper," he roared. He slapped Billy's face with the front of his hand and then the back. Billy screamed.

Somebody banged furiously on the other side of the thin wall.

"What the fuck's goin' on in there?" a man shouted. "I'm tryin' to get some sleep. You want me to come in and settle it? And turn that fuckin' TV off."

Booker rolled off Billy who jumped to his feet. Booker stayed on the bed, not bothering to cover his genitals.

"Go on," he said. "Get the fuck out of here, you ungrateful little bastard. You've lost your chance to join the Klan."

Billy was out of there before Booker could change his mind. He went back to the cafe and, outside, found a trucker stepping up into his cab. He talked his way into a ride and got to Meridian, Mississippi, after midnight. From Meridian, he jumped a freight train. He didn't care where it was going.

Billy Waddell was standing over the trooper, the .38 that had killed Ferret in his hand. His shot had blown off the back of Vaughan's head and the trooper's hat was drenched in blood.

"Goddamned, mother-fucking nigger," he said. He looked for a moment at the .38, then stuck it in his belt.

"You stupid bastard," the Teacher said. He turned as a car went by on the highway. It kept going, but they listened until distance had swallowed the sound of the engine.

"He had it coming," Waddell said. "He whacked Ferret. A fucking nigger."

"You goddamned fool," the Teacher said. "Kill a cop and you drive 'em mad. They'll have the sheriffs and the feds out, every trooper in the state, saturating the area. Christ . . ."

"They won't stop us now," Waddell said. "A few more hours . . . We can still do it, the two of us."

The Teacher was bending, picking up Vaughan's

heels. "Get his shoulders," he said. "We'll dump him in the woods."

Trying to avoid the bloody mess above the shoulders, Waddell lifted the corpse awkwardly from the side. They carried it deep into the woods and dropped it in a gully before hurrying back to the layby.

"What about Ferret?" Billy Waddell's voice was full of resentment. He didn't care what the Teacher said. He had done the right thing.

"Check he has no ID on him." Not once throughout the episode in the layby, not even when anger made him tremble, had the Teacher raised his voice. They carried Ferret into the woods and dropped him near the gully. In death, Ferret's face was as unemotional as it had been in life.

"Give me the .38," the Teacher said. Reluctantly, Waddell handed it over. Bending, the Teacher put it in the trooper's limp hand. "Maybe confuse 'em," he said. "It's the best we can do. We can still pull it off without Ferret. Come on."

Back at the layby, the Teacher threw a swift glance around. The cruiser was a dark, broken outline behind the scrub and saplings. Tire marks and beaten down undergrowth showed its path, but it was only noticeable if you looked for it.

A few minutes later, when they passed the neon doughnut sign outside the Crossroads Diner, the stolen Taurus was doing the regulation 55 mph and the Teacher was driving as circumspectly as if they were heading for church.

23 ◄

Fifty minutes out of New York, Paige said, "What's wrong with this sentence: 'We're fifty minutes out of Grand Central Station'?"

Lady Jane said nothing and he glanced over at her. She had let her *Town and Country* magazine fall into her lap and was staring at him with her unblinking eyes narrowed to slits.

"Even when I do this," she said, "you don't look anything like Cary Grant."

"Never did," he said. "Why?"

"Listen, I look on this as a rerun of *North by Northwest*, with us hot on the trail of the killers. I fit the role of the glamorous blonde who makes whoopee on the train with Cary Grant. But you look more like a sheepdog that's slipped its leash."

"Never mind that. Answer the question."

"I haven't the slightest idea what's wrong with that sentence, darling. I expect you'll tell me."

"Grand Central Station is the post office. The

place where the trains come in and out is Grand Central Terminal. Not many people know that."

"Fascinating. D'you remember in the movie when the train goes into the tunnel just as their romance is flowering on the bunk that lets down from the ceiling? Very suggestive. I expect we'll be coming to a tunnel soon."

Paige looked out of the window. At this point, the Hudson narrowed between rolling, timbered hills. Across the water, the austere gray battlements of West Point were coming into view. A huge barge was being towed upriver while a speed-boat full of teenagers buzzed around it like a wasp trying to bother an elephant. The Amtrak gave a long toot and the tug replied with its foghorn.

"Here's another one," Paige said. "Why is New York called the Empire State?"

"Come on," she said. "It's time."

"Time for what?"

"You know perfectly well." She took his hand and led him toward the toilet at the end of the car. Paige looked around at their fellow passengers. Most were either reading or asleep, but two little girls in the front seats looked up and watched them.

"Damn," she said. It was occupied.

"We can find another one," he said, getting into the spirit, but as he spoke a lank-haired youngster came out accompanied by a gust of cigarette smoke. "All yours," he said, heading south down the car.

"Isn't there supposed to be a smoke alarm, like

they have on airplanes?" Lady Jane said, wrinkling her nose.

"Evidently not," Paige said. "You want to find another one?"

"No, this'll do." She held the door open to evacuate the smoke, then led the way in and locked the door. The toilet was tiny, with barely enough room for two. The operation required Paige to sit on the toilet bowl while Lady Jane, who as if by design wore a loose skirt for the occasion, maneuvered herself into position above him. Paige thought it was all pretty weird, but Lady Jane giggled and whispered, "First on a train, first on a train . . ." as she pumped up and down. He hardly heard her because she was gripping both his ears like a bridle to steady herself. Afterward, she said, "We didn't go through a tunnel did we?"

When, their clothes readjusted, they emerged they found a conductor approaching. He was sniffing the air suspiciously.

"You been smoking in there?"

"We don't smoke," Lady Jane said virtuously. "It was a young man who came out a few minutes ago."

"Yeah, but what were the both of youse doing in there?"

"The usual," Paige said.

"At the same time?"

"She needs help," Paige said. "An unfortunate medical condition." The two little girls were whispering together, holding their hands over their mouths.

Back in their seats, Paige touched his tender ears and said, "That was one of the least satisfactory . . ."

"Oh, pish. The point is, I did it. I'm already a member of the Mile-High Club and now . . . I wonder what they call doing it on a train. The swaying made it quite interesting."

"The Loco Club?"

When they reached the stop for Albany, they found they really were in Rensselaer, a characterless community across the Hudson. It seemed that the tracks bypassed the capital city and they had to take a taxi. They checked into the Omni, a bland, modern hotel down the hill from the state capitol. Paige set off for the Albany Medical Center while Lady Jane headed off to inspect the "Million Dollar Staircase" in the capitol which she had read about in a brochure in the hotel room. "Although it can't be much of a staircase if it only cost a million," she said. "Sometimes, Americans are quite bizarre."

Paige was paying off the taxi outside the red-brick bulk of the hospital when he saw vanAllen coming out.

"Hold it," he said to the driver. "I may need you."

VanAllen looked shaken, haunted, her features drawn and white. She said, "I need a drink." For once, she was wearing a skirt and Paige checked out her legs. Okay. Above it was a blue, gold-buttoned blazer and a tight-fitting white sweater.

In the cab, she took out a mirror and repaired her makeup. Paige had read somewhere that the Hudson at Albany was only about ten feet above sea level and the air was drenched with humidity. The cab had no air-conditioning and he opened the windows.

"You look terrible. Been crying?" Paige said.

"You know that cops don't cry."

"Well, I knew a narc, Flaherty, up in the four-four who used to shed a tear when a skell beat the rap."

"Right now, I can do without your flip lines, Paige."

"Sorry. I'd have thought you were used to this sort of stuff now. You saw the Morgan woman?"

"I did. She's in a pitiful state." The cab was moving past fast-food joints, dingy bars and run-down apartment buildings that didn't seem to live up, to Rockefeller's expectations for the capital city.

"She must be shattered."

"You believe in evil, Paige?"

"I guess I do."

"Well, I just saw the result of it." Finished with the rehabilitation work on her face, she tossed the mirror and makeup into her purse and snapped it shut. "When I hear these oily friggin' defense attorneys moaning about their clients being the victims of their upbringing and the culture of deprivation . . ."

"She talk to you?"

"She's got two black eyes and a split lip. But, yeah, she talked. She was just coming out of sedation."

VanAllen had been alone at the bedside. The
woman doctor said that physically Mrs. Morgan
would be okay. Psychologically was another matter.

Outside the door, male investigators from the
sheriff's office and the Albany PD were camped out.
She could hear the rumble of their voices. They were
angry that vanAllen was doing the initial interrogation, but a call from the NYPD chief of detectives to
the fourteenth floor of One Police Plaza in
Manhattan and from there to the governor's office
had cleared the way for vanAllen. The suits at police
headquarters liked to flex their muscles; they insisted
it was their case so they had first dibs. During the
time that she sat there waiting for Mrs. Morgan to
recover consciousness, the men kept poking their
heads around the door to ask if everything was all
right, if she needed any help. Finally, vanAllen told
them to fuck off.

She had been waiting more than half an hour,
sometimes going to look out of the window at the
brutal architecture of Rockefeller's state buildings,
when Mary Morgan woke up and whispered, "Who
are you?"

"I'm Detective Lieutenant vanAllen from the
NYPD, Mrs. Morgan. I hate to question you at a time
like this, but I have to."

The woman just looked at her with eyes almost
hidden by the swollen flesh pressing in around them.
The room was small, sparsely furnished, antiseptic,
no flowers, no baskets of fruit. On the wall at the end
of the bed, a black TV screen stared down like a

Cyclops eye. VanAllen disliked hospitals intensely. She had spent too much time in them. She remembered the hours, the days, she had spent in a Bronx hospital with her mother, waiting for her grandmother to die. Then, there was all the time she had spent waiting to take statements from wounded victims . . .

"Where's my husband?" For a moment, vanAllen thought in dismay that the woman didn't know the full story, thought he was still alive.

"I mean, his body."

"He's being examined. Can I get you something?" The woman ignored the question.

"Have you caught those murderous degenerates? Oh, Christ, what's happened to me?" Her voice was despairing. She turned away from the detective and faced the wall. Her heavy shoulders, under the blue hospital gown, shook as she wept. VanAllen took her hand and stroked it gently.

"I should have done something," the woman wailed to the wall. "I should have fought them.

"It would have done no good, Mrs. Morgan. There were too many."

"I should have died with Joe." The guilt of the survivor, it was always the same.

"You have children. They'll need you."

The tears slowed. She gulped and turned back to vanAllen. Her face was a distorted mask, soaked in unchecked tears.

"Have you got any dark glasses?" VanAllen hunted through her purse and handed a pair of Ray

Bans to her. With trembling hands she slipped them on. She wanted to hide more than her wounded face.

"The children . . ."

"They've been told. They're on their way here."

"Where's here?"

"The Albany Medical Center. You've been under sedation."

"You're not local."

"No, I'm from New York City. You're not the first victim of these degenerates. They killed three, maybe more, in Manhattan."

"And a woman is better at questioning a rape victim. Is that it?"

"That's the theory."

"What d'you want to know? I already talked to the cops who found me."

With frequent prompting, she described the horror of the nighttime invasion at the lakeside house, the three men, their guns, their ski masks. "They made me get up and leave Joe and go with one of them to the children's bathroom. That's where he did it to me. When I struggled, he hit me, kept hitting me, in the face, until all I could do was let him. My hands were tied behind my back. He was still doing it when the shots came and I knew they'd killed Joe. He just laughed.

"Then he locked me in and I guess they all left. I didn't hear their car. If they had one, they must have left it some distance away. There's nobody living close to us there."

VanAllen was still holding her hand. "Did he say

anything, anything at all, while you were in the bathroom?"

"Just those horrible grunts. He was like a grotesque animal."

"He didn't speak?"

"Just about what he was doing to me. Oh . . . and he said this wouldn't be the end of it. Something about a plan. I don't know. I was out of my mind, still am."

With her bound hands, Mrs. Morgan had turned on all the faucets until the water ran under the door and down the stairs and under the front door. "I knew the water would run there," she said, "because the pipes burst one winter when the furnace died and flooded out under the door."

"You're a very brave woman," vanAllen said.

"No, I'm not. I'm bereft. I've lost everything. I don't know what to do."

"There are the children. Life goes on . . ."

"Not for me. Joe was my life, my sun and my moon. And he's gone."

"Would you recognize these men?"

"I don't know. Their heads were covered."

"Did they have accents?"

"The one who . . . who assaulted me sounded Southern. The others, I don't know, they just had ordinary voices. The one who seemed to be the leader, his voice was cultured, educated."

VanAllen was silent, her head bent over her notebook.

"Wait a moment, I think they called him, Teach or Teacher, something like that."

"Was he tall, short?"

"Average, all of them were average. He was, maybe, a hundred and eighty pounds."

"You can't think of anything else they said?"

"They were after Joe, I don't know why. That bastard raped me because I was available, a bonus . . ."

Paige said, "What was she like?"

"Probably a nice woman. By the time she stopped talking, I was in a pretty bad state, too." She drew in a deep breath and it came out as a sigh.

Paige spotted Lady Jane sauntering down State Street, staring at people like Marie Antoinette taking a break from Versailles to see how the vulgar throng lived. Her expression was so haughty that some people were staring back at her. Paige admired her long, well-shaped legs, now back in stockings, and remembered the way they had rippled and tensed on the train as she achieved her baroque ambition. She was weird, but there were consolations. He ignored her.

The cab pulled up outside the hotel and they went in.

"Order me a vodka and tonic," vanAllen said. "I have to make a couple of calls."

The bar off the lobby, all dark wood and brass rails, was freestanding and square, decorated with small green lamps. At two corners, TV sets were offering numbers for a Quick Draw lottery. No takers. The woman behind the bar was putting the drinks on the counter when Lady Jane strolled in. She looked at the vodka and said, "You must be a mind-reader, just what I want."

"It's not for you, but help yourself. I'll order another."

"Who's it for?"

"A cop, a Detective Lieutenant vanAllen. Be here in a minute."

"Those stairs, I'd rate them as worth less than a quarter of a million."

"Cost of living, etcetera."

"It's such a strange town, all those gigantic slabs of buildings by the capitol."

"Rockefeller's last erection."

"I'm hungry."

They got a menu from the bartender and were pondering it when vanAllen joined them. She looked better, with more color in her cheeks, but Paige had the sense there was an edge of hysteria underneath her calm. It made him wonder. He introduced the two women and they smiled while their eyes inventoried each other, first the face, then the figure and the clothes.

Paige braced, waiting for the outbreak of hostilities like that around the swimming pool in Connecticut. But Lady Jane said peacefully enough, "Charmed. Pray tell, is your first name Chloe?"

"No," van Allen said, looking puzzled.

"Let's eat," Paige said. They took their drinks into the dining room, almost deserted at this early hour.

"You're a policewoman?" Lady Jane said when they were seated. "How fascinating."

"It's a job."

"I've sometimes thought about getting a job." VanAllen arched an eyebrow at Paige.

"But then I'm so busy with other things. What made you join the police?"

"My father—my stepfather, really—wanted to be a cop, a detective. But his parents made him go to law school. He told me about it and I suppose I tried to make up for it by becoming a cop. I guess I was trying to win his approval."

"Didn't you have any brothers who could become policemen?"

"Two. One's a park ranger in Montana and the other's in the navy, a flyer."

"All in uniform anyway, then. Was your father pleased with you?"

"He's a lovely man. If I'd become a garbage collector he'd have been happy for me so long as it was what I wanted to do." Paige stared at Lady Jane. She had got more out of vanAllen in five minutes than he had in five years.

"My father's a federal judge in Connecticut," Paige said. "He keeps trying to persuade me to go to law school, follow in his footsteps, but I reckon I should stick with what I'm so good at."

They didn't seem interested. After they ordered food, Lady Jane said, "I don't think I could do it, throw questions at somebody who's just been raped and lost her husband like that."

VanAllen said, "It's hard. They don't want to talk about it, but maybe it's best that they do, get it all out."

"In England," Lady Jane said, "a Frenchman tried it with me. I got a grip on his cojones and had him squealing for mercy. I felt like Wellington at Waterloo."

"It's not always that easy."

"I know."

Before the food arrived, vanAllen's beeper went off and she checked the number.

"I have to return this one," she said, and left them.

When she came back, she was looking at her watch. She tossed some money on the table and said, "I can't stay to eat. There's been another killing. It has to be them, but they've broken the pattern. No connection to the Wilderness. It's a state trooper. He must have spotted the scumbags. They shot him and dumped him in the woods, the bastards."

"You sound as though you're taking it personally," Paige said. VanAllen looked as haggard as when she left the hospital.

"Where did they dump him?" Paige said.

"About halfway between here and Hamillton."

"They're on their way to the Wilderness."

"Right. It has to be part of their plan. The end game."

24 ◄

Approaching from the east, the Teacher and Billy Waddell drove into Hamillton at midafternoon. Up here in the mountains, it was cool and cloudy with a few vagrant raindrops dampening the summer's dust. Already there was a smell of autumn in the air. Only a few people were about as the Taurus moved down the main street toward the prison. A normal day in Hamillton.

"You reckon they found Ferret and the nigger yet?" Waddell said.

"Doesn't matter much now," the Teacher said. "We're here."

"Pigs, douche bags," Waddell said, staring sullenly from the passenger seat at the scattering of people on the sidewalks. Then his eyes went to the right, to the thick walls hiding the ugly mass of the prison annex that once had been a hospital for the criminally insane. He had spent twenty-two years locked up there and in the pen, when his total sentence for armed robbery had been only eighteen years, even without parole. His features constricted bitterly. Those years had completed the poisoning of Billy Waddell's mind.

"We should blow it up," he said. "Put dynamite under it and bring it all down."

"We'll do better than that," the Teacher said. They were coming to the wall on the right now, massive and grotesque, looming over the little town. The penitentiary behind it covered more acreage than the entire town it dominated. Guards were lounging in the glass-sided watchtowers that allowed them a view of the prison buildings one way and of their homes the other. The only arms in the prison were stowed in the watchtowers. It was from the towers that, thirty-five years earlier, guards had machine-gunned desperate, mutinous convicts in the yard. Ray Bliss had told them about the slaughter.

"Remember Savage and his collections?" Waddell said.

First as assistant principal keeper under Crain and then as full PK, Savage had developed a collection system among the inmates. When a prison official retired, the convicts were expected by Savage to contribute toward a going-away gift from the few cents they made laboring in the prison workshops.

Even five cents from each of 3,000 men could buy a handsome gift. Savage said it showed they had the correct, cooperative attitude. From the start of his time in the Wilderness, the Teacher had refused to hand over a penny. It had been enough to

draw the PK's attention. He ordered the Teacher to
pay up, and when he refused again, that was enough.
The Teacher appeared before the PK's court and the
doctor, Campbell, was brought in and the Teacher
disappeared into the madhouse.

"I remember," the Teacher said flatly. "Why
d'you think I chose Savage as my target? Now it's
collection time for us."

They didn't stop. They drove at the same unremarkable pace clear through the town until wooded
hillsides took the place of the modest clapboard
houses that clustered around the prison.

Both the Teacher and Waddell had been back in
Hamillton a number of times since their release.
They knew the layout well, the eight square blocks
that constituted the town's viscera, the stores along
the main street, the brick Catholic church with a
statue of the Madonna outside, the little cinema, the
Splendide, open only in the evening, the town's
administrative offices standing directly across from
the main gate of the prison. And they knew where
Savage lived, down by the firehouse.

On the western edge of the town, with the
cemetery on the left, the Teacber found a spot in the
road wide enough to turn and they began to drive
back along the main street. So might a disguised
patrol scout enemy territory.

"Jesus!" Billy Waddell was staring down
Rancie Street which ran at right angles to the main
street. "No, don't stop. Jesus!"

"What is it?"

"Outside Savage's house down there. There's a state police cruiser just pulling up. I saw it, Teach. They're on to us!"

"Cool it, Billy." The Teacher's voice was even, dispassionate. "There was always that chance now we're coming to the end of it all. Maybe they found the trooper, maybe they're putting it all together. It won't stop us."

"They must have found the nigger."

"Perhaps, but I doubt it," the Teacher said. "If they found him and connected the whole thing to Hamillton, the place would be swarming with cops."

"But that fucking trooper outside Savage's place . . . they must be on to us." They were moving back past the prison annex again, and even in the midst of his agitation Billy Waddell stared at it with hating eyes.

"It could be anything or nothing," the Teacher said. "Some of the troopers are pals of the stinking guards, all the same stripe. It could be just a friendly visit. Listen to me. We got this far and they're not going to stop us now. We'll just take it as it comes, Billy." Feeling the power of the Teacher's leadership, Waddell sank back into his seat.

"Okay, but we gotta dump this heap," he said. "And quick. God damn that flat tire and God damn that nigger. He screwed us up good. I don't care what you say, I still think I did the right thing, Teach. He killed Ferret and now there's only two of us to do the whole job. It's not the way we planned it all those months. No Jackie and now no Ferret."

"It was good we found out about Jackie in time. We had to take care of him and of Ray Bliss. Ferret, well, he was just unlucky."

At the eastern edge of town, the Teacher turned right and drove down a narrow road for a quarter of a mile. They were both silent, both conscious of rising tension, for the next few minutes could be crucial.

Twisting in his seat, Waddell stared back through the rear window at the empty road unwinding behind them. There were no houses here, just trees pressing close to the road. They crossed a bridge over the summer-dry bed of a stream, turned a corner, and there it was. The Hamillton Junior and Senior High School. The car passed between two stone pillars and headed along a short asphalt driveway toward the modern one-story building set down in a pasture with hills all around. Four yellow school buses stood parked at the side.

"Nobody about," the Teacher said. "You see anything?"

"Nothing," Billy Waddell said. He was still studying the area behind the car through the rear window. The school and its grounds and playing fields were in a natural sylvan bowl overlooked by nothing but silent woods. It was a tranquil scene, the one town resource out of sight of the prison. The town fathers had done that much for their children.

"You're sure there's no caretaker, Teach?" Waddell said as the car moved around the school buildings to the rear and pulled up at a loading bay.

Now they were out of sight of the road and the driveway.

"I'm sure," the Teacher said coldly.

With Jackie and Ferret gone, Waddell had begun to show signs of presumption, as if he had as much authority as the Teacher. He had shot the trooper as if he was equal to the Teacher in decision-making. Madness. The Teacher wouldn't mind killing a battalion of cops, but the task came first and to carry it out he had to be in complete charge. Afterwards . . . the Teacher didn't expect there was going to be an afterwards, not after what they were going to do to Hamillton. And to Savage.

"Yeah, you're sure," Billy Waddell said. "But how do we know some guy isn't sitting inside right now phoning the troopers?" There was a needling note to his voice.

"I checked and double-checked," the Teacher said. "When the kids are on vacation, the place is locked up and left alone. No caretaker, nothing. People in Hamillton are too cheap to hire a care-taker. They reckon all the burglars are behind bars and they reckon they're all too law-abiding to bust into a school, and that goes for their kids, too." His voice was savage with contempt for the town and its people.

At the loading bay, they moved swiftly. Reaching back into the well of the Taurus, they took the four Kalashnikov rifles and the spare magazines from under the towel that had concealed them. They dumped them all on the loading platform. They

opened the trunk and pulled out the cans of gasoline
they had bought on the thruway before hitting
Morgan. They put the cans with the assault rifles.
Although they had eaten the roast beef sandwiches
in the car, there was still some cheese and fruit and
root beer, enough to keep them going until nighttime. Billy Waddell had wanted to pick up a bottle
of Southern Comfort, but the Teacher had vetoed it
peremptorily. There would be no drinking until the
task was completed. Time enough for that afterwards. The food went with the guns and the gas.

While Waddell went to examine the door that
led from the loading bay into the school, the Teacher
slid back behind the wheel of the Taurus. There was
a path made by the kids into the woods and he drove
the car along it. Gunning the engine, he moved up a
slope and into the trees until the car was deep in the
cool shadows, invisible from the school.

The Teacher switched off the engine and sat for
a moment thinking. They were in position, ready,
just as they had planned during the months when
vengeance beckoned them on. Crain had been like a
test run and it had gone off beautifully.

After that, they had been almost ready to finish
the job, one after the other in quick succession
before the authorities had time to recognize the pattern, see what was coming down.

But then Ferret, who had never mentioned the
pain, went into the hospital and the doctors confirmed what he had already guessed. Cancer.

It had been a rough period, more than five

months of waiting. The Teacher made the others wait, overruled their impatience. If there was a chance that Ferret might get out to join in the task then, by God, he was going to get that chance.

They used the time to make sure that nothing would go amiss, to produce a blueprint for justice. Covertly, they had studied the town of Hamillton until they knew it almost as well as if they had grown up there instead of suffering behind its bars. They had watched Campbell in New York, discovered the steps from the drive to the park which allowed them to appear before their victim as if by magic and to disappear with equal facility. When the cop showed up above the ramp, it was the Teacher who had ordered the seizure of the children.

They had reconnoitered so that they would know where to find Mahoney and Morgan when they wanted them. They had gone to a warehouse in the back streets of Baltimore and cut a deal for the four AK-47s.

It was during those months of waiting that the Teacher had seen what must be done to complete the task.

Ray Bliss. He had been a problem. Billy Waddell had a grudge against him, no doubt of that. Something to do with young prisoners and a remark that Ray might or might not have made about Southerners. It didn't matter much what was behind it. Whatever Ray's role in the closing of the hospital, Billy Waddell wanted him dead. He had a point, too.

They should never have mentioned the compact to Ray. They should have known he didn't have the strength they had. He had turned them down. He was interested only in his law books. It meant, though, that he had the knowledge to blow them and their plans out of the water.

Ferret had seen that clearly enough when they talked about it at his hospital bedside. Ray Bliss, he said, was a loose cannon. He had to be secured. So Ray became part of the task. So, eventually, did Jackie.

None of it mattered compared to what they had accomplished and what still lay ahead. They were on track and moving forward. If the Teacher had one regret, it was that Ferret, not Billy Waddell, had died in that layby. Ironic that a bullet, not the cancer, had taken him. Ferret was smart. Close-mouthed, dedicated, and far-sighted. He had seen where the whole thing would lead them, the inevitability of the ending. Talking privately to the Teacher a few weeks before the cancer in his stomach went into remission and allowed his release, he had shown his knowledge and accepted the finality. Billy, now, Billy Waddell was different. They would escape in the confusion, Billy said, head into the mountains, lose themselves, get over the border into Canada.

Sure, Billy.

Behind the walls, the Teacher had won his nickname because he had taught at Columbia before the killing and the conviction. Inside, he used the library, read heavy old books, and helped inmates with their letters and with their appeals. They looked up to him because of his intellect, these men of little education, and his power was reinforced by the strength of his personality.

His earlier life had done nothing to prepare him for the years locked up, but he had survived them and that, he thought, was a triumph of sorts.

That earlier life now was like a dream, so far in the past that it was hard sometimes for the Teacher to recall separate episodes of what had happened and the emotions that spurred the events. Sometimes, even his real name seemed unfamiliar, for now it was always Teach.

At Columbia, he was an assistant professor, teaching nineteenth-century American literature, specializing in Melville. He had little money, no tenure, but he was young and it was enough that he did work he enjoyed and, away from Columbia, in the apartment in safe and peaceful Washington Heights, there was always Janet and the treasure they shared, little Serafina, just seven.

When the call came, the call that would distort his life, he was finishing up with a student who embarrassed him and knew it. He would remember it as his last moment of serenity. The girl's bell-bottomed jeans were so tight that they outlined the thrust of her pudendum. The buttons on her shirt were undone enough to demonstrate that she wore no bra. He was used to women students flirting with him, maybe hoping for better grades, but this one's approach was so blatant that he was made uncomfortable by it. Her offering was too crude for him to be seriously tempted, and he was not about to forget his devotion to his family. She seemed amused by his discomfort, sometimes standing over him to point out something in *Moby Dick*, lightly leaning against him and speaking so close to his ear that he could feel her breath. He had heard that she was living with one of the student leaders who had led an invasion of the dean's office to protest the war in Vietnam.

A woman from the college office put her head around the door and said that he was wanted immediately at the stationhouse two blocks from his apartment. She vanished before he could question her.

Without a word he left, the student staring after him. He debated trying to find out more at the office but instead, his mind whirling with questions, drove straight to the precinct. At the desk, the sergeant told him to go up to the detectives' squad room.

Janet, six months pregnant, was standing by a railing beyond which were desks and men in shirt-sleeves with holstered guns at their waists or under their arms. A phone was ringing and nobody answered it. Her pretty features were pale and stricken. With her was a fat man smoking a stub of a cigar.

"It's Serafina," his wife said. "She's been attacked. Oh, God, it was my fault."

"She's been hurt? Where is she?"

"She's all right," the man said. "But we're having trouble getting a statement from her." He said he was Detective Humphrey Prince—"Call me Bogey."

"Oh, Charley," Janet said, "it was some sort of sexual assault. And she's not all right." Now she was looking at him with something, perhaps guilt, in her blue eyes.

His daughter was down the corridor in a small bleak room with a uniformed policewoman who looked up, shrugged at the detective and left. The place, graffiti on the grubby walls, reeked of cigarette and cigar smoke. Serafina was curled up in a chair, her legs under her, her arms wrapped around her little chest. There were tear marks on her face, but now she looked frozen. She wouldn't look at them, wouldn't talk, not at first.

It took more than an hour for them to get the story, but the Teacher remembered all of it as if it had been burned into his synapses. She had been left alone napping in the apartment while her mother went to the store. Waking, the girl had unlocked the door and gone in search of Janet.

At the bottom of the stairs on the ground floor, a door had opened and a man had appeared. He talked to her, asked where she was going, said she could wait for her mother inside. She didn't want to, but he took her hand and led her into the apartment. And that was where it happened.

She said that at first he was nice, giving her cookies and turning on the TV for her. But then it started. She said he took her in his lap and kissed her. He ran his hands over her, lifted her skirt, pulled down her panties, and put his fingers in her. He kept doing it, kept hurting her. When she cried out, he slapped her face and told her to shut up. She wept silently. She was still crying when he lowered his trousers and made her touch him. She began to scream. Again he slapped her and made her put her hand back on him until he was satisfied. He said she shouldn't say anything about what had happened. It would be their secret. Finally, he let her out and closed the door behind her. When her mother found her on the street, she was incoherent, almost babbling about what a man had done to her.

The precinct house was near and her mother took her directly there and the police called Columbia.

As the Teacher listened, a cold rage spread through him. He thought afterwards that he changed, became different. He knew who the man was. Gerry Evans. There were only two apartments on the first floor. One was occupied by a young couple, both of whom worked in midtown Manhattan. The other was occupied by Evans. He was a bluff, red-faced widower, a member of the city council, and a power in local Democratic circles. There had been whispers about him and his interest in children.

"I want him arrested," the Teacher said.

Bogey looked doubtful. "I don't think we can do that right now," he said.

"The man's a sexual monster. Look at my daughter. He has to be arrested."

"Well, there's a problem with that."

"What are you talking about?"

"It's just that . . . it's her word against his. Tough case to prove. Hold on." He went away and returned with a smooth-faced, smooth-talking young man he introduced as an assistant district attorney visiting the precinct on another matter. This attorney, Peters, listened with a poker face as the matter was explained to him. At the end, he asked who they were accusing.

When they said Evans, a curious expression crossed his face and the Teacher knew he recognized the name. The lawyer said he had to make a phone call and went out.

When he returned, he said they should go home and they would be contacted. The Teacher knew then. He and his family were nothing. Evans was influential, had lines into city hall, controlled a large block of voters, and an election was coming up.

They took the girl to a hospital and she was examined. The doctors said it was inconclusive.

In the days that followed, when Serafina turned from an outgoing, eager child into a withdrawn, zestless stranger, the detective called Bogey became difficult to reach. Finally, the Teacher went and waited at the precinct until he showed up.

"Look," Bogey said, "I know it's tough to take, but it's out of my hands. The DA doesn't think he can get a conviction, not on the word of a six-year-old."

"You mean nothing is going to be done about this evil bastard?"

"If we had some real evidence beyond what

your daughter says . . . and she would have to testify. Would you want that?" He was clearly embarrassed. The Teacher left the stationhouse and set about finding a gun. It took him three days but, for $300, he ended up with a 9mm Smith and Wesson semiautomatic, its number filed off.

It was easy. He simply knocked on Evans's door, and when the pervert opened it, the Teacher gave him long enough to recognize him. Then he shot him in the face. The Teacher stood over him and put another bullet into his crotch. Then he went to the front steps and waited for them to come for him.

The Teacher never saw his daughter again. Janet never came to visit him in the Wilderness. She wrote that, for the sake of her little girl, she must create a new life in which he played no part. The words were cold, perhaps driven by guilt. He wrote to her three times, and each time the letters were returned unopened. When the Teacher finally accepted that she had abandoned him, the tectonic plates of his life shifted dangerously. He changed—changed irrevocably.

Years later, long after she divorced him, she wrote once more. She said that she was getting married to an older man in Pennsylvania, a good and kind man. It was for her daughter's sake, she wrote. Sure, it was. He didn't reply.

In the days after he was released from the hospital, the Teacher thought of trying to find them, thought of seeing his daughter. But he did nothing. Personal entanglements might dissipate, divert, his determination to punish Hamillton. Hamillton had become the focus of his life.

When the Teacher got back to the loading bay, Billy Waddell had forced the lock of the rear door with a tire iron. They carried the rifles and the banana-shaped magazines and the gasoline and the food inside. The place smelled of chalk and floor polish. A tiled hallway led into a modern kitchen with stainless steel sinks and big ovens. No food had been left to attract mice during the summer recess.

In one corner was a huge blue refrigerator, its power plug hanging loose.

"Maybe they turned off the power for the summer," Waddell said. But after they reconnected the refrigerator, it shuddered and hummed into life. They put their food and drink on the shelves.

"We ate like rats in the Wilderness and in the hospital, and their kids live like princes," Billy Waddell said bitterly. "Lookit, microwave ovens, blenders, china plates, everything."

The Teacher went to explore the school. Class-rooms, offices, a teachers' lounge, a small gymnasium with a stage so that it could double as an assembly hall, a dining area with serving tables. In the principal's office, there was a radio and a TV set. He turned on both, searching for news programs.

Nothing. Talk shows on TV, music on the radio. There had been nothing on the car radio either about the trooper's death or the design that lay behind it.

From the windows of the principal's office, the Teacher's eyes commanded the approach to the school. He turned the big leather chair behind the desk so that it faced the windows and sank into it. Looking at his watch, he saw they had about seven hours to wait.

25 ◀

VanAllen called the state police headquarters, just off the thruway on the outskirts of Albany, and was told that if she got there in twenty minutes she could get a ride with a helicopter going to the Wilderness. She hurried off.

Lady Jane was tackling her food, commenting unfavorably on its character. Carrying a hamburger on a bun, Paige went to use a landline to call his office and found himself talking between chews to LaFleche. The city editor had a message for Paige and he sounded affronted at his role. Savage, he said, was in the air—"wheels up," he said, playing the pro—and due to land in Albany in half an hour. Paige was to meet him at the airport, rent a car, and drive the managing editor north.

"What's this all about, Paige?" LaFleche said in aggrieved tones.

"Gotta go."

"I order you to tell me what is going on."

"Sorry. Can't hear and there's somebody waiting

for the phone." Paige put down the receiver on
LaFleche's angry protests and went back to Lady
Jane.

"This fish," she said, "wasn't caught. It put up its
fins and surrendered."

"Come on," he said. "We have to go, unless
you'd prefer to stay here."

"Where do we have to go?"

"Up north, the Wilderness."

She put down her knife and fork, pushed the fish
aside, and said, "If we go any farther north, we'll be
rubbing noses with Nanook. What about our room?
That bed looked comfortable enough."

"We'll have to leave it. Come on." They went
out and found a cab which took them to the airport.
Paige was filling in the paperwork for a car when
Savage appeared at his elbow. He had no luggage. He
looked worried. When he was introduced to Lady
Jane, he shook her hand and said nothing about her
unexplained presence with his reporter.

"You know about the trooper?" he said edgily to
Paige.

"Our gang, right?"

"Has to be. I'm going to call my father, then
we'll get on the road."

There was no answer at the house on Rancie
Street. Savage wondered if, as promised, a trooper
was stationed outside the place. A serpent of fear
slithered up his spine as he thought of the ruthlessness and cunning of the killers. He was sure his father
was a target.

At first, Paige drove, but after fifteen minutes an impatient Savage took over and increased the speed. Lady Jane went to sleep in the back.

"What d'you want me to do when we get to Hamillton?" Paige said.

"Do your job. Be a reporter. Interview my father when we catch up with him." Savage's voice was harsh and tense. The night before, he hadn't slept well and his eyes felt sore as if they had been sandpapered. The fear was spreading and consolidating like a tumor. Under the restless urging of his foot on the accelerator, the car's tires were squealing on tight bends.

"Interview your father?"

"That's right. When we find him. Talk to him like you talked to Bliss. Get his side of the story." Paige saw nothing but disaster. Once, on another paper, he had interviewed a distant relative of the publisher on a subject he had long since forgotten. Afterwards, there had been a stream of complaints, about his appearance, about his manner, about his questions, and about the resulting story. Paige had left the paper shortly after the incident.

"Couldn't you talk to your father?" he said hesitantly. "He would open up far more to his son, don't you think?"

"You're the reporter. I'm merely going up to make sure he's all right."

"Yes, but it could be a tad difficult, even for me. I mean, accusations have been made, serious and unpleasant accusations. It might be embarrassing."

"That's why you're going to do it, Paige. It's very difficult to embarrass you." Paige pondered this, not sure whether it was a compliment.

"Your father," he said, "what's he like?"

"He's getting on. He can be a bit testy." Oh, great, Paige thought. Why did this sort of thing always happen to him? Savage's old man sounded like his own. Whenever they met, the judge asked Paige when he was going to find a respectable job. His irritating father was one reason Paige suspected he might have been abducted from an English peer's cradle and mysteriously shipped to the U.S.

"Leave it to me," he said dismally. "Old Paige will come through as usual. You think we're safe, going at this speed?"

In the distance, Paige could see the dark line across the horizon that was the southern foothills of the Adirondacks. They'd be in Hamillton in an hour or two. Perhaps Savage's father wouldn't be around. Perhaps he had gone on vacation. Perhaps he had suffered a stroke and was in a hospital. Perhaps he had been struck dumb. Perhaps the hit men would get him first.

At the wheel, Savage was quiet now. His concern about the safety of his father had deepened into another anguish, a fear that his father had taken part in something iniquitous. He sensed that whatever else lay ahead, he and his beliefs would be tested as never before.

Over the years, Savage had developed a code that he believed a newspaperman should follow.

Words like truth, accuracy, fairness, they sounded trite these days, were easily mocked and subverted. Yet if he didn't believe in them, what had his life been about? Newspapers had given him a lot. Maybe there was a debt to be paid.

"What made you decide to get into this racket, Paige?" he said. They were off the Northway now, heading west into the mountains. Paige stirred warily. He didn't much like his managing editor probing his background any more than he liked the speed they were doing.

"Oh, I don't know," he said. "It certainly wasn't the money. As a matter of fact, I wanted to talk about my salary. I have a lot of commitments and—"

"We'll talk about that some other time. That wasn't the question."

"Well," Paige said uneasily, "newspapers, I suppose, are my natural habitat. As far as I can tell, in most jobs there's a lot of bullshit. There's not so much in newspapers, if you exclude LaFleche, perhaps because it's a reporter's job to see through it. Anyway, there wasn't much else that I could do so superbly and have so much fun at the same time.

"You know and I know that every politician without exception is a pandering scoundrel and occasionally we're allowed to point it out. A newspaper pays you to study the absurdities and bullshit all around, I guess, to expose the crooks and poseurs, to shout that the emperor is wearing nothing. It's a pretty good deal."

They drove into Hamillton in the early evening.

On the way, there'd been a couple of showers, but now the air was clear and dry, so that the surrounding mountains, their wooded sides a blurred plaid of green and smoky blue, seemed to be pressing in on the little town.

"Weird-looking place," Paige said as they drove down the main street. "What's that?"

"The hospital where they locked up Bliss and the rest of them. And this is the prison." Passing below the wall, Savage felt a curious mix of emotions. Inevitably, there was some affection for a place where he had grown up happily enough. There was the little cinema, the Splendide, that had transported him to the Western plains, the foggy streets of London, the canyons of New York. There was the drugstore where he had first held hands with a girl. Some of the buildings had second-story balconies that Savage had never seen used except for storage. These were the streets where he had learned to drive his father's car. Through the window of the town's single grocery, he caught a glimpse of Mr. Shell, old now, who sometimes used to give him an apple to eat on his way home.

And yet the recent disclosures about the hospital had given another dimension to the familiar streets and buildings. Savage felt confused, almost disoriented. Underneath the placid surface all the time there had been an undercurrent of secret knowledge about the men in the hospital, Hamillton's Gulag.

"I'm hungry," Paige said. "I had to leave my food in Albany to answer the call of duty. I need, let's see, a Scotch, and then maybe another one, and then a sirloin steak with baked potato and butter and a salad with blue cheese, and then ice cream on—"

"Paige, give me a break and stop thinking about that stomach of yours," Savage snapped. "We have work to do." He was about to turn down Rancie Street, and the tension that had been building within him during the journey from New York was reaching a peak.

He stared through the windshield. There was the house. No trooper, no radio car. No sign of his father's Buick. Nothing. Jesus, where was he?"

"Sorry," Paige said, hurt. "Naturally, I'm prepared to starve, go down to skin and bone, if it's for the good of the paper. It's just that I do my best work if I eat regularly."

"Okay, okay," Savage said distractedly. "We'll eat a bit later." He wondered if his father would agree to talk to Paige about the hospital. Savage couldn't interrogate his own father; there was too much authority in the relationship. A form of moral cowardice maybe, he thought, but he quailed at the thought of appearing to sit in judgment on his father.

Beyond that, there was the question of publishing the interview. If an assassination team was at work, then it was all bound to come out eventually one way or another. He was caught in a vise.

He braked at the curb outside the old house. The garage doors were open. No car.

"We'd better start talking to the neighbors," Savage said. "You take that one and I'll take the one on this side." They were getting out of the car when a black Buick, his father at the wheel, turned down the street toward them. Immediately behind him was another car, a dusty, brown Chevrolet.

But Savage was staring at his father's passenger. It was Kit.

It was by design that Savage and Paige saw nothing unusual when they reached Hamillton. The Bell JetRanger helicopter, fitted for law enforcement use, with vanAllen and a few ranking state police officials on board, had caused a flutter of excitement among the children of Hamillton, but then it sank out of sight behind the prison walls. It stood in the yard, cleared of prisoners who were now in lockdown, its rotor blades still turning. A half-dozen plain-clothed state troopers and investigators had arrived in unmarked cars with instructions to keep out of sight and monitor traffic.

The first of them entered the town forty minutes after the Teacher and Billy Waddell went to ground at the school. Some of them were setting up headquarters for the Bureau of Criminal Investigation inside the Wilderness while others watched the streets from shop windows and from the prison watchtowers. They noted Paige's rental car, ran the license, and swiftly traced it to the Albany airport.

By canceling leaves and stripping highway patrols, Albany was able to assign seventy-three troopers to the town. While some were in plain clothes, others did not have time to change out of their uniforms. All were armed with M1 carbines.

On a large-scale map pinned to the wall of a requisitioned office in the Wilderness, small red stars indicated the homes of potential targets, retired or still in the service. In the belief that the assassination team was interested only in the higher ranks of the Corrections Department, the BCI major in charge in Hamillton left the homes of ordinary guards and attendants unstarred. Protection of every house in the town with a prison connection was impossible. After some discussion, it was decided not to alert the townspeople at this time to the danger they faced for fear of provoking a panic. The NYPD, because of the Campbell and Mahoney killings, was promised it would be kept informed and vanAllen was with the BCI major.

By the time the full complement of troopers and investigators was in position, some assigned to surveillance, some held in reserve inside the penitentiary, it was growing dark.

Billy Waddell was watching a gangster movie on the principal's TV set when the Teacher suddenly sat upright in his chair and rasped, "Turn that off." Catching the tension in the order, the Southerner, who had been sitting on the edge of the big desk, leaned forward, flicked the switch and the picture faded. He turned and stared through the windows.

Three youngsters, all boys in their midteens, had

ridden their bicycles through the gates and onto the grounds of the school. They were playing Follow the Leader, circling and zigzagging as they maintained their positions. None of them showed any interest in the school buildings, but the Teacher and Waddell withdrew toward the middle of the principal's office, where they could watch unseen from outside.

"Get the rifles," the Teacher said. They had left their weapons with the gasoline cans in the hallway outside the office. Waddell slipped away, returning a moment later with two of the AK-47s. Without taking his eyes from the cyclists, the Teacher stretched out a hand for one of the guns.

"Little punks," Waddell muttered. He lifted his weapon and aimed, squinting, at the lead kid. "Bang, you're dead," he said. He giggled.

"Stop that," the Teacher said. "This could be trouble."

"The little bastards are just messing about, Teach. They'll be gone in a minute. And if they don't . . ." He fingered the trigger.

"If they go around to the back . . . if they spot the car in the trees." Even as he spoke the boys began to move out of sight. They were heading towards the rear of the school.

"Little punks," Waddell said again. The Teacher was already through the door, across the corridor, and into a classroom that overlooked the rear area. The boys had abandoned their bikes. They were on the swings in the playground, laughing and jeering at each other as they swung higher and higher.

"Go check the door," the Teacher said. "Make sure it's closed." His thoughts were turbulent with anxiety that at this last moment the boys might arrest the flow of his design. They only had to approach the loading bay, look at the school, to see the splinter marks where Waddell had forced the lock. Or wander into the woods and stumble across the car. They'd be off immediately to report what they'd seen.

The Teacher's hands tightened around the Kalashnikov. He wouldn't hesitate to cut them down if need be. They were part of the sewer called Hamillton. Grown up, they would become guards, ready in their turn to brutalize a new generation of prisoners. But the thunder of the AK-47s almost certainly would be heard in the town.

Tiring of the swings, the boys climbed to the platform atop a slide. One of them played Tarzan. He thumped his chest and shouted, "Jane, where are you, Jane? Tarzan wants to screw Jane." On top of the slide, he was looking down into the school windows, and the Teacher thought for a moment that he was staring in at him. But then the youngster whooped and ran, waving his arms, full-tilt down the slide.

"Get away. Leave," the Teacher urged under his breath. His nerves were strung tight. Another hour and it would be dark and they would be safe and they could move out and start what they had come so far to do. He lusted for the dark as if it were a woman.

"Door's closed okay." Billy Waddell was back.

Two of the boys were wrestling on the grass now, rolling and shouting, raising a little cloud of dust. The third watched for a moment, a superior smile on his face, then turned and walked toward the woods, to the left of the spot where the Teacher had left the car. He was a thickset youngster with a baseball cap tilted back on his head.

"What the hell is the little slimebag gonna do?" Waddell sounded angry, as if the boys were deliberately mocking him with their presence.

"Go and wait at the door," the Teacher said. "We may have to take them out." If the boy looked to his right with any intensity, he would see the car, had to see the car. Swearing softly, Billy Waddell went off. Barely breathing, the Teacher stared at the spot in the trees where the boy had entered the wood. They would have to shoot them down.

Zipping up his pants, the boy reappeared. His expression was tranquil. A moment later it was over. They climbed on their bikes and, again following the leader, rode through the school gates.

Savage's father had been to Lake George to pick up Kit from the New York bus.

Getting out of the car, the youngster, in blue jeans ripped at the knees and a Chicago Bulls T-shirt, was equally surprised to see Savage, but before they had a chance to talk, the brown Chevrolet had pulled up behind the Buick. In it were two men and they both got out. One of them was carrying a carbine, holding it so that the barrel ran down the side of his leg.

"Everything okay here?" the other man said.

"Who the hell are you?" Savage's father said. The man pulled a wallet out of his pocket and flashed a badge.

"State police," he said. "And you?"

"I live here. My name's Savage. This young fella is my grandson and this is my son. Don't know who he's got with him."

Paige fumbled in his pocket and brought out a grimy NYPD press identification card.

"Jesus," the man said. "The press here already?" He looked into Paige's rental car at Lady Jane who was still asleep, sprawled across the backseat.

"This a rental?" he said, nodding at the car.

"Yeah, we picked it up in Albany," Savage said.

"What's all this about?" Savage's father said.

"Just routine checking," the man said shortly. "We'll be on our way." Both stalked off back to their car.

Shrugging, Savage's father went to put his car in the garage. Paige pulled his, Lady Jane still sleeping in the back, onto the little driveway. The old man led the way into the house. It was just the way Savage remembered it, even the smell. They went to the kitchen and the old man filled a coffeepot. His dog, Jasper, watched them from his basket, but didn't stir. Sitting at the table by the window, Savage could see the wall looming over the town, the guards looking down from catwalks outside the watchtowers.

"What the hell are you doing here, Kit?" he said.

"I thought Mom was going to call you," the boy

said. "I phoned Grandpa just to say hello and he invited me up. Hadn't seen him for a while, so I thought I'd jump on the bus, come up for a couple of days." Savage suspected the visit was as much to escape his mother's tearful concern over the boy's plight.

To Kit's question about his presence in Hamillton, Savage said vaguely, "We might have a problem. Nothing's clear yet." Sitting in these familiar surroundings, the concept of a gang of hit men stalking his father seemed absurd, unreal. He introduced Paige, who was uncharacteristically subdued in the presence of his managing editor's father. The old man was still formidable, Savage thought. Over six feet tall and broad-shouldered, he had lost none of his stiff-backed air of command.

"It has to do with your phone call, I suppose," his father said, putting out cups. "You'd better tell me what's going on."

Savage went through the sequence of events, starting with the kidnapping at the Sutton Place park and the death of Duncan Campbell. When he came to Ray Bliss and said that the ex-con was still alive, the old man scowled.

"That's a bad one," he said. "We knew all about him, a wife-murderer, and now he's killed again because they let him out."

"He says he didn't do it," Paige ventured. "He says it was a setup." The old man looked at him as though he were feebleminded.

"Sure, oh, sure. And there'll be people ready to

believe him, just like those judges did. He's so cunning, they'll end up giving him a medal."

"He could be charged with murder," Savage said. "As soon as he's out of the hospital." His father shook his head angrily.

"He'll get out of it somehow," he said. "He'll find one of those soft-headed, soft-hearted judges, and he'll walk away laughing. Just you see."

Savage described the murders of Mahoney and Morgan. Morgan had been killed with rounds of the same caliber that struck down Campbell. "Both men had links to the prison hospital, admittedly distant. You can't ignore the possibility of a conspiracy to kill certain officials of the State Corrections Department. And now we've got a trooper killed not far from here. I talked to the superintendent of state police, and they're taking it all very seriously." Kit was silently listening, fascinated.

"Bliss," the old man said. "He has to be part of it." Paige thought that he seemed obsessed with Bliss.

"Maybe," Savage said, "but Bliss was in the hospital when the last murders were committed. Even if he's involved, there are at least three other men at large."

"You think they're coming here? After me?" Now his voice was tight with anger.

"Listen, Dad. You said you thought it was strange that the PK before you, Crain, died in a hunting accident. Okay, you thought it might have been suicide. But suppose he was one of the targets. Suppose they killed him and made it seem like an accident to give themselves time to get around to others. You could be next on their list. Maybe some of them blame you for the time they spent in the madhouse. It's possible."

Savage's father got up from the table and went to stare out of the window. His eyes were on the wall.

"Let 'em come," he said. "I can look after myself. I've spent most of my life among killers and rapists and thieves, and I know how to handle them."

"Dad, these are shrewd, ruthless men. They've proved that already. You can't just stay here and wait for them to come and kill you." His father swung around, his heavy body outlined against the gathering dusk.

"What d'you want me to do?" he demanded. "Run and hide? Maybe go and lock myself in a cell where they can't get at me? If these men are from the hospital, then they're insane, and I'm not going to run away from three or four crazies."

"I'm not suggesting that you run away, Dad. I couldn't reach you during the day and I got worried and that's why we came up here. Now, all I'm suggesting is that you take some precautions. It wouldn't hurt for you to go inside the prison where they couldn't get at you. Give the authorities time to run them down."

"No way am I going to hide from these dirtbags inside the prison."

"At least, be on your guard until the police catch up with them. Keep your doors locked. They're bound to find them soon."

"Perhaps they've already caught them," Paige said. "I'll go call the state police."

"No," Savage said. "I'll do it. I've already talked to the deputy superintendent in Albany. Even with your tremendous interviewing techniques, Paige, I might get more out of him." Ignoring Paige's expression of disbelief, Savage picked up the receiver from the wall phone. He was put through to the deputy superintendent almost immediately.

When he put the phone down, he looked concerned and his father said, "What is it?"

"It's off the record, but the state police are sure the bastards are heading for Hamillton, if they're not already here. There was another body with that dead trooper and they've identified him as an inmate of the hospital."

"What are they doing about it?" his father asked. If there was any fear in him, it didn't show. He looked more angry, Savage thought, than scared for his life.

"They said they're taking precautions, whatever that means. He wouldn't say much more, except that this house is under surveillance. He pointed out that there are a number of potential targets in Hamillton, you among them. They're doing the best they can." Savage shrugged.

"They haven't identified them all?" Paige said.

"If they have, they're not telling me. He says his intelligence people have been going through the files. Oh, he did say something else. They've sealed off all means of access and exit here. If the gang's not already in town, they'll have a tough time getting in."

"Maybe they were scared off after running into the trooper," Paige said. He wasn't sure he liked being in a house that might be the target of a bunch of crazed killers.

Savage's father left the kitchen. When he returned a few minutes later, his face was impassive.

"There's another car outside," he said. "You can see it from the front window. A gray Toyota with a guy at the wheel."

"Probably a trooper," Savage said. "The superintendent said they'd be in plain clothes in unmarked cars."

"This is crazy," his father said. "A couple of guys with guns and they act as though the town is under siege."

"Dad, it is. All it takes is one man with a gun. Remember the Kennedys, Martin Luther King, the Pope. That's the way it goes nowadays."

"And John Lennon," Kit said. "They shot John Lennon." He was on his knees, petting Jasper.

"That's what I mean," his father said. "You can have all the security in the world and you won't stop the crazies." Savage looked at the old man with concern. The anger had been replaced with a weary fatalism.

"I'll go and check with that trooper outside," Savage said. He wanted a break from his father, a chance to think.

"Suppose nothing happens," his father said. "Suppose those bastards just sit and wait. The troopers can't stay here forever."

"Let's just take it as it comes," Savage said. He went out to talk to the man in the car. The street was quiet as he approached the Toyota, which was parked directly outside the house, facing up the slight incline. Bending down, Brand peered into the interior. It was empty.

He was straightening up, puzzled, when he felt something hard jab into his back. A man said, "Freeze." Oh, my God, he thought. They're here. His back arched with fear and automatically, as if he were in some film, his hands went up. With a kind of detached interest, he knew his hands were trembling as if with an ague.

"Hands on the roof and spread 'em," the man said. "Identify yourself." Relief swept through Savage. These were the hard, authoritative orders of a cop, not a hood. Still, his voice was shaky as he explained who he was and finally was allowed to turn and face the burly plain-clothed trooper who had been keeping watch from the side of the house.

As Savage turned to go back inside, Lady Jane emerged from Paige's car. She looked around and said, "Where the hell am I?"

26 ◀

Beyond and above the western range of mountains, there was a skeletal line of light in the sky, but in the deep bowl that held Hamillton it was dark as midnight. A steady breeze out of the north palpitated the leaves in the woods around the school and set the wires holding the school flagstaff humming.

"You reckon they found Ferret and that fucking nigger yet?" Billy Waddell asked again. He had used crayon he found in a classroom to blacken his face and hands like a commando. The dark wax accentuated the glitter of his eyes. The Teacher didn't bother with a ski mask or wax. The time for secrecy was just about gone.

"It doesn't matter if they found them, not now," the Teacher said. "You almost ready?" The moment to strike was here and he felt no excitement. He was composed, almost serene. After all the lost years of bitterness and frustration when he had dreamed of this time, nothing would stop them bringing justice to

Hamillton. Other men might think of it as revenge. He knew it was justice.

"Ready," Waddell said. He sounded tense and the Teacher glanced at him. Probably thinking about his trek through the mountains to the Canadian border, slipping across to freedom. Let him have his fantasies as long as he fulfilled his part of the compact.

They had finished the food, but they left the big refrigerator running. When it was all over, investigators would discover too late where they had been holed up.

Each carrying an assault rifle in one hand, a five-gallon gasoline can in the other, they slipped silently out of the back door to the loading platform. The other two AK-47s they carried slung across their backs. Spare magazines weighed down the Teacher's pockets. Pausing to let their eyes adjust to the darkness, he felt the wind on his cheeks and drew a deep breath. Around the school, the night was silent. Everything was going their way.

"From now on," he said, "no talking, no sound, unless it's vital. You got everything straight in your mind?" Waddell grunted assent. After the weeks of planning, they both knew what they must do and how to do it, as if they had rehearsed it a hundred times. Billy Waddell put a hand on the Teacher's shoulder.

"Whatever the fuck happens," he said, "I want you to know, Teach, even if we don't see each other again . . . Aw, I'm no good at this sort of stuff."

"I know," the Teacher said softly. During their time together, he had learned something of Waddell's history. Sometimes he thought, for all their violently contrasting backgrounds, both he and Billy Waddell were victims in their different ways of child abusers. "We've been through a lot together, Billy, and we never let each other down. Same now. If something happens to one of us, the other must go on and finish it. That was the deal."

"We'll do it together, Teach. Hey, can you imagine what'll happen with the guys in the Wilderness when this goes down? They'll go ape."

"Maybe. But they're all locked up in their cells by now. Not much they can do except rattle the bars. Let's go."

They padded quietly across the rough grass around the school, two men drawn by hatred and bitterness toward the town that had spawned their righteous wrath. At the treeline, the Teacher took the lead on a path that paralleled the road to the school. Slowed by the weight of the gasoline cans, they moved with delicate precision, halting frequently to listen. They had all the time in the world; patience was something they knew about.

Once they froze in midstep as something stirred the dry leaves on the ground to their right, then skittered off. A squirrel or a chipmunk. They pushed on.

Faintly, through the thinning trees and brush, they saw the first lights of houses. Beyond, where the town lay waiting them, there was a feeble blush in the night sky. Not far now.

Silently, the Teacher gestured ahead and to the right. They moved along a treeline until they faced the mouth of a lane. Wide enough for only one vehicle, it ran past backyards directly into the heart of town. The only sound was their steady breathing and the gentle sloshing of the gasoline in the cans at their sides. They went forward.

The Teacher took one side of the lane, Waddell the other. Bending from the waist, staying close to the fences that bounded the end of the yards, they could have been guerrillas launching an attack on an unsuspecting enemy. As they moved down the lane, they could hear the occasional sounds of domesticity from the nearby houses: the clatter of dishes, music, a burst of raucous laughter. Hamillton was relaxed, at ease. That would change soon enough.

At the far end of the lane, their way was blocked by a row of buildings, the shops and offices that faced the main street. Beyond them, across the road, was the wall and the Wilderness. Just as they were about to break out from the lane to reach the buildings, an eerie howl erupted from behind the fence against which Billy Waddell was crouching.

A second later, a heavy body thumped hard against the fence. Furious barking and whining broke out and they could hear claws digging frenziedly into the high wooden fence. For a moment, they were immobile. The Teacher recovered first. He dashed out of the lane and threw himself into the shadows under a porch at the rear of one of the main street buildings. Waddell, shaken and wild-eyed, came after him, and they squatted listening to the angry barking from behind the fence.

Beyond it, a light came on and a door opened. A man growled, "I'm gonna get rid of that goddamned pooch once and for all. I'm sick and tired of the neighbors complaining." Some of the animal's fury seemed to have passed. It was barking steadily now as if in time with a metronome.

"Stop that, Max!" It was a woman's voice, much closer. "Everything's all right. There's a good dog." She was almost crooning to the beast. "Come inside, Max, and I'll give you something to eat. Oh, please stop that barking." She had to be pulling the dog back toward the house. The barking slowed, became weaker, more distant. Finally it stopped. A door slammed and the light went off. Faintly they could hear an argument inside the house.

The Teacher looked around. They must be behind the vegetable store. There were wooden boxes and tissues from oranges, and he could smell the sickly sweetness of rotting fruit. Crouching there, the silent Billy Waddell alongside, he calculated. He pictured the main street, the shops and cinema and the building used for town administration. The administration building must be three doors down to the right.

Now there was silence except for the occasional murmur of a car moving along the main street the other side of the buildings. There was slightly more light here than in the woods, reflection from house and streetlights. He touched Waddell's arm and jerked his head to the right. He thought he could see sweat on his companion's face, but it might have been the wax.

They slipped through the area at the back of the shops, evidently used by trucks for deliveries. Yes, there was the administration building, a sort of town hall that ordered the lives of people outside the Wilderness.

Cautiously moving a few feet out from the building line, the Teacher looked up. No lights. Like most of the structures facing the main street it was deserted at this time. Only the cinema might be occupied.

Returning to Billy Waddell, he whispered, "Okay." It was the first time they had exchanged a word since they had left the school. While the Teacher crouched, listening and staring into the darkness, Waddell climbed the five steps that led to the rear door. He had taken gloves from his pocket. A few moments later, there was a muffled cracking noise and the sound of splinters of glass tumbling to the ground like the jingle of coins. This would have been a job for Jackie Baum, but Jackie was gone. The Teacher kept his vigil. He imagined Waddell reaching through the broken window, unlocking the door, stepping inside, but for nearly five minutes he didn't move. He strained to hear any reaction to the break-in. Nothing.

Finally, silent as a wraith, he turned and went up the steps. The door was open and Billy Waddell was waiting inside. Leaving the door ajar, they stood listening. There was nothing but the sound of a diligent wall clock in an office immediately to their right.

The Teacher's haggard face was visible now in the faint glow of light coming through the building from the lamps along the main street. He led the way into the office, where the unheeded clock registered the last moment's of Hamillton's tranquility. There were desks and tables and a counter, all bearing piles of forms and letters. They began.

Before swallowing it, Paige held some icy beer in his mouth so that his teeth ached pleasantly. He was sitting at the table staring at Lady Jane who, announcing that she was hungry, had come into the kitchen with Savage a few minutes earlier.

She looked as sleek as she had before bedding down in the back of the car. But now she wore a white apron and was bending down to reach into the refrigerator.

"You know how to cook?" Paige said in disbelief.

"There are two places where I'm expert," she said, "in the bedroom, which you know about, and in the kitchen. I'm a cordon bleu chef, well, almost . . . I failed in the dessert department. It was when Mummy fell for a race car driver in Paris and she wanted to get rid of me for a bit. She sent me to work under the chef at Charles' Le Petit Veau. Those Froggy chefs are a sexy lot. All they think about is food and fucking."

Savage glanced at Kit, who was grinning at her. Her freewheeling language in front of the kid made him uncomfortable, but he liked this fleshy Englishwoman with the unblinking gaze who treated Paige like an overgrown wayward child. If she was aware of the tension in the kitchen, she didn't show it, and that helped relieve it.

Now she was demanding that his father produce various ingredients and, meekly, he did his best to find them for her. Watched by the men, she took a packet of Uncle Ben's wild rice and spilled it into a pot of water. Into the rice went tarragon, a chunk of butter and a pinch of salt. She took a bottle of Thomas's sauce from North Carolina, examined the label, shrugged, and poured some into the rice.

Using a wooden mallet, she tried to beat peppercorns into four frozen chicken breasts but the peppercorns bounced off the hard surface and she said, "Merde." She slapped the chicken pieces into a pan, tossed the peppercorns onto them and lit the gas. On the chicken, she poured some salad dressing and a slug of cream. She chopped up onions and some shriveled mushrooms she found at the back of the vegetable compartment and tossed them into the pan. Into the concoction, she dropped some horseradish sauce and Vermont maple mustard. Pondering the result for a moment, she poured in some white wine, then some more.

Savage nodded at Paige, and he knew question time was here. He fortified himself by taking another swig of beer. It helped, but not much.

"I talked to Ray Bliss before the knifings in Harlem," he said to Savage's father. "He claimed that hundreds of men in the hospital were perfectly sane, the majority of them. He said they were dumped there, buried, merely because they created difficulties inside the prison."

Savage's father said, "Did you believe Bliss, that murdering bastard?"

"It's not my job to believe or disbelieve," Paige said primly. "I just look and ask questions and listen and report what I see and hear. Bliss said that in all the time he was in the madhouse he never received any treatment, neither did any of the other inmates." Paige wished he were back in New York, even in Suffolk County. Notwithstanding his journalistic grace and expertise, he was finding it damnably awkward to question the father of his managing editor. The only consolation was the intriguing aroma beginning to curl from the pan on the stove.

"Bliss was lying," the old man said. "He always was a liar and nothing's changed. Campbell was in charge of treatment in the hospital and there were visiting psychologists."

"Did you ever go into the hospital, Mr. Savage?"

Lady Jane, who had poured some of the New York State wine into a glass, turned the chicken breasts, and more pungent smells spread around the kitchen. She drank from the glass and graciously masked a grimace.

"Not more than once or twice in all my years in the department. My responsibility was the penitentiary, not the hospital."

"So you really don't know what went on inside?"

"I know Dr. Campbell was a good man who took

his duties seriously. He was a good man and a good physician."

"But not a psychologist?"

"I believe he had a degree in psychology or some mumbo-jumbo like that. He certainly knew when somebody had mental problems. What is this, the third degree?" The old man was staring at Paige with growing hostility, and Paige took another gulp of beer.

"Dad," Savage said, "we're not the only ones who are gonna be asking questions. I suspect, with all the killings and what may lie behind them, there'll be an investigation, maybe a public inquiry. It wouldn't hurt for you to get your side of it out. Paige here is just doing his job."

"On your orders."

"Yes. I want to know the truth of it all."

"You think I'm lying? You believe Bliss?"

"I didn't say that. I'm trying to find my way through all this. After all, the judges believed Bliss, didn't they?" His father shrugged dismissively and took a piece of avocado from the board where Lady Jane was throwing together a lettuce salad.

"There's nothing to hide, no mystery," he said. "If a prisoner acted strangely, was brought in front of the PK's court, then Campbell was asked to examine him. If he decided the man was mentally sick, then the prisoner was transferred to the hospital. That was the system, had been for years. Once they went next door, I had nothing more to do with them."

"It must have helped deal with a lot of problems," Paige said. The old man stared at him coldly.

"Mental illness is a problem," he said.

"Did you really believe the men Campbell certified as lunatics were all insane?"

"I don't have a degree in psychology, any more than you or Ray Bliss. I wasn't in the position to argue one way or another. That was the doctor's responsibility, not mine."

Paige said, "Bliss claims the reason he was sent to the madhouse was simply that he tried to file a deposition about corruption in the Wilderness. They got rid of him by sending him to the hospital."

"That's his story and it's bullshit. I wasn't PK then, but I know it was bullshit. Everybody knew. The man was paranoid. The man is still paranoid, a paranoid killer with blood on his hands."

"The court that convicted him of killing his wife decided he was a killer, that's true. But it was Hamillton that decided he should be held for thirty years beyond his sentence."

"He wasn't fit to be released. When he knifed the other man in Harlem he proved that. He's incorrigible."

Savage stirred. "Paige," he said, "take a walk. Take Lady Jane with you. Go get a drink. You'll find a tavern up the street on the corner. And, Kit, why don't you go upstairs and wash up? I want to talk to my father. Alone."

Paige looked at Savage in dismay. "What about the chicken?" he said. "It'll be ready in a minute." He was ravenous.

"More like thirty minutes," Lady Jane said.

"Come on, Paige. I want to take a look at this prison."
Paige got up from the table and headed for the door.
Kit vanished upstairs.

"You want me to check in with the rag?" Paige
said. "Maybe give them our number here. LaFleche
will be worrying his warty head about us."

"Do that," Savage said. He sounded preoccu-
pied. "Call them from the tavern and tell them I'm
with you. Find out if there are any messages." Lady
Jane turned the chicken breasts in the simmering
sauce, put a lid on the pan, and led Paige out of the
kitchen. She was still wearing her apron like an aris-
tocratic housewife.

"You gonna take me on yourself, boy?" Savage's
father said when they had gone. His back was to
Savage as he took plates from a cupboard. "You
going to get the truth out of me, is that it?"

Savage's voice was harsh with anger now.
"Listen," he said, "I made a mistake. I didn't want to
put these questions to my own father. So I told Paige
to do it. It didn't work. You gave him a load of bullshit, and you know it and I know it."

His father turned and stared at him. "Be careful,"
he said. "You may be a big newspaper executive in
that cesspit, New York City, but up here you're
nobody, nobody at all. You think you can come back
up here after turning your back on Hamillton, and
you think you can interrogate and accuse and blacken
the names of the people who work in the penitentiary."

Savage started to speak, but his father plunged

on. "You can't because you don't know what you're talking about. You don't know how it is in the prison and how things are done, have to be done. You're a naïve simpleton and I don't have to answer your damn-fool questions."

Like a physical blow, Savage could feel the authority of a man who once had ruled the lives of hundreds of criminals. But his anger only grew and he had to struggle to control himself.

"In the last few days," he said, "I've been getting a pretty good idea of how things were done in the Wilderness. And don't give me any crap about the doctor deciding whether a man was insane or not. You just brought in Campbell to legitimize your burial of troublemakers, didn't you?

"You probably didn't have to say a word. Just tell Campbell you think a man might be mentally disturbed and he knew what you wanted. You wanted a certificate and you wanted the man out of your hair. He obliged."

His father said, "It would be very easy for me to tell you to get out of this house. I'm an inch away from doing just that."

Their eyes were locked. "You think that would solve anything?" Savage demanded. "You think the questions would go away, just like me? You're going to get tougher people with tougher questions coming at you." Savage's father stared at him with a strange expression in his eyes. Savage thought it could be contempt. They were lacerating each other and he didn't know how to stop it.

"You always thought yourself too good for Hamillton, didn't you?" the old man said. "You looked down on men worth ten of you, doing a dirty job that society doesn't want to know about. So you walked away with your nose in the air. Don't think I didn't know what was going on in that prissy, sanctimonious head of yours. Your mother knew, too."

"My God, I hope she never knew what was going on in the Wilderness. I hope she didn't know you were burying people alive if they wouldn't toe your line."

"You know what you're saying?"

"Yeah, and it makes me wonder about that riot all those years ago. I looked up the newspapers. They talked about brutality and outright slaughter of prisoners."

"All lies, all of it. I was there."

"Yes, you were, weren't you? Doing your duty."

"Damn you. Damn you and people like you who have no inkling of what it takes to control some of the most evil bastards walking the face of the earth. No, it's very easy to sit back and throw mud when you're outside the walls, when you don't have to deal with the freaks inside."

"Nobody forced you to take the job."

"Yes, they did."

"Who?"

"You. Where d'you think the food on the table, the clothes on your back, came from? There were no complaints about my work then, were there? You took it all as your right."

"Good try, but no cigar. I'll do you a favor. I'll tell you one of the questions they'll be throwing at you. Let's talk about Ray Bliss. You know that Bliss tried to plead insanity when he went on trial for killing his wife?"

"That weasel would try anything."

"You don't see it? You don't see that the court and its psychologists decided he was sane and sentenced him accordingly. Yet you and Crain and Campbell knew better. You decided he was mad and away he went into the hospital and there he stayed until the federal courts stepped in and said you were running a Gulag up here. Same with the others. Funny how they were sane when they arrived at the prison, certified by the courts, and then they run across you and suddenly they're mad and have to be put away."

"You'd better leave before this goes any further."

"That's all you have to say?"

"I don't have to say a word, boy. I know we did nothing wrong, whatever those damned judges may have decided. The bleeding hearts are always ready to condemn others. Never the criminals, oh, no. Forget the victims. Just remember the poor misunderstood killer and arsonist and rapist and try to understand him and help him. Forget the guards who have to deal every day, every night, with the shit they pour into the prisons. Condemn them, and feel better. Lousy hypocrites, the lot of you."

Savage's father walked heavily to the door and held it open.

Savage said, "I guess you just answered my questions. You felt you had the right to bury men because they were killers and rapists and arsonists, never mind what the law said. You were the law up here."

"Get out. I don't want you in this house. All I can do is thank God your mother's not here to listen to this rubbish."

It was ironic, Savage thought, moving to the door. That was what he had been thinking earlier. He looked back. His father was standing quite still, staring into the darkness outside the window. In the unforgiving glare of the electric light, he looked suddenly old and tired. Savage started to say something, shrugged instead, and walked out of the house.

The trooper's car was moving, turning to head up toward the main street. Savage stopped on the sidewalk and sniffed the night air. There was a smell of burning. He heard pounding feet, and the next moment Paige, panting, was in front of him. For a moment, he struggled for breath.

"They weren't after your father after all," he puffed aloud finally. "They were after the town. They've set it alight!"

At first, Savage's thoughts were so mired in the scene he had just left that he didn't take it in. But then he looked up at the night sky, and he saw a growing brilliance above the houses and, carried on the wind, he heard the roar and crackle of conflagration.

◀   ◀   ◀

In the central office of the town administration building, the Teacher and Billy Waddell picked up armfuls of paper and carried them out. In the corridor, they piled the paper in the recess under the flight of stairs that led to the upper floors. They worked together like a well-drilled team. Finally it was done and they stood back. The Teacher uncapped his gasoline can and the sweet fumes flooded their nostrils.

He splashed gasoline onto the paper. When the can was half empty, he turned and laid a liquid trail into the office from which they had taken the paper. Inside, the Teacher sprinkled the remaining gasoline on the floor and counter and walls before throwing the empty can away. The place, he thought, smelled like a refinery. Starting in the rear of the building, the fire, the burning of Hamillton, would be well started before the alarm could be given.

The line of main street structures facing the prison were jammed side by side with nothing to act as a firebreak between them. They had checked them during their visits. All were wood, old dry wood.

The Teacher picked up the second gasoline can. They would have to move fast now. His blackened face intent, Waddell struck a match, touched it to a spill of paper. When it was well alight, he tossed it into the mounds of gasoline-soaked paper. The Teacher was already out of the rear door and going down the steps when the fumes exploded into fiery ignition. A line of fire raced across the hallway into the office. Suddenly there was a *whoosh*! like the passage of an express train as flames erupted out of the piles of paper. By then, Billy Waddell was also out of the rear door, running down the steps.

"We've done it, Teach," he shouted triumphantly. "The whole thing's going up like a furnace." Grabbing the remaining can from the Teacher's hands, he moved swiftly to the rear of the next building. After the time of silence, he was giggling uncontrollably, whooping and capering.

The Teacher knew he couldn't quiet him now and he didn't try. It didn't matter anymore. For a moment, he watched as Waddell splashed gasoline on the door and walls of the building and on cardboard boxes strewn on the ground.

"Fire purifies," he said.

A match flared. Flames leaped up the exterior, reaching for a ramshackle balcony on the second floor. The northerly wind seized the flames and threw them further. Billy Waddell whooped crazily. Frolicking and laughing, he looked with his blackened face like some manic devil come from the nether world to bring the creed of flame and fury to the little town.

Moving away, the Teacher turned once to look back. The windows of the administrative building were cracking and bursting like pistol shots, and through them he could see that the fire was now a maelstrom consuming the interior. The second floor was ablaze and the roof was glowing.

He wasn't finished yet. He turned and slipped away.

At the third building to be torched, the vegetable

store, Waddell threw wooden boxes against the wall and splashed the last of the gasoline on them. Perhaps it was a vagrant spark drifting with the wind into the fumes. He would never know.

The wooden boxes suddenly burst into flame as if a blowtorch had been turned on in their midst. The vapors carried the evil bloom of brilliance over Billy Waddell, enveloping him, his hair and nostrils and arms and his clothes, and in a moment he was a Roman candle, alight from head to foot.

If he had flung himself down and rolled in the dirt, he might have had a chance. Not much, but a chance of survival.

But Billy Waddell ran. He ran screaming, blinded, a human firebrand, until he slammed in a frenzy into the fence where the dog had scrambled to get at them, and the flames loved him more, crawling over every inch of his body in a blistering embrace.

Turning, he tried to run again, and the wind sent the flames licking over him until he was a horrifying, blackened, gurgling burlesque of a human being, now on his knees, now writhing on the ground.

Drawn by the fire bursting out of the row of torched buildings and then by the hideous screams of the man who was on fire, people came. Some ran for water, but even as they ran, they knew it was hopeless. Billy Waddell had brought fire to Hamillton and it had cremated him.

◀　　◀　　◀

Outside Savage's father's house, Paige said, "Jesus, the whole town's on fire. It started in the building across from the main gate of the prison . . ."

"The administration building."

"Right. That's already just about gone and it's spreading all along the block. Everything could go."

"Is it arson?"

"That's what they reckon. There's no way it could spread so fast unless it was set. Christ, what a story. Suppose the prison catches fire; there are sparks all over the place."

Savage and Paige were moving now up the incline toward the main street. The smell of burning was stronger and Savage could feel the heat coming from the fires.

"Did you call the office?" he said.

"Yeah, but that was before I realized the town was burning."

"Okay, get back to them and tell them to see if they can organize a photographer. There might be a stringer in Lake George." The streets were coming alive, with people running, shouting. Mixed in with the tumult of the fires, Savage heard sirens and bells. And, as they reached the main street, there was another sound that he remembered from years ago. It was the prison whistle, shrill with its belated warning.

27 ◄

With the fires at his back, with one of the Kalashnikovs in his right hand, the Teacher moved across backyards and lawns and vegetable patches. Sometimes he had to climb over fences, but he went in a direct line as if following a familiar path. He made only a cursory effort to be silent; the night now was full of noise. Once, clambering over iron railings, the AK-47 slung on his back became entangled on a point of the railing and he landed awkwardly, twisting his ankle. But, limping, he pressed on.

He felt suffused with satisfaction, an epiphany of long-sought justice. Whatever happened now, Hamillton was burning. There was only one more task to be completed, and he was possessed with an absolute confidence that nothing would stop him carrying it out. He heard a rising clamor behind him and he smiled in the darkness. They'd be rushing around and falling over each other like rats from a disturbed nest.

He reached the backyard he wanted. Ahead was the house that was his target. Crouching with the rifle across his knees, he examined the white clapboard building. There were lights on the ground floor and he thought he could see shadowed movement behind the curtains. He flicked off the safety catch and, both hands around the AK-47, he went forward.

The Teacher started firing from the waist as he walked steadily toward the back door. The weapon tried to leap and jerk in his hands, but he held it firmly, the rounds slamming into the old door in a fury of clattering thunder. There was smoke and splinters and spurts of flame and the door burst inwards as if smashed by a giant's fist. Taking his finger off the trigger, the Teacher jerked out the magazine, tossed it away, and slapped in another. Then he went in after his bullets, through the smell of cordite.

The man he wanted was standing by the sink staring appalled at the wreckage of the door. He held a can of beer as if frozen in the act of drinking by the sudden cannonade. After passing through the door, one round had hit the photograph of a solemn-faced woman hanging on the wall. It had penetrated her left chest as if fired by an executioner. The Teacher went deeper into the kitchen. He was smiling.

An old yellow dog with gray whiskers was standing in his basket, barking. The Teacher shot it and the animal was flung back out of its basket against the wall.

"Hello, PK," he said. "It's been a long time."

The old man, pale and tense, slowly put the can of beer down on the draining board. Behind him the chicken breasts were gently simmering in their pan. He stared at his dead pet, then at the Teacher.

"You murdering psychopath," he whispered. "What do you want?"

"More than you can give. But we'll manage." There was a terrible calm to his voice.

"You killed Crain and Campbell." It was a statement.

"More than them, PK. They were just part of it. Anybody else in the house?"

"You going to kill me, too?"

"Anybody else in the house, I said."

"My grandson's upstairs."

"Sure he is. So why hasn't he come running?"

"The police. He'll have gone for the police. You'd better get out of here and quick." The tone of his voice showed that he didn't really expect the invader to believe him. His hands were trembling, and he put them behind his back so that he seemed to be standing at a petrified parade rest.

"You know what's going on outside?" the Teacher said.

"What?" The old man's voice was dull. He cared nothing about anything happening outside this kitchen.

"The town's on fire, PK. The stinking town is burning down. We put the torch to it, me and Billy Waddell." Savage looked through the shattered remains of the door. Across the backyards and fences, buildings were blazing. Even as he looked, he heard the shriek of the prison whistle.

"My God," he said, momentarily forgetting, in the enormity of it, his perilous position. "There are people in those buildings, innocent people. Women and children."

"There are no innocents in Hamillton, PK. Everybody here is part of what was done to us and they must pay for it."

"What are you going to do with me?"

"I could kill you right here in your own kitchen, couldn't I? Just fill you with bullets and go. Out there, they're too busy with fires to try and stop me. Saving their own skins." The Teacher smiled. His finger was on the trigger again. "But I'm going to give you a chance, PK. I'm going to give you the chance to save your life."

"What d'you want me to do?" Dear God, the man was insane and he had a gun and he hated Savage. The hate was there in his eyes. He'd killed Crain and Campbell and thought nothing of it. Now he'd come for another enemy. Savage wondered where the rest of the maniacal gang was, what they were doing. Jesus, where were the troopers?"

"We're going for a little walk," the Teacher said. "We're going to the Wilderness, and when we get there, if you want to live, you're going to tell the world the truth about the hospital and the men who were sent there. Let's go."

He motioned with the AK-47. At first, Savage seemed to be obeying. But, suddenly, he wheeled and went at the man with the gun. He was about a yard away when the Teacher fired. He got off a quick burst that slammed the old man in the chest and sent him reeling back against the wall. He stood against the wall for a moment, then his legs collapsed and he crumpled to the floor. The Teacher knelt to feel for a pulse. There was none. God damn his soul. Even in death he was wrecking the Teacher's plans.

As he stood up, the Teacher saw a boy standing in the doorway. He was staring at his grandfather, at the blood leaking from the sprawled body.

The Teacher put the AK-47 on him and said, "You're his grandson?" The boy, stunned, still looking down at the corpse, said nothing. His eyes went to the dead dog, then he looked at the Teacher. The Teacher thought the boy might offer salvation.

"Why?" the boy said in a whisper.

"Because he had lived long enough," the Teacher said. "He owed too many people too many years. What's your name?"

"Kit."

"Okay, Kit, you're gonna do what you're told, or you'll end up like the old man. You understand?" Kit looked as though he understood nothing. His face was white and tears were trembling in the corners of his eyes.

"Answer me, you little bastard." The boy nodded.

"We're going to walk out of here and we're going to the prison," the Teacher said. "There won't be a moment when this gun isn't on you. You disobey me just once and you're dead. Understand?"

"Yes," Kit whispered.

"All right. Let's do it." They went, the boy in the lead, the weapon at his back, through the house to the front door. Stepping outside, Kit saw that the trooper's car had gone. With a town to save, they had no time for anything else.

"Move!" the Teacher said.

The most fabled, or notorious, chief of the NYPD's Internal Affairs Division was Sydney Cooper. Patrolmen and detectives, narcs and sergeants, knew he was watching them, trying to catch them out, and they despised him for it. Once, at the PBA's annual convention in the Catskills, he stood on the dais and pretended to peer through an all-seeing periscope at the ranks of cops before him.

They booed him heartily. He just grinned at them.

But Cooper, his big bald head and his searching eyes, were long gone. Now the assistant chief in charge of Internal Affairs was Gary Lopes, and nobody hated him because hardly anybody in the rank and file knew who he was or what he did, which wasn't much.

Lopes believed that rugs and dirt belonged together. You used the first to hide the second. The department was always caught in a contradiction. The brass proclaimed that they wanted corruption rooted out, but they didn't want headlines like the Knapp Commission and the Mollen Commission had produced. Therefore the temptation was to get

dirty cops quietly out of the department with no
criminal charges filed, no publicity. Better to let
them have their pensions. Lopes understood this
and acted accordingly.

He knew that he was going no higher in the
department. He reckoned that if he kept his head
down, drew no attention, he would be able to retire in
six months at full pay and without being despised by
the thousands of cops he left behind. If he caused no
waves, there was a job heading up security for a
department store waiting for him.

The whole vanAllen mess had been dumped in
his lap because the other chiefs smelled nothing but
trouble. It was, after all, an internal affair, they said.
Let Lopes use his skills to push it under the NYPD's
rug. He didn't like it one bit, but Lopes was too far
down the hierarchy to protest.

The buzz about vanAllen had started in the
Organized Crime Control Bureau after the four men
from the Wilderness had been tentatively identified. It
moved swiftly up to Assistant Chief Joseph Bu-
chanan, and then had been passed to the chief of operations, who had looked around and decided Lopes
was the man to run with it.

At One Police Plaza, in a white-Formica-walled
conference room overlooking the traffic jams on the
FDR Drive and the Brooklyn Bridge, it was on top of
the evening meeting's agenda. Just before the Teacher
and Billy Waddell put the torch to Hamillton, Lopes
cautiously briefed the gathering of chiefs and their
acolytes.

"There's no doubt about it, it all fits," he said unhappily, shuffling the file on the oval table in front of him. "She's up at the Wilderness right now. She linked up with the state police and got a ride up from Albany aboard one of their choppers."

"And what the hell is she doing up there?" asked Chief of Operations Boris Shamsky. "She's way out of her jurisdiction. What is this, she's gone national like the fuckin' Feebs?"

"My information is that she got the go-ahead from the chief of detectives on the grounds that she was pursuing a New York investigation, the shooting in the park and the other killings in Manhattan." There was a thoughtful silence. Chief of Detectives Clarence Davis was black, shrewd, hard-working, and generally considered to be vanAllen's rabbi. Davis was notably devoted to his wife and family so, with no hard evidence to back them, rumors of a more intimate relationship had almost died out. Davis would have been at the meeting, but he had just gone into Columbia-Presbyterian for an operation.

"You got her personnel file there?" Shamsky said. "I'd like to know how the hell she got in the department in the first place."

"She was checked out by . . . let me see . . . a Lieutenant John Duffy, now retired. No problems. College education, a good degree in law enforcement. Clean record. No organized crime connections. There was only the matter of her family, which was noted at the time, and that was not considered significant enough to keep her out. Otherwise her background was outstanding, so she was accepted. Did well at the academy and even better afterward."

Rowlands, the chief of the Personnel Bureau, said, "I've checked her F-file. She's clean."

"Clean . . . Jesus," Shamsky said, thinking about the situation in Hamillton and the commissioner's reaction to it. "Somebody's gonna get flopped over this. Anybody talked to Davis?"

"He went under the knife tonight. Prostate."

"Beautiful."

"We have to be careful, chief," Lopes said. "Her being a woman and all."

"I know she's a fucking woman. What's that got to do with anything?"

"Well, it's just that the women's groups are ready to file suit at any hint of complaints about unfair treatment from a woman in the department."

"Fuck 'em."

"Yes, chief."

"Women, they should never have been allowed—" started a deputy chief who believed he should have at least three stars.

Shamsky silenced him with a look. "That's bullshit. This could have happened with a man. It's simply a matter of terrible judgment. Are we in contact with her?"

"Yeah, through the state police. They've got quite a situation on their hands up there. There doesn't seem much doubt that these ex-cons are hanging around the Hamillton area bent on God-knows-what mischief."

"Mischief! Christ. Are those press rattlesnakes on to it yet."

"Nothing so far."

"They will be."

Lopes said, "If we get her back before anything happens, we can make it all go away. There'll be nothing for anybody to make a fuss about."

"Right," Shamsky said. "Get hold of vanAllen immediately. Tell her to drop everything, I don't care what she's doing, and get her pretty ass back here tonight. You can tell her she better have a good explanation."

"Right," Lopes said. "It may be difficult to contact her. I have calls in, but the state police seem to be in some sort of panic."

"Back-country hicks. They get into a panic over a two-car fender bender. I want her back here tonight. And I want her in my office in the morning before I go to the fourteenth floor to face the music."

The Teacher and the boy, captor and captive, moved into the middle of the road and started up the gentle incline that led to the main street. As if salved by the fires, the pain had gone from the Teacher's ankle and he no longer limped. The flames were only two or three blocks away and spreading fast. All around, the night was vibrant with the sound of sirens, fire bells, and intermingling with them, shouts and screams. The Teacher stepped closer to the youngster's back so that the barrel of the AK-47 was brushing his T-shirt.

"Don't even think of stopping," he said. "Whatever anybody else says or does, don't stop unless you want your back blown open. I won't hesitate." He had to raise his voice to make himself heard above the uproar of the fires and the men trying to fight them.

At first, on the side street, nobody seemed to notice the two marching steadily in the center of the road. People were too busy with their own concerns, evacuating their homes or rushing to join the fire-fighters. But as they turned into the main street it was different.

There were people on the sidewalks, looking toward the fires. Mostly they were women and older children. The Teacher saw them begin to stare and point at the strange two-man parade, at the gun that linked the pair.

"Keep moving," the Teacher said. They went forward toward the flames and fire engines and hoses and ladders and straining, sweating men. Both their faces were bathed in the orange glow of incandescence thrown from the burning buildings. An old man stepped from the sidewalk toward them. He was wearing a red, peaked cap and soiled overalls.

"Hey," he said, "you can't go any closer. They want us to stand back here."

"Tell him," the Teacher said, jamming the Kalashnikov hard into Kit's back.

"Stand away," Kit said. "He's got a gun on me."

"And an itchy finger," the Teacher said. Now the man in the red cap saw the assault rifle and his eyes opened wide in almost comic astonishment. His mouth formed an O. His eyes fixed on the weapon, he backed away toward the sidewalk. The boy and the Teacher went on.

On their right was a three-story structure with a hairdressing salon on the ground floor. It was well alight. On their left was the prison wall. Glancing up, the Teacher saw guards on the catwalks around the watchtowers. One man was gripping a machine gun as he stared down. The scene must have looked like something out of World War II, with a POW being marched to a camp through a newly assaulted village. Another guard was talking urgently on the telephone inside his glass-walled eyrie.

There were hoses on the ground and pumpers, one from inside the prison, hook-and-ladders, and men in helmets who had attention only for their immediate enemy, the flames. With a roar and a shower of sparks, the roof of a building collapsed and burning debris hissed as it landed in the water that had gathered on the ground around the firefighters. The Teacher saw that the administration building was completely destroyed. It was nothing but a blackened, smoldering pile of broken timbers almost abandoned by the flames that were eating their way further along the block.

Two uniformed troopers, both carrying M1 carbines, came out of the small door alongside the main gates of the prison and stood waiting for the Teacher and his prisoner. Instead of their usual soft campaign hats, they wore black helmets with visors.

Ten paces away from them, the Teacher ordered Kit to halt. The barrel of the AK-47 was tight against the boy's back and the Teacher's finger lay alongside the trigger.

"What's going on?" one of the troopers called. The Teacher looked up to the top of the prison wall. One of the guards on the catwalk was leaning over, his machine gun covering the Teacher.

"First," the Teacher said, "tell that clown to step back. I don't want to see him. Otherwise I blow the kid away." The trooper hesitated, then waved away the guard. A man in civilian clothes came out of the door and joined the troopers. Tall and graying, his blue eyes glittered in the reflection of the fires. In his right hand was a cel phone.

"I'm Major McGuire," he said. "What d'you want?" He started to move forward.

"Stay back."

The major stopped. "What the hell is this?" he said. Then, to the Teacher, "Who are you?"

"The talking comes later," the Teacher said. "Right now, I'll tell you what I want. I want to go inside the Wilderness. You bring up anybody behind me, they can get me, but I'll get the kid as well. You gun me down and I'll take him with me. Understand?"

"You want to come inside. What for?"

"I want to pay a visit. See the old place again."

The major stared at him. It didn't make sense, but nothing much in Hamillton this night was making sense. He shrugged. At least, if they came into the prison there could be some control of the situation. Outside, it was a shambles of fire and smoke and confusion.

"You the firebug?" he said.

"Fire cleanses," the Teacher said. He wondered briefly what had happened to Billy Waddell. Probably in the mountains now, his task done, heading north for the border.

"Where are your compadres?" the major said.

"Don't waste my time with foolish questions. Just get out of the way."

"Okay," the major said slowly. He could see sweat on the boy's pale face and hoped it was from the heat of the fires. A hostage who couldn't control his emotions was an erratic element in an explosive situation.

"How d'you want to do this?"

"You and your men go back inside. Slow and steady. We come after you. We'll take this one step at a time. No tricks. You upset me in any way . . ." He gestured with the rifle. "The safety catch is off."

The major nodded and muttered an order to the troopers. The trio turned and withdrew through the narrow door. It was the same door the Teacher had used so many years ago when he had been transferred down the street to the hospital. This was one of the most hazardous moments, this walking into the spider's web.

It was the major's best chance. Grab the kid as he came through the door, jerk him to one side, blast the Teacher. But they hadn't expected any of this, hadn't been given the time to work out tactics. They'd wait and see.

Jabbing Kit with the gun, his finger curled tight around the trigger, the Teacher went through the door. Nothing. Above them, a surveillance camera recorded their passage. The area was like an airlock with another door ahead. There was a metal detector that buzzed in outrage as they went through it. The Teacher and Kit passed through the second door. Again no unexpected movement. They were doing what officials always did best: nothing.

In the yard beyond, a squad of troopers was drawn up, some in orange overalls, all in black helmets. The major was standing in front of them.

"Now what?" he said grimly. Flashing a look around, the Teacher saw a group of guards to his right, all staring at him. He wondered if any of them had been in the Wilderness all those years ago when he had been held in C Block. Other guards were manning a prison fire truck, spraying water on the roofs of buildings close to the wall to douse any flying sparks.

Floodlights on the walls splashed the yard with light as bright as if the sun were overhead. From the cells beyond, there was a rising clamor. The Teacher smiled. Reacting to the conflagration, prisoners were rattling metal cups against the bars, shouting, hammering pipes.

He could hear a chant: "Burn, Burn, Burn!"

Soon they would know everything. There were no secrets in the joint. They would know that the men of justice had come back to Hamillton. "Tell the guards to come down from the southeast watchtower," he said to the major.

"I can't do that. You know I can't." The Teacher nodded.

"Get the warden. And quick."

The major turned and gave an order to one of the troopers who nodded and trotted off toward the fire truck. A moment later, he came back with a portly, bespectacled man wearing a fedora with a feather in the band. His rimless glasses glinted from the arclights on the walls. He wore a gray suit and a blue-dotted bow tie that looked frivolous in this scene. The civilian and the major conferred, then the fat man moved in front of the Teacher and Kit. He looked exasperated, like a high school football coach preparing to scold his team. The Teacher had never seen him before.

"This is no good," he began "Dammit, we have enough on our hands without all this."

"I want the southeast watchtower cleared," the Teacher said.

"The hell are you?" The Teacher suspected they knew exactly who he was, probably had his picture and rap sheet lying on the warden's desk.

"I'm the man with the gun," he said. "Clear the tower."

"Why don't we talk this over? We can go to my office." In the cellblocks, the din from the prisoners was increasing. The state police major was looking away as if rejecting any further responsibility.

"I'm not a patient man, warden. You want me to blast the boy?"

"He killed my grandpa. And his dog," Kit said.

"Who the hell are you, anyway?"

"He's PK Savage's grandson," the Teacher said. "Now he's my ticket to the tower."

"You were up here, in the Wilderness?"

"Until you bastards put me in the madhouse."

The warden looked at the major, but he only shrugged and then stalked off. The warden shook his head disapprovingly, but he moved toward the southeast corner of the yard where two guards were looking down from the catwalks.

"Cunningham, Randall, come down here," he shouted. "Bring your weapons with you." The men moved off the catwalks and vanished into the glass-walled tower.

"Anything else we can do for you, sir?" the warden asked sarcastically. "Maybe some iced champagne?" His voice hardened. "You know you're not gonna get out of here, not alive. I've got a cell that will suit you just fine. And an electric chair."

"Is the loudspeaker system still hooked up to the towers?" Looking puzzled, the warden nodded.

"You gonna campaign for office up there?" he said. "I'll tell you right now, you won't get my vote." The guards from the tower, both carrying machine guns, emerged into the yard from the tower steps.

"Move," the Teacher said, and he jabbed the AK-47 into the boy's back. The stupidity of the old man had wrecked his plans, but he could still carry them out. He had almost done it. Once they were up in the tower, he would have control. The toughest part had been stepping into the yard, but he had pulled it off. He could taste the approaching triumph.

The troopers and guards watched silently as the Teacher and his hostage went toward the steps. On the other side of the wall, the sound of ambulance bells diminished down the street. There were twenty-five steps, and their feet made the steel risers ring out in the enclosed stairwell. The Teacher remembered the steps leading up through the darkness to the Sutton Place park.

Then there was flickering light and they were in the glass-sided chamber that overlooked the prison on one side and on the other, Hamillton, now ablaze.

The Teacher slammed shut the trapdoor through which they had emerged and looked around. Kit was standing with his back against one of the glass walls. The Teacher kept his AK-47 trained on him. There was a metal table, a chair, and a telephone. A rack for machine guns was empty. On the table was a sheet of paper, headed ORDERS OF THE DAY, a much-thumbed copy of *Popular Mechanics*, and a paper cup half full of cold coffee.

At first, he couldn't see the microphone connected to the loudspeaker system, but then he spotted it under the table. Obviously it was rarely used. The main purpose was to broadcast a warning should a prisoner try to scale the walls.

The Teacher put it on the table and flicked the switch at the base. It came alive with a resonant hissing. He tapped it with his fingernails and heard the sound amplified through the speakers along the walls.

He pushed the chair toward the youngster. "Sit down," he said. "Put your hands flat on the table and keep them there. We're going to be here a while."

He looked east. There it was. The hospital. All the stolen years, all the mindless brutalities. Whatever they used it for now, it must be filled with the ghosts of all those lost men. Well, he was about to bring succor, some peace, to those restless phantoms.

He looked again at the kid and wished it were Savage, the old man responsible for so much pain. The Teacher looked across to the other towers. In each one of them, guards stared back at him. In the yard, he could see the major surrounded by men in orange overalls. The warden had vanished. The major had his cel phone to his ear and was talking earnestly, once gesturing toward the Teacher's tower as if his listener could see it.

The Teacher took the phone off its cradle, picked up the microphone, and flicked on the switch.

"Listen," he said, hearing his voice blaring out from the speakers. "Listen, all of you. My name is van-Allen. Charles vanAllen. They call me the Teacher."

28 ◀

Paige, his press card hanging around his neck, was standing alongside a pumper talking to a white-helmeted fire chief when Savage found him. The chief was in the midst of a brief battle report. The fires at the west end of the block were nearly under control now, but here, at the east end, they were still raging under the spur of the north wind, swallowing building after building. After devastating the shops and offices and the cinema, leaving the block smoking and blackened, the flames were advancing down a line of houses at right angles to the original blaze.

"We've lost at least eighteen structures," the chief said wearily. "They were all wood and we couldn't hope to contain it."

"Arson?"

"Had to be. The interior of the administration building stinks of gasoline and we found a couple of cans back there. They must have soaked the lower floors."

"How many dead?"

"Sixteen, so far. There may be more. One of them was the firebug, we reckon. Found him around the back with a couple of AK-47s near the corpse. Stank of gasoline, must have gotten too close to his work. Good riddance to the bastard."

"Has he been identified?"

"Probably never will be. He's a crisp. You can hardly tell it's a body. He was roasted."

"What about the locals?"

"Most of the dead were in the cinema, men, women, and four children. Thank God it was a lousy film and nobody wanted to see it. Some bad burns among the survivors. Two hospitals on full standby, but the closest is forty minutes away. A couple of the volunteers have smoke inhalation problems." He gestured to where three firefighters were sitting slumped against the prison wall, sucking oxygen from metal tanks.

"How long before you bring it under control?"

"Jesus, I don't know. This is a pig, the worst I've seen." He turned away to rejoin the battle.

"Did you talk to New York?" Savage said.

"Yeah, there's a photographer on the way from Glens Falls, but it'll be a while before she gets here."

"Any messages?"

"A couple for you, but they didn't sound urgent, nothing that can't wait until you call in." They stepped back as two firemen carrying a hose pushed by them.

"Have they got enough equipment and men to handle this?"

"The chief wants more, but he reckons they might manage. He says they've got volunteer fire-fighters and ambulances from fifty miles around and they're still coming in. By the time they get it all under control, though, there's not going to be much left of Hamillton."

As they talked, Paige was scribbling in his tattered notebook. "Funny how we were worrying about your father," he said, "and all the time they were planning to burn the town. You get ready for an upper cut and they come at you with a left hook. Did you eat the chicken?"

"No, I was talking to my father."

"Sorry I wasn't more effective with him. Did my best."

"It wasn't your fault, Paige. It was a difficult situation all around."

Above them, in the light of the fires, an enormous column of mustard-colored smoke was heaving up until the wind bent it and drove it south. Savage felt battered by wave after wave of depression. He sensed that the foundations supporting his life were giving way. The paper, his family, even the uncertain relationship with Sarah vanAllen . . . it felt as though they were being swept away like that smoke before the wind. Leaving him, he thought, with damn little except the shards of a life. The shadows of failure that recently he had glimpsed at the periphery of his vision seemed to be moving closer, thickening.

"Where's your Lady Jane?" he said.

"Last I saw of her, she was drinking martinis and flirting with a couple of old geezers in the tavern on the corner. She seemed to think all this was arranged for her amusement. Hey, the thugs are here."

Savage looked around and saw that a mobile TV unit was maneuvering among the fire trucks, rolling over hoses and edging past sweating firefighters, the driver ignoring angry shouts to be careful. Standing on the roof of the big truck like an old-time newsreel operator, a cameraman was panning his lens across the flames while he stamped on the roof in a vain demand for steadiness.

"They got here fast," Savage said without interest.

"Probably on some other job in the area," Paige said. "The gorillas have everything we don't: radio communication, electronics, mobile telephones, money. Mostly money. They think they own the world, and sometimes I think they're right."

Down the street, the way they had come from Savage's father's house, some sort of commotion was going on. Paige turned and moved with deceptive speed to investigate. It seemed to be at the prison gate, but when he reached the area, the gate was shut.

He asked some of the onlookers what had happened, but they stared back at him with closed faces as if he had no right to be here amidst their pain, let alone to ask them questions. It was definitely a weird place, Paige thought. He shrugged, made some more notes, and headed back toward Savage. Along the way, he saw two people with press credentials stuck on their chests. Both upstaters. It was too early for the New York pack to arrive, and when they did, they would have nothing like his story.

A fire captain, unimpressed by Paige's press card, tried to make him join the spectators. They were still arguing when the prison began to talk. At least, that was the way it seemed until Paige realized it was the loudspeakers up on the walls. Glancing around, he saw that Savage, a few steps away, was staring up as the voice boomed out.

". . . the Teacher," it said. "I was a prisoner in the Wilderness until 1966, when I was transferred to the hospital. With me in the tower is the grandson of Principal Keeper Savage, the man who had me transferred, even though he knew I was perfectly sane. He was the man responsible for my being detained fifteen years longer than justice demanded. I've settled with him, and now I'm going to tell you why."

Following his managing editor's eyes, Paige saw that the speaker was immediately above them in the southeast watchtower. Moving back a little and to his left, he could make out a pale-faced man, a weapon slung on his back, speaking into an old-fashioned microphone. If there was anybody else up there, he was out of sight.

On the roof of the TV truck, the cameraman had swung around to focus on the glass-walled chamber at the top of the tower. Alongside him now, a reporter was talking into a microphone as if in imitation of the man in the tower. Typical, Paige thought morosely.

The TV morons, from their perch, had the best position.

". . . you to know," the loudspeakers said, "that your town is burning because it was Hamillton and its people, like Principal Keeper Savage, who allowed, encouraged, injustice to flourish. Some of the men who suffered at your hands have returned, not for revenge, that is too easy, but to expose and cleanse this evil place . . ."

"Jesus, it's one of the firebugs," a firefighter muttered at Paige's side. "He must be out of his mind."

During the first few minutes of the broadcast, the efforts against the fires had slowed as the firefighters allowed themselves to be distracted, but now they returned to their first enemy as if the man in the tower was of no consequence, merely a bizarre interlude. The onlookers, though, the reporters and cameramen, continued listening, staring up, as the words spilled out of the loudspeakers.

". . . hundreds of us were held in the hospital illegally, far beyond our legitimate sentences, in barbaric conditions. The people of Hamillton, not only the guards and attendants, must have known it. There cannot have been an adult who did not know that something diabolical was being perpetrated, yet not one of them tried to . . ."

Paige was taking notes again. It was, he thought, the weirdest story he had ever covered in the weirdest town. Darting a look around, he saw that Savage was no longer with him. He was walking swiftly toward the prison gate.

◄   ◄   ◄

At first, they wouldn't let him in. But then he told them the hostage in the tower was his son and they told him to wait, then a state police major in civilian clothes came and escorted him inside the walls.

"It's your kid? In a Chicago Bulls T-shirt?"

"Goddamit, yes." For Savage, it was like staring into a black pit. He couldn't get control of his thoughts. "Why the hell did you let him take the boy up there?"

"Because he was threatening to blow him away. Would you have preferred that?" He looked hard at Savage and said, "Look, if you're gonna be a loose cannon, I'm gonna have to lock you up until this is over."

"Okay, okay. I'm all right." Savage took a deep breath and looked around. In the yard it was astonishingly calm. Troopers and guards stood looking up at the tower, but there was little activity. A helicopter stood off to one side, its rotor blades motionless. At first, the major was impatient with the emotional turbulence of a nonprofessional like Savage, as if he were nothing more than an unnecessary distraction. When he learned that Savage was a newspaperman, his irritation seemed to deepen. Finally, though, staring at the tower, he said slowly, "Maybe you can help after all."

"How?"

"I'm not quite sure. It's all happening so damn fast. He's got us by the balls at the moment. We're trying to reach him on the internal phone to open up a dialogue, but he's not answering. All the asshole wants to do is spout that rubbish over the speaker system."

"You can cut him off, can't you?"

"That's your son he's got up there. You want us to make this maniac feel mean, frustrated? Maybe take it out on the kid?" The major had a faint striation on his right cheek, like a dueling scar, and he kept running the tip of his right forefinger up and down it as if he were trying to erase it.

"Jesus, we have to do something," Savage said. Again he was remembering Kit laughing, jumping into the waves at the shore, running across a baseball field.

"What we have to do is be calm," the major said. "Right now, we have to let him get it off his chest."

"I suppose it can't hurt."

"I don't know about that," the major said grimly. "I don't know what's going on in the town, but the guards in here don't like it one bit, all this stuff about corruption and kidnapping prisoners for the hospital. There could be a riot, and I'm not talking about the inmates. You think the guards don't want to storm the tower and stop him talking?"

"Maybe it's true, what he's saying up there."

"I don't give a flying fuck whether it's true or not. In our situation, truth is not exactly the big issue." There was a deep, edgy anger below his professional calm, and Savage remembered that one of the victims was a state trooper.

"We've got a town on fire and a wacko busily

insulting everybody who lives in it. We don't need Socrates. We need somebody who can talk sense into this guy, stop his ravings." A conventionally uniformed trooper came up and handed the major a sheet of fax paper. Holding it in the glare of the floodlights, the major flicked his eyes over the message.

"This just in," he said. "Okay, it's confirmed. A homicidal maniac named Charles vanAllen. He was inside on a murder rap. He's quite right about one thing. He was held in the Wilderness until he was transferred to the hospital in 1966."

"VanAllen?" Sarah's name. It had to be a farfetched coincidence, but Savage remembered her reluctance to talk about her family. She had talked warmly once about her stepfather, a Philadelphia lawyer, but steered away from any mention of her biological father.

"Right."

"Where was he from?"

"Doesn't say."

"Why was he put in the hospital?"

"According to this, paranoia. He thought everybody was out to get him. Wouldn't cooperate with prison authorities, antisocial behavior. That, he's displaying right now."

"Like Bliss."

"Who?"

"It doesn't matter. Does he have any relatives who can talk to him? That's the usual thing, isn't it?"

"No time for that. Anyway, we can't reach him. The phone in the tower has been off the hook since he

went on the air. He seems to have other things on his
mind besides chatting with Mom." The major gestured behind him. "You want to move to that tower,
alongside the gate? Maybe we can come up with
something."

Savage nodded. They went to the watchtower
by the main gate. They climbed up the steps and
emerged in the glass chamber. There were half a
dozen men, some troopers in orange overalls, some
guards, atop the tower, spilling out of the doorway
onto the catwalk.

"Any luck on the phone?" the major said. A
black-helmeted trooper with a phone to his ear shook
his head.

"He's still got it off the hook," he said. "Just
wants to blather through the loudspeaker."

"Okay," the major said. "Let's get this organized. First, I want all the correction officers out of
here. This area is now in state police jurisdiction. Go
and report to your superior in the yard." Two men
moved toward the steps. One of them threw a last
angry glance at the southeast tower, then they vanished through the trapdoor.

"What d'you want me to do?" Savage said. He
thought he could make out Kit in the other tower.

"We'll see." Savage realized the major was
studying him with appraising eyes. "At least your son
might be able to spot you. It might help him, know-
ing you're on the scene."

◀   ◀   ◀

". . . and some men were killed in the hospital simply because the attendants didn't like them. One man was held for forty years beyond his time and he was sane, like nearly all of the men in the hospital . . ."

The Teacher's amplified voice was steady, almost matter of fact, as if the injustice had gone on so long that mere speech could not convey the depth of his bitterness. Below the walls, on the street, the TV camera had swung back toward the fires, which finally seemed to have lost some of their fury as the firefighters concentrated their efforts on stemming any further advance down the side street.

"This boy's grandfather," the Teacher said, motioning with his AK-47 towards his captive, "was responsible more than most for the theft of years of men's lives. That upright, respected stalwart of the community . . ."

"Let me go and try to talk to the bastard," Savage said. "We can't just stand here."

"I don't know. We need a professional, a trained negotiator, for this. There's one on the way, but God knows when he'll get here."

"Well, for Christ's sake, we've got to do something now. The bastard could pull the trigger any moment."

The major suddenly made up his mind. He gave Savage a yellow cap with a long peak. "Put this on," he said. "That way, we'll know who's who."

Savage stared along the catwalk at the other tower.

He could see the man with the microphone; his son was no more than a shadow slumped against the table. Absurdly, he remembered the problems at the paper that had dominated his thoughts for so long. They seemed childish and futile now. From the moment he had decided to come north, he had felt somehow that the journey and its ending would define his future.

"Let me do it," he said.

"Okay," the major said slowly. "I guess it's our best, maybe our only, bet. Now, as you can see, there's a catwalk running along the walls between the towers. See how close you can get to him along the catwalk." The major was talking to Savage as if he were a child. "Tell him you're the PK's son, the hostage's father. Tell him we'll do what he wants. Tell him anything. Get him talking. Tell him we want to negotiate. Open him up. Okay?"

The major stared at him for a moment, then continued, "You sure you're up to it. I could try it with one of my guys."

The troopers in the tower were pretending not to listen. But one of them stirred and said, "Major, I'll give it a try, see if I can talk to him." He was young, fresh-faced. Savage glanced at him. He looked like a boy just off the farm.

"What the hell would you say to the murderous bastard?" he demanded. "I have to do it."

"If there's another way, it escapes me," the major said. "I'm afraid I'm clean out of ideas."

"All right," Savage said again. The major reached into his pocket and produced a silver flask.

"A drink?" Savage wondered if flasks were standard issue among the troopers. He shook his head. The major stared at him, nodded, and punched a number into his cel phone. He spoke for a few moments so quietly that Savage couldn't hear the words. Looking along the catwalk, Savage estimated the distance at about fifty yards. A nice little stroll. The major closed up the phone and said, "Ready?"

Savage tried to grin. A nice little stroll with an armed maniac waiting to welcome him. He went to the edge of the wall and looked down. The words were still spilling out of the loudspeakers, but they didn't penetrate; they were just noise. But the TV camera was aimed again at the southeast tower. Savage could see Paige, notebook in hand, staring up at him. Savage gazed bleakly down and turned back to the major.

"Ready," he said.

As Savage stepped out on to the catwalk, the major flicked open his telephone again. At first, Savage felt awkward, like an actor who hasn't been given his lines, yet the spotlight and the audience awaited. A deep feeling of loneliness seized him. A couple of steps along the iron work, he hesitated, holding on to a handrail. He was conscious of men in the yard staring up at him and of the steaming black timbers left by the fires to his right.

From this height, he could see the whole town; it looked as though the firefighters were winning their battle now. He thought he heard the major say, "Good luck," but it might have been imagination, might have been just part of the major's telephone conversation.

Straightening his shoulders, Savage began to walk steadily along the catwalk. There was a sour taste in his mouth and a muscle in his right eyelid kept twitching distractingly. He kept his arms away from his sides, hoping the man in the tower would see he was unarmed.

He hadn't been listening to the sense of the words coming from the speakers, but he realized that suddenly they had stopped. The man had put down the microphone and come to the door facing him. They were maybe forty yards apart. Savage continued walking forward.

Detective Lieutenant Sarah vanAllen sat on a cardboard box well back from an open dormer window high in the building that once had held Ray Bliss and the Teacher and hundreds of other men certified as insane. Now it was used as an administrative center and to store old files from the penitentiary.

From her position, she had a panoramic view of the burning town, the prison, the walls, and the southeast tower. She was motionless as she stared down. Except for a shudder deep in her soul, she felt numb, as if her emotions had iced over. Once her thoughts, particularly about the desolate woman, Mary Morgan, lying in her Albany hospital bed, brought an involuntary moan.

Before leaving the prison, vanAllen had stripped

off her outer clothes and put on an ill-fitting set of orange coveralls with STATE POLICE inscribed on the back. They were too big for her and made her feel like a child. She suspected the major had sent her up here to get rid of her. As an NYPD lieutenant, she was not completely under his control, and he probably saw her as a distracting nuisance. But, as two men came to the doorway of the gate tower, a man in a peaked yellow cap and then the major, the cel phone they had given her buzzed. It was the major.

"This nut in the tower, his name's like yours. Strange."

"Isn't it," she said flatly.

"I'm sending you a weapon," he said. "You any sort of expert with a rifle?"

"Managed second last year in the all-state thousand-yard tournament," she said without pride.

"That was you? I heard about it. You pissed off a couple of our marksmen." He sounded impressed. "We'll have three other shooters, but you're in as good a position as any of them."

"What d'you want me to do?"

"We'll see. I'll get back to you," he said. "Listen. If you have to shoot, make sure and check what else might be in the line of fire. We don't want the round to take out anybody else." He hung up. A few minutes later, a burly trooper, breathing heavily from running up the stairs, came in. He had a fleshy, sour face and a drinker's nose. He had the look of a man who had married three or four times and enjoyed the divorces more than the marriages.

"You the lieutenant from the city?" VanAllen
thought he sounded hostile, as if he resented having
to fetch and carry for a woman. She looked at the
three rifles he was carrying. "One of those for me?"

"Right. The major sent them." He let her examine them, shifting impatiently as he waited. One was
a Fusil F1 sniper rifle equipped with an image-
intensifying sight. The others were Remingtons. All
were branded on the stock: PROPERTY OF NEW YORK
STATE POLICE. She chose a Remington 700 Varmint
with a Leupold scope. He said, "They been test fired
couple of days back," and handed her a box of .223
shells. He took the other rifles and left her alone. But
then he poked his head back around the doorframe
and said, "Hey, good huntin'." Maybe she had mis-
judged him.

VanAllen checked out the Remington, sighted
through the scope, and opened the ammunition box.
She loaded it, thinking about the one time she had
killed in her career with the NYPD.

That had been in the angry heat of a sudden
shootout during a buy-and-bust on the Lower East
Side where there had been no time for thought, only
action. This was different.

Fending off her thoughts, she pushed aside the
cardboard box on which she had been sitting and
moved a filing cabinet into position. Standing behind
it, the rifle was supported okay but pointing a little
high. She turned the cabinet sideways and further
back, and now she could look down on the walls, the
catwalks and the towers. The southeast tower and the

man with the microphone were about seventy-five yards away. She put the open ammo box on the cabinet, ready for a fast reload. Impatient with the coverall, she rolled up the sleeves to her elbows.

VanAllen wondered what was going on in New York. By now, they must have discovered the truth about the situation. She could imagine the reaction. Even now, she could walk away from it. But she stayed behind the filing cabinet, staring through the scope at the catwalk and the tower. The dormer window was a couple of floors higher than the walls, so she easily commanded the area outside the glass-walled chamber.

The man in the peaked cap was moving along the walk to the southeast tower. VanAllen couldn't be sure, but she thought it might be Savage.

"Stop right there!" The Teacher stood at the doorway, his automatic rifle thrust forward, pointing at Savage's stomach. Savage slowed, but he continued walking. His body was chilled and he realized it was fear. His hands went up level with his shoulders. Another twenty yards, about twenty paces. But what then?

"I want to talk," he said. His voice was tight with tension, and he realized the man couldn't hear him above the commotion around the burning buildings. Louder, he said, "I have to talk to you." As he spoke he was drifting closer.

"You can save your ass by turning around and

getting out of here. Who the hell are you? You want to commit suicide?" Savage could see the man's finger was around the trigger of the AK-47.

Only fifteen yards, fifteen paces. Savage stopped.

"My name's Savage," he said. "I have a personal interest. That's my son you've got in there." His voice was stronger now, as if somebody finally had prompted him with his lines. He wanted to look for Kit, but he didn't dare take his eyes from the man with the gun.

"Your son? The PK was your father? You proud of him, your father? D'you know what he did, him and the others?"

"I know." Savage took another slow step.

"His work was stealing people's lives. You know that? They paid him to kidnap men and bury them. Right there, next door. Like gangsters, only nobody would do anything to stop them."

"I know."

"So?"

"So, he's a human being who went along with the system. The world's full of people who do that. You killed Crain, Campbell, and the rest of them?"

"The state wouldn't give us justice . . ."

"The state is human beings, fallible human beings. The killing has to stop."

"Bullshit. You're a guard, too? A cop, maybe? The PK's son has to be on the public tit."

"That's another reason I'm here." Keep him talking, open him up, the major had said. "I'm a newspaperman." Another pace forward. Savage could see the man's face more clearly now, the hollow cheeks, the sunken eyes shadowed by thick eyebrows. The gun barrel went down fractionally, and Savage knew he had caught the man's interest.

"Where?"

"New York. I'm the managing editor of one of the biggest papers in the country. Our stories go on the wires through a syndication relay to a hundred other newspapers." Two more paces. "Release my son and I'll make sure your story is told. Everybody will know what happened to you, not just the people up here."

"I already have the press," the Teacher said, nodding toward the TV truck below.

"TV? TV won't tell your story. They think two minutes on the tube is an in-depth investigation. We'll tell the whole story."

"Sure. Cute. And when you've got your son back, not a word appears."

"Listen to me. I'm leveling with you. We've been working on this before today. I've got a reporter down there. We know just about all of it, the insanity certificates, Campbell, Bliss's legal work . . . and the killings. I doubt if I could stop the story running if I tried. A newspaper is worth a million loud-speakers."

"How about your father and what he did?" Savage shrugged.

"He's part of the story."

"Show me some ID." Savage reached carefully into his hip pocket and took out his wallet. He found an out-of-date police card and, taking two more steps, offered it to the Teacher.

"Stay where you are!" The Teacher didn't emerge from the doorway. Now he showed no interest in the card, as if he accepted that Savage was who he said he was. Savage let the card fall to the catwalk.

"And you'd tell everybody what your father did?" Savage nodded.

"Why?"

"I want my boy and I want him alive. There have been too many killings. Let it end."

"That's the deal? I let your son go and you publish the truth? You swear?"

"I swear." At the edge of his vision, Savage saw movement behind the man with the gun.

"And what happens to me?"

"Give yourself up. You've done what you set out to do. It's over . . ."

Again that movement behind the Teacher, and this time Savage's eyes went to it. He knew it must be Kit, almost forgotten, ignored, while the bargain had been struck. The Teacher started to turn, but then the youngster was on him.

Behind her filing cabinet, vanAllen balanced her weapon with her left hand and answered the phone with her right. It was the major again. His voice was tight with tension.

"You see it all, lieutenant, the way it's developing? It's probably gonna be our only chance."

"I see it." Her voice was flat. Through her scope she zeroed in on the two figures on the catwalk who had suddenly become three.

"You've got the best view up there," he said. "You have to take out the wacko."

"I can't talk any more," she said, and put the phone down. With both hands firmly on the Remington, she stared through the Leupold at the eruption of action on the walkway.

Savage saw arms wrap around the Teacher's biceps and chest, pinning the gunman in a position that left the AK-47 pointing at Savage's feet. Frozen, he watched as the two staggered forward out of the doorway. He heard a furious snort, the sound of air being forced violently from lungs. There was a harsh scraping of feet on the ironwork, and then the weight of the two carried them forward so that the handrail pressed against the Teacher's belly.

They were locked together as if bound by love, not enmity. The Teacher let go of his rifle, let it clatter to the catwalk, and reached back behind his head to feel for the boy's neck, his jugular. He still carried the other Kalashnikov slung across his back.

Savage darted forward, picked up the weapon, and held it awkwardly pointing at the struggling men.

"Kit," he shouted, "let him go. It's finished. I've got his gun." His finger found the trigger. He would have fired, but at this angle he feared he

might hit Kit. The boy's grip slackened. It was what
the Teacher wanted. Turning, he stepped back from
the relaxing arms and then stepped forward again,
his hands reaching like claws for the youngster's
throat.

Before he could find it, there was a whipping-
sighing noise followed by a crack and a round
slammed into his chest. It threw him back against the
handrail. The Teacher's eyes went to Savage, standing there gripping the Kalashnikov, and it seemed to
Savage that there was an anguished plea as well as
shock in the gaunt face.

He was still trying to read the message in the
haunted eyes when the sighing noise was repeated
and this time the round exploded the Teacher's head.
The features burst into a pulpy mess, blood spraying
in a fine mist over Savage, and the force of it threw
the body over the handrail and the wall and down to
the ground outside the Wilderness.

At the sound of the shots, the clamoring prisoners
in their cells had fallen silent. Down below the wall,
a woman shrieked. The TV cameraman was zeroed
in on the broken body.

"My God," Savage said. Kit went to lean against
the rail, his lungs heaving, staring down at the broken
body below.

"Son, you okay?" Savage went forward and Kit
turned and they put their arms around each other. The
boy's face was tear-stained and white, and his body
was shaking as he clung to Savage.

"He killed Grandpa," he said. "He came into

the kitchen and he shot Jasper and he shot Grandpa. He made me go with him." He paused for breath. "Oh, Dad, when I saw you coming for me, it felt so good, so . . ."

"Awesome?"

"Totally. But I couldn't leave it to you. I had to do something."

Savage put a hand to his splattered face and looked at the blood on his fingers. He stretched an arm around Kit's shoulders and they started walking wearily back toward the major who was standing halfway along the catwalk, looking down at the Teacher.

"Crazy as a coot," the major said, delivering officialdom's epitaph for the corpse at the base of the wall. The major grinned at Savage and reached forward to clasp his hand as if some sort of victory had been won.

29 ◄

When Paige reached the top of the stairs, a trooper was coming out of a room carrying two rifles with scopes attached.

"You the shooter?" Paige said.

"Inside," the trooper said, nodding over his shoulder and heading down the stairs. Paige walked into the room. It smelled of dust, old papers, and cordite. There were a couple of ancient computer terminals in one corner and gray filing cabinets lined the walls, one on its own near an open window. A cel phone lay on the top. With her back against the cabinet, vanAllen was sitting on the uncarpeted floor in an orange jumpsuit, the sleeves pushed up to her elbows. She was staring blankly ahead and at first she ignored Paige. He would have said that she had the thousand-yard stare except he suspected that scribblers reaching for dubious authenticity used the expression more than combat veterans.

He crouched down beside her and said, "You shot him?"

"I had to," she said. "The killing had to be stopped." To Paige, it sounded as though the words had been rehearsed.

"Like, destroy the village to save it?" Paige was pissed off that he would never be able to interview the madman in the tower. He had gone looking for the shooter in the hospital as a poor substitute.

"It wasn't like that."

"You know his name was vanAllen, the same as yours?"

"I know."

"Weird coincidence. A vanAllen shooting a vanAllen."

"Coincidences happen, that's why there is such a word. He was my father. I had to shoot him, Paige. I had to." She got slowly to her feet, and when she seemed about to crumple, Paige went forward to hold her. She held on to him and he could feel her body quivering.

"I know why they gave me the gun, why they wanted me to take him out," she said. "It was political. It suited them fine. Best for me to do it, no connection with a state agency, to cut down a lunatic shouting his hatred of the state. They didn't know it was my dad."

"Jesus," Paige said. He fell silent, considering the enormity of it. Then, still holding her, he said, "It was your father? Down in Albany, I seem to remember you told us your father was a lawyer."

"My stepfather is the lawyer. Not that it matters. I told a lot of people a lot of things that weren't true."

At first, Paige didn't know what to say. The story was becoming too complex.

"When did you realize the lunatic was your father? Jesus, I'm sorry. I didn't mean that." She stood back from him and said, "I want to see Jake Savage."

Outside, the flames had died down along the main street, but firefighters were still pouring water into the smoldering ruins of the town. The major was giving a press briefing in front of the TV camera and a small group of reporters at the prison gate. As they went by, Paige heard him say, ". . . two shooters, one up in the old hospital who fired the first shot, another on the prison roof. She blew the bastard's head off . . ." The Teacher's body had been removed.

They found Lady Jane at the bar in the tavern at the end of Rancie Street. She was playing a gambling game with three old men who appeared more interested in her cleavage. She didn't seem to mind. The game involved hiding matchsticks of different lengths in closed fists. Lady Jane was winning; she had a pile of dollar bills in front of her. The place was full and the atmosphere was strange: a mixture of excitement and exhaustion as if the people had not yet come to grips with their losses.

"My dear," Lady Jane said, turning to vanAllen, "you look dreadful. And that orange outfit isn't you at all."

"Stow it," Paige said.

"If you say so, darling," she said.

◀   ◀   ◀

When Savage and Kit got to the house on Rancie Street, two troopers were carrying out a black body-bag to their cruiser.

"Sorry about your loss," one of them said awkwardly. "The coroner's been and gone but there are no ambulances available. We'll take him to the morgue in Lake Placid. You should contact them about burial arrangements. There's a dead dog in there as well."

Savage put out a hand to touch the rubbery material of the sagging bodybag as they carried it past him. Beyond the sense of loss was the sickening realization that now he would never be able to make his peace with his father. Perhaps the chasm between them would have been too wide, but he could have tried. Savage and Kit dug a hole in the backyard and buried Jasper.

They found the others in the tavern. VanAllen was sitting alone at a corner table without a drink and Savage went to her. "Jake," she said, "can you get me away from here?" Her voice was a flat monotone.

"Sure," he said. Paige came over and Savage said, "Give me the keys to your car."

"Okay, but how the hell am I going to get out of here?" He handed over the keys to the rental. "I didn't see a Hertz office . . ."

"You can stay long enough to clear up the details, start to put a story together. Look after Kit while you're at it. Buy him a beer if he wants one. I'll be back in a few hours. Come on, Sarah."

Savage put his arm around her shoulders, steered

her through the crowd and out of the tavern. Her body felt rigid with stress.

"You gonna be okay?" he asked as they headed for Paige's car.

"Yes," she said flatly. "I just want to be away from here. I've been ordered back to New York."

"I'll drive you to the airport in Albany. You can get a flight from there." VanAllen got into the passenger seat and he reversed from the driveway into the street. He knew a way to get out of the town without going along the main street. Even so, he had to maneuver past fire trucks and ambulances clogging the back streets before they reached the open road.

She was silent at first, staring ahead at the bright headlights cutting a path in front of them. He left her alone. But then she started to talk. She sounded as though she was trying to get it all straight in her own mind.

She told him about her shot from the aerie in the hospital; that she knew it was her father on the wall with the microphone; that she had known since Albany, from things that Mary Morgan said, that he was one of the marauding assassins. She fell silent, but then she told him about the sexual assault, her father's reaction, and his imprisonment. He reached out and took her hand.

Perhaps it was being away from it all in the intimacy of the car moving through the darkness, perhaps it was the lifting of a long-carried burden, but at the end, she sounded stronger.

"Oh, Jake," she said, "I should never have come

upstate. But, once I started, once I began to suspect, I had to follow through, find out the truth of it all. Then, he was in my sights and I thought about all the killings, the misery they caused, the rape . . . And all the time, I was thinking as well that he had gone to prison for all those years because of me." She waited, as if for him to hand down his verdict.

"We all have secrets," he said. "Our secrets collided. You saved my son. You saved him by killing your father. I don't think I can take it in yet."

They were silent as the car moved south, and when he looked at her again, he saw she was asleep still holding his hand, curled up in her coveralls like a little girl. Once he saw a trooper, lights flashing, who had pulled over a speeder; things were getting back to normal. Two hours later, as they approached Albany, she came awake and began to talk again.

"When I was little," she said, "I was weighed down with so much guilt. I felt responsible for everything going wrong."

"No way was it your fault."

"I know, but when you're a kid you don't think things through, don't always think logically. I was an imaginative child, I suppose. So I began to make up stories about my father. Other kids, they talked about their fathers being city workers or firefighters or salesmen. I couldn't tell them my dad was in prison for murder. Sometimes I would get mixed up, saying that he was a cop when before I'd said he was in construction. Eventually, I learned to put a story together and stick to it. I knew I was all screwed up. One time

I was going to see a therapist about it. I turned away on her doorstep." The words came spilling out and Savage wondered if they were helping her find some sort of armistice with herself.

"I drilled my brothers until they got their stories the same as mine. The twins didn't care as much as I did. They were born after he went away and they never met him. It got better when my mother met my stepfather. I could talk about him as if he were my real father.

"Anyway, by the time they finally decided to get married, I was on my way to college and I thought it was all behind me."

"What was your mother's attitude?" Savage said. "It must have been even harder for her."

"She dealt with it. She tried to forget him and devote herself to us kids."

"I'd like to meet her. She must be special."

After another silence, Savage said, "For Chrissake, why did you decide you wanted the NYPD? You must have known they investigate candidates, their backgrounds, everything about them."

"I don't know. It just seemed right. Probably I had some vague idea about doing good, helping people. I knew I needed structure in my life and the military didn't appeal. I reckoned that if, even with a father in prison, they let me in, I would have a chance to put it all behind me. This lieutenant came poking around, but he was only interested in the mob, whether I had any relatives who were connected. He knew my dad was in prison, but it didn't seem to bother him."

Ahead was the turnoff for the airport, and Savage pulled out of the stream of traffic heading south. "Let's get something to eat," he said.

"I'm not hungry."

"Some coffee, then."

"Listen," she said, "I keep talking about myself, but I haven't been fair to you, have I?"

"You did what you had to do. You know about my father?"

"I had time to listen to the broadcast from the wall." She squeezed his hand. "Both of them, my father and yours, were caught up in the system and, in their different ways, went bad."

"It's terrifying. They were both monsters. How much of them is in us?" They were parked now outside the airport buildings, people moving around them. "Maybe we can help each other."

"Jake, this isn't easy for me to say and maybe now's not the time for it. The world is turned upside down for both of us. But the hell with it. D'you think we could start all over again? See where it takes us?"

Savage lifted her hand to his lips.

"I want that," he said. He guessed she was struggling to deal with her crisis by trying to look to the future. He turned off the engine and said, "After all this, anything's possible." In spite of everything, he felt pretty good. But then he realized she had not asked if he was going to include her and her history in the story he planned to publish.

30 ◀

Savage got out of the cab on Third Avenue and looked up at the gray, art deco facade of the paper's offices which once had commanded the street but now was dwarfed by the huge featureless blocks that had been thrown up in the eighties. When he walked in through the glass doors, he saw immediately that the Skipper's picture no longer hung in the lobby alongside the roll of honor of employees who had lost their lives in America's wars. He could see the outline delineating where it had hung, but the portrait had gone.

As he stood there, a guard came over. It was Joe Delgardo, a retired city cop who limped slightly, the result of an encounter with a holdup man who specialized in delicatessens in Queens in the mid-sixties.

"Where's the picture, Joe?"

"Orders from the editor's office, Mr. Savage. They've moved it somewhere up there, I expect to the Skipper's office." Nobody used the Skipper's office on the ninth floor. It was the same today as it had been when he died. The papers, the pens, the paperclips, they lay frozen in time, undisturbed except for the weekly dusting.

"Who decided on that?"

"Not sure. I don't know why it had to be moved. I used to like looking at it. You know, remembering him and the way he was."

"Hello, Savage."

He turned and saw it was Brompton, the circulation chief. Brompton nodded at the bare wall and said, "I wondered how long it would be before they got around to that." They walked toward the elevators.

"Joe thinks it's in the Skipper's office," Savage said.

"Out of sight, out of mind."

"How's circulation?" Savage sounded, he thought, like an anxious hospital visitor asking a doctor about a relative's condition. Brompton must be sick of the question.

"Up a little," he said. "Must have been that prison story up in Hamillton. Should give us more like that."

"I'll do my best. That was just a taste of what's to come." They entered the elevator. The only other occupant was an old messenger carrying a leather-bound layout from one of the advertising agencies. He was deep in a mumbled conversation with himself.

"Let's have a drink sometime soon," Brompton said. He was an old hand who claimed he remem-

bered the circulation wars of the thirties. He told stories of street fights between circulation men who
sometimes carried guns and sometimes used them.

"Sure. Friday maybe?"

"Fine. A word to the wise. They're after your
ass, Shannon and the rest of them. You know that?"

"The thought has occurred to me."

"They want to clear out the Skipper's men. Put
out a different kind of paper. I'm glad I'm retiring at
the end of the year."

Savage stepped out at the eighth floor and
walked past the editorial reception desk, staffed by
the widow of one of the paper's travel writers. She
was dealing with one of the crazies who somehow
had gotten past the guards in the lobby. She rolled her
eyes at him. He grinned at her and kept going.

The newsroom was quiet at this early hour. The
copy desks were deserted, and only a handful of
reporters, leftovers from the night shift and early
arrivals on the day turn, were at their desks. No sign
of Todd Paige, of course. He had done a decent job
on the Hamillton story. A good reporter, and he made
Savage laugh when he wasn't irritating the hell out of
him.

Savage looked with distaste at the video terminals that had replaced the typewriters with which he
had grown up. He still missed the urgent clatter of the
typewriters, the satisfaction of a well-written story in
black and white on paper that you could hold in your
hands. He missed the hard reality of metal type in the
composing room below and he missed the steady

skill of printers doing the work their fathers and grandfathers had done.

Now, the words, green on black, floated like phantoms on the video screens and you pushed a button and they were set in type a second later and it was all modern and clean and Savage said to hell with it. There had been an excitement in the old days as the deadline approached and the clamor of the typewriters surged toward a climax that was almost sexual. In those days, reporters and editors talked, argued, laughed, and swore as they worked. Now they stared at their screens as if hypnotized and talk was sparse and the atmosphere was sadly different. More like a bank, he thought. He wondered if he had become an old fart.

Savage was heading for his office when his secretary, Mandy Lyttel, who wasn't at all little, turned from the newsroom coffee machine to stop him. She looked at him oddly and said, "Good to see you back, Jake. You're wanted in the editor's office right away."

He nodded and thought, The secretaries always know first and here it comes. He had been expecting it and now that it was here he found he didn't care so much. He would find something else to do, maybe write the book he had never gotten around to.

At the desk outside Shannon's office, the editor's secretary flashed him a smile and said, "Go right in, Mr. Savage. You're expected."

He walked in and, closing the door behind him, stared at the woman sitting at Shannon's desk. He looked around, but there was no sign of the editor. For a second, standing there, he was so bewildered that he wondered if he had come to the wrong office. The woman, dark-haired, plump, stood up and laughed out loud at his expression.

"Come on in, Jake. You don't remember me, do you?" She put out her hand and he went to shake it.

"I'm afraid I've put on a bit of weight since you saw me last," she said. "You still don't remember?" He shook his head.

"Victoria Hewitt. My latest married name. I used to come here when I was a girl and you were a reporter. Remember now?" Jesus, the Skipper's daughter. She had been a handful, always in the discos, jetting around with Eurotrash, whispers of drugs and—what?—three marriages, as many divorces. The last one had been to an Australian, a surfer from Bondi Beach. During her vacations from Vassar, she had worked at the paper, in editorial and then in advertising. The Skipper wanted her to take over when he was gone. Once she had helped Savage on a serial murder case in Queens and he thought she showed promise. Certainly she had common sense, humor, and initiative. But she had drifted off into a different, gaudier world. When the Skipper died, as his only child she inherited a majority interest in the paper, but she left it to the board and got on with her fast-track life.

Savage grinned at her and said, "How the hell are you, Vicky?" She wore an expensive dark power suit, but it couldn't quite conceal the over-generous curves of her body. He remembered her as slim and lithe. Alongside the desk, a wire-haired fox terrier lay in a patch of sunlight, watching Savage with its head between its front paws. At her elbow, a cursor blinked on a computer screen.

"Sit down, Jake," she said, "and let's talk." As he turned to find a chair, he saw that the Skipper's picture from the lobby now was hanging on the wall directly in front of his daughter. They looked alike: the same aggressive jaw, the same commanding stare.

And Shannon's pictures, knickknacks, all evidence of him, had gone.

"Shannon," she said, "has taken early retirement. There's going to be some reorganization. I've been watching what's been going on and I finally decided I had to step in. I've awarded myself the title of publisher. I guess I'll learn on the job."

"You've been watching? Where from? Monte Carlo? Gaastad? You could have fooled me."

"I've been back for some time and Sue Chandler has been keeping me informed. We're old friends." Jesus, Sue Chandler was supposed to have been her father's mistress.

As if she could read his mind, she said, "I know. I resented her at first, but over the years, as I got over my public foolishness, we became close. She's a nice woman and she loved my father. These things happen. Anyway, she was my pipeline into the paper. Through her, I learned the way things were going. What I'm getting around to, Jake, is that I desperately need your help. The board and I want you to be editor. Not like Shannon. You'd be a hands-on editor, really running the paper. You'll get an increase in your news budget so that you can do the job properly. What d'you say?"

It was all coming too fast. Savage got up and walked to a window overlooking Third Avenue. Another traffic jam. A cop, ignoring the confusion of traffic, was writing a ticket for a driver parked next to a hydrant.

"Here's the deal," she said. "The board is willing to let me take over as publisher so long as you become editor. They were unhappy with Shannon and there was talk of bringing in an English sleaze-meister to run it. I talked them out of it, but that doesn't mean there aren't conditions, and you're one of them."

"There are complications," he said, turning back to her. "I'd take the job in a minute, but there are things about me and my family you don't know."

"You're talking about Hamillton and your father? I don't see the problem. Your man, Paige, wrote a fascinating story, we beat everybody else and that's it. Incidentally, what are they going to do with the bodies, the one who called himself the Teacher and the one who burned?"

"They're going to be buried in the prison cemetery. Full circle. They end up where it all began."

"It's finished, then."

"There are things that haven't come out yet. Todd Paige wrote some of it, a good story, about the events of that night, but there's a lot more behind it."

"Involving your father?"

"He did terrible things and they were at the heart of the burning of Hamillton." He told her about the years of corruption in the Wilderness, the burial of prisoners in the hospital, his father's part in it all. He thought about Sarah vanAllen's role, but did not mention it.

"Paige is putting it all together, the background, making a series out of it. I want to run it as soon as possible, starting Sunday at the latest."

She looked at him, sighed heavily, and said, "I don't understand this. I don't understand why you want to rake up old history. Surely it's over and done with."

"I made a promise."

"To who?"

"To the Teacher, vanAllen, when we were up on the wall, when my son was a hostage, just before vanAllen was killed."

"You don't have to keep that sort of promise, Jake. It was made under duress, right? You can promise a kidnapper anything. but that doesn't mean—"

"It wasn't like that. I made the offer and he accepted it."

"It was still made to a criminal, a killer who took more than twenty lives, trying to save a life."

He shrugged and said, "I'm sorry. I feel we have to publish it, the truth. If we don't, somebody else will." She was silent for a moment, then she looked at her watch.

"It's just fifteen minutes and we have our first

disagreement," she said. "All right. I'm not going to tell you that you can't run the story if it means a lot to you. I'm not going to take decisions like that away from you. But maybe I can persuade you that you're making a mistake. It seems to me it does no good, only harm."

Savage thought again of vanAllen. She had called him just before he left his apartment. She had been quietly suspended, told to drop out of sight for a couple of weeks. After the wounding interrogation on the fourteenth floor, Chief of Detectives Clarence Davis, still in the hospital recuperating from his operation, had told her unofficially that as things stood, she would be able to resume her career eventually. There would be a note in her file and she could forget any ambitions for moving higher in the department. But she would survive. Brush it all under the rug.

Savage knew that if he identified the Teacher as her father, if the paper revealed that she had shot him down, she would be finished. Since Hamillton, his emotions had been too chaotic to sort out. He felt deeply tired, disoriented.

"I don't know about your relationship with your father, Jake," Vicky Hewitt said. "But I do know that you would wound his memory if you published the whole story, and I don't think it's justified. After all, most of it is already out one way or another, what happened in the Wilderness in the past, what happened the other night. There isn't going to be an inquiry, too embarrassing all around. It's finished."

For a moment, Savage had a flash of the Teacher

mortally wounded on the wall, the anguished question in his eyes. It was followed almost immediately by Sarah vanAllen's white, haunted features. Son of a bitch.

He was silent. She said, "You know, Jake, I wonder how much of this is selfishness, you thinking that the truth and some promise you made in a crisis situation are more important than the peace of mind of people close to you. An English writer once said that if he were forced to choose between his country and his friend, he hoped he'd have the courage to choose his friend. Choose your father, Jake."

And Sarah vanAllen, he thought.

Maybe, somehow, she recognized his impasse. "I'll tell you what I think I'm going to do, Jake," she said. She looked at the picture across from her. "I think it's what my father would have done. I'm going to take the decision away from you. In spite of what I said before, it's my paper and it's not your decision. It's mine and I've decided that we're not going to publish Paige's series."

Just like that, the decision was taken from him. So was the burden sitting on his shoulders.

"The man is dead, Jake," she said. "You're alive. We should be concerned about the quick, not the dead."

"You gonna make a habit of this, persuading me I'm wrong?"

She just smiled at him. When he left, he turned at the door and said, "I think maybe you're gonna be a helluva publisher." And he flicked a salute at the picture of the Skipper.

◀   ◀   ◀

Todd Paige was coming out of a deep sulk. The Johnny Walker Black Label in his fist was helping. So were the smells from the kitchen, which were reaching him even out on the deck. At his suggestion, Lady Jane was repeating the dish she had made in Hamillton, a dish that was never eaten as far as Paige knew.

He thought about Savage. Benedict Savage. The man was supposed to be a straight shooter, and he had betrayed Paige as casually as tossing away a hotel pillow mint. Paige had spent hours hammering out the series on the background of events in Hamillton. It was Pulitzer Prize stuff, Paige's big breakthrough.

And then the bastard had told him to forget it. Savage, now editor, said he had decided that they had devoted enough space to the Wilderness and what happened there. He told Paige to take a couple of days off, relax, and then he could come back to work in Manhattan.

Shit. Still, he told himself, he was a naturally cheerful fellow who could handle setbacks. Look on the bright side.

For one thing, so far, Lady Jane had said nothing about the money she had loaned him. He had managed to score another $200 from her on the way back from the Wilderness. Perhaps she considered it all a gift. Should he pay her back when the goddamned accountants got around to his expenses? He was noted for his integrity, like Philip Marlowe, a

Galahad of the gutter, but on the other hand he had provided extensive services of various kinds for her. He would have to give it some thought.

The next plus: he was going to work back in Manhattan where he belonged. Maybe Savage would fix LaFleche. He owed Paige big-time. So did vanAllen. There had to be other consolations if he could just think of them.

Lady Jane floated out to the deck, sipping a glass of white wine. She was barefoot and wearing a gauzy, ivory-tinted gown cut low enough to allow him a peek at what she called her bristols.

"Fifteen minutes and it'll be ready," she said, sinking into a chair alongside him. "Now, the dinner party is tomorrow night in Manhattan. So far, I've got Mary the man-eater, that scribbler Mickey McGovern, a woman from New Zealand as a conversation piece, and Dominick Dunne. We'll need a few more."

"If this man-eater is so offensive, I don't know why you hang out with her."

"She makes me feel superior. She'll be so jealous when she hears about my adventures in Hamillton."

"I don't know what adventures you had other than getting pissed with a bunch of hoary old geezers with straw sticking out of their mouths." Paige wasn't completely out of his sulk yet.

"It doesn't matter, darling. All they want to do is listen to themselves talk anyway. What a vulgar sunset. It looks like a fried egg." The day had been very hot, but now, at dusk, a cool breeze was coming off the water. Paige drank more Black Label and felt even better. He had recovered his old car and his possessions, now parked outside Lady Jane's beach place. Perhaps he'd be able to fiddle with the odometer and sell it.

She was staring out across the water at a sailboat beating its way back to port.

"I'll tell you what I want you to do tomorrow," she said. In bed or out, she still ordered him around as if he were her goddamned liveried footman. "Use your investigative techniques to find a yacht we can rent for the day."

"I don't know how to sail."

"You don't have to. We'll just bob around in the harbor. I've been serviced on a big liner, but never on a little sailboat. It's time."

Paige said nothing. Lady Jane was wearing him out and he had more important things to do with his energies. As soon as they had gotten back from Albany where he wrote the series, she plonked him in the Jacuzzi as if to wash him off, allowed him one Scotch while she made some calls, then ordered him to bed for a "cocktail-time frolic."

He was pretty sure he could remember the phone number of the woman from the Fifty-seventh Street bar, Chloe. He wondered if she had a garage where he could park his Chevy.

But then he looked at Lady Jane's ample bristols and thought, On the other hand . . .